DOO WOP

Voices of God

Karen Gottlieb

ISBN: 979-8-218-08903-0 (print)

Printed in the United States of America

ACKNOWLEDGEMENTS

This book would not have come into being without the magic literary midwifery of Deena Metzger, the encouragement & insight of her original Monday Night Class, the invaluable friendship & genius of Joan Tewkesbury, & the great heart & generous spirit of the incomparable Matt Fogel, a true earth angel.

I am especially grateful for the unconditional love, support, and patience of my husband and soulmate, Leonard Krosney, who brought the Doo Wops into my life again, and stayed with me every step of the way, read every word, of every sentence, of every paragraph, of every page, of every chapter, of every draft, even before there was a draft, and talked over everything endlessly with me, all those years of nights we walked our dogs in the park and sat on that magic bench, dreaming this story together.

With Special Acknowledgement

To the songwriters, who created the heavenly melodies and timeless portraits of love that conjured the images which blossomed into the *Doo Wop Voices of God,* with gratitude for the inspiration:

This Magic Moment
Words and Music by Doc Pomus and Mort Shuman © 1960 (Renewed)
Mort Shuman Songs LLP and Pomus Songs
All Rights for Mort Shuman Songs LLP
Administered by Warner-Amerlane Publishing Corp.

Sh-Boom (Life Could Be a Dream)
Words and Music by James Keyes, Carl Feaster Floyd Mc Rae, Claude
Feaster and James Edwards © 1954
(Renewed) UniChappell Music Inc

Since I Don't Have You
Words and Music by James Beaumont, Janet Vogel, Joseph Verscharen,
Walter Lester, Lennie Martin, Joseph Rock and John Taylor Copyright ©
1959 by Bonnyview Music Corp.
Copyright Renewed
All Rights Administered by Southern Music Pub. Co. Inc.
International Copyright Secured
All Rights Reserved.
Reprinted by Permission of Hal Leonard LLC

This I Swear
Words and Music by Joseph Rock, James Beaumont, Janet Vogel, Joseph
Verscharen, Walter Lester, John Taylor and Lennie Marti.
Copyright © 1959 by Bonnyview Music Corporation
Copyright Renewed.
All Rights Administered by Southern Music Pub. Co. Inc.
International Copyright Secured
All Rights Reserved.
Reprinted by Permission of Hal Leonard LLC

Dedication

To my mother, Marian, who told me that I would never know my true capacity for love until I had a daughter of my own, and to my daughter, Alexandra, who proves my mother right every single day. I am blessed to be my mother's daughter and my daughter's mother. Someday, I hope to be as wise as you two have always been. And, to my father, Benjamin, the embodiment of unconditional love, in whose eyes I could do no wrong.

The three of you are the heart and soul of my story.

Something in the ad caught Miggsy's eye.

"Perhaps because there is no price, which means it's probably worth nothing," an irritating voice observed coolly, in his head.

Miggsy ripped the ad from the paper. But he knew he was grasping at straws. And so did the voice.

"You're not *seriously* pinning your hope on *this, this* pathetic little cry for help. Surely, you haven't sunk this *this, this, this—low*," it stuttered, as tongue-tied as a voice in one's head can be.

But, atypically tongue-tied or not, the ruthless inner critic Miggsy had long ago dubbed Noel Cowardice, because it popped up to provide withering commentaries on the worst moments of his life, but never stayed long enough to suffer the consequences, had hit the nerve right on its ending, once again. If you put it *that* way, or *any* way, he supposed, he *had* sunk that low. He had awakened—was it just yesterday—to the terrible realization that he had reached a depressing milestone. It had been ten years since the accident. But even after *that* long, even after ten never-ending years, he was still as raw as when it had happened.

He was just getting accustomed to the inescapable conclusion that the loneliness and remorse showed no signs of ever letting up, when another insight grabbed him by the arm like a madman with whirling eyes. And, in an aching flash of clarity, it struck him that ten years was nothing compared to what lay ahead, that he'd just had no way of knowing, when he tore himself away from his loved ones forever—propelled by the bravado of despair—how much time it would take to feel like forever would never end. That morning, he woke up and knew. And it terrified him.

He warned himself not to give in, to keep in mind that even in his worst moments after the accident he had not allowed himself to break down. He fought against tears again that morning, refusing to cry for all the mornings he would wake up and remember everything as if it were yesterday.

That afternoon, to remind himself to stop wallowing, because no matter how miserable he felt, there were so many others out there so much more deserving of his pity, he reluctantly but resolutely left the security of his apartment. Often, when he was overwhelmed with self-pity, he would trudge uptown to St. Mary's, a small, virtually forgotten storefront church he had stumbled upon in his aimless treks up and down the city's most desolate streets. He'd felt an immediate affinity to the church because, like him, St. Mary's was a lost cause; paint was peeling from its walls, the altar cloth was irreparably frayed, and yet, the truly kindly priest welcomed anyone in need. Father Joaquin had seen Miggsy outside, shivering inside his massive coat on a particularly frigid winter day, and immediately ran out, his cassock insufficient protection against the chill. The old man's body was dissipating with age, and his face was a roadmap of wrinkles. But Miggsy immediately saw that he was not as fragile as he looked. His long, thinning white hair, illuminated by the wintry afternoon sun as he approached Miggsy, gave Father Joaquin an aura of sanctity, and Miggsy could not shake the feeling that a slightly rickety angel was coming for him. Believing himself underserving of kindness, he turned to beat a hasty retreat. But before he could escape, the surprisingly agile Father Joaquin ushered him in and handed him a hot cocoa, thinking the young man was too embarrassed to ask for assistance. And in a way, he was right, though for the wrong reasons. For the last decade, Miggsy had deliberately depended on no one, reached out to no one, bore his pain and guilt alone. And he knew that would never change. But basking in the warmth of Father Joaquin's simple generosity, sipping his hot chocolate inside the little church, which was so poor, the altar was a table and the pews were folding chairs, he realized that his own desolation didn't mean he couldn't lend a hand to others in need. And how could he not help out this well-meaning church? First, secretly donating money to help keep the lights and heat on, then returning to help Father Joaquin in any way he could, even sweeping the floors, if necessary. But not today. Today, he couldn't face the pity in the old father's wise yet guileless eyes; they only intensified his loneliness.

So, hunched inside his deliberately oversized coat, blending into the anonymity of the city, he trudged downtown to Hughey's News & Smokes. He wasn't looking forward to seeing Edwin H. Hughey, a burnt-out ex-reporter, who fancied himself an overlooked Hemingway, but only resembled the great writer in alcohol consumption, beard, and girth. Having drunk himself out of a job decades before, Hughey never had a kind word for anyone. But there was nothing to be done. Hughey's one saving grace, as far as Miggsy was concerned, was that, while he seemed to hate everything and everyone, he had never lost his love of newspapers and the smell of newsprint. Holding court, even when no one was listening, discoursing like a cross between a mad prophet and an enraged grizzly bear on the multiplicity of ways the world had gone to shit, the crusty curmudgeon had managed to keep his grimy shelves crowded with a hodge-podge of newspapers, X-rated magazines, and suspicious looking smokes, which made Hughey's, seedy as it was, the only newsstand in the city that still stocked local papers—or what was left of them—from all around the country. Luckily, Miggsy was able to sneak in and out of the claustrophobic, hole-in-the-wall store that was hardly bigger than an actual newsstand, dropping more money on the counter than his purchase was worth, while Hughey was mercilessly berating someone cowering in the shadows for turning his stand "into a gaddammed lending library!"

Once home, Miggsy tore away at each paper, section by section, desperately searching for the classifieds where some personal ads might be hiding in plain sight. And when he did find those few remaining remnants of hope and despair, he found the same thing: an invisible army of lost souls, fighting their losing battles for their lost causes, struggling—like he was—to maintain the slender, brittle balance between abject hopelessness and the flimsy will to live. Riveted, forgetting to eat, unable to sleep, feeling kindred spirits reaching out to him from the pulpy, inky pages, he hurtled from curiosity, to sympathy, to an overwhelming longing to lift them all out of their despair. But then he remembered he couldn't even help himself.

In the end, his "dive into the quicksand of the worst-case scenarios of the human condition," as Cowardice, his derisive doppelganger had cruelly couched it, only served to remind him of the heartbreaking capriciousness of fate, and the one thing he'd been trying to forget: the great heights from which he'd fallen, not once, but twice.

He looked down at the ad he'd been seeking without knowing it and wondered at its odd hold on him. Cowardice was right. It was so small and indistinct, he practically needed a magnifying glass to decipher it. This meant something, Miggsy knew. But it could have been anything, from the obvious, that "ma" didn't have a lot of money to spend on an ad (which was why she was selling her erstwhile establishment), to the Shakespearean, that maybe ma wasn't so sure she wanted to sell *ma's,* and was perhaps, having a Hamlet moment (which explained why she put her ad in the personals, not the classifieds). But, unbeknownst to him at the moment that ad was misplaced in that paper, "ma" wasn't having a Hamlet moment. She was having an AHA! moment.

Had Miggsy broken his own rule and allowed himself to peruse the news section of *The Daggett Gazette*, the paper from which he had extracted the enigmatic ad, his "fatal ad-traction" as Cowardice snidely, if somewhat banally, labeled it, he might have seen, hidden in plain sight, another piece of the puzzle which, had he put it all together—and how could he not with his superior brain power and nothing better to do besides leap over mountains of used books—just might have helped him uncover the remarkably simple, yet simply remarkable, reason for the sudden sale of the rundown relic. Regrettably, though, he refused to break the vow he'd made to himself at the very beginning, not to look at anything that might carry any gossip, news, or rumor that might remind him in any way of his past life, which is why he eschewed any technology that could connect him to it. Still, had Miggsy just bent his unbreakable rule ever so slightly, he would have been at least somewhat enlightened by a tiny tidbit of extremely local news. Instead, he remained in the dark.

LOCAL WOMAN RECUPERATING

Norma Walters, long time resident and unofficial founder of the now defunct town of New Nebo, who was struck by lightning during a freak thunderstorm two months ago Thursday, is still alive if not yet kicking, or maybe kicking, if not still alive. Miss Walters is known in the area as "Mama," owner of "ma's Café"—a must-stop off Route 66 in its hey-day both for its food and its hospitality. The almost forgotten local personality was reportedly singed but otherwise unharmed, except for a slight scalp wound. According to her long-time companion and business partner, John Nash, she is on the mend and resting quietly in seclusion. Little else is known about the condition of the woman who once gave so much to this area and all the travelers who passed through it—although there have been uncorroborated sightings of smoke blowing from the general direction of her head.

Had Miggsy read this tidbit, instead of lining his garbage pail with it, he might have had second thoughts. Had Norma Lee Walters, the no longer mysterious "ma," read it, she would have laughed and said, "Well, that's one way of looking at it," meaning that unlike beauty, truth wasn't necessarily in the eye of the beholder, unless, of course, it was. This was something Mama had learned recently, although she may have known it forever. It was hard for her to tell these days, since, ever since a certain flash from above, time was beginning to take on a new meaning. It was more or less slipping through her fingers. In both directions.

Mama knew, of course, somewhere in her mind's backyard, that indeed, she was Norma Walters (although no one had called her that in years), that she did, of course, own the once famous, now failing, *ma's Café*, and that her partner in love and life was, without a doubt about it, John Nash, although she had only ever called him "BJ" for Big John, because as far as she was concerned, he was a giant among men in every way. She knew, too, that if she was anything, she was a resourceful woman, who had, somehow, used up all her and BJ's resources just trying to keep *ma's* going, and that they'd do it all again, if they could only figure out how. Because even now, when all was just about lost, strangers still wandered in, some with old Route 66 guidebooks falling apart in their hands, all looking for a good meal and maybe something more, something that reminded them of times gone by, knowing they could find those gentler days again at *ma's*. So, how could Mama not believe in the soul of her heart and the heart of her soul, from the front and back yards of her mind, that *ma's* would always be there to give weary travelers—however few and far between—a place to rest and catch up with themselves, whether or not they had the means to pay. Even if they were only hungry for a little conversation, some company, or just a few kind words. Lightning-struck or not, Mama knew all this for sure from some bone-deep place on her insides. Her outsides, however, were another matter.

Geographically, Mama knew she was where she always was, ever since lightning had enlightened her: in her actual backyard, pretty much singed around the edges, more or less melted into her favorite lounger, except for a minor side-effect of her meteorological mishap. Every so often, and always when least expected—as if anyone would ever expect this—something inside her hiccupped, and shock waves of leftover lightning jolted her out of her lounger, keeping her aloft for a shimmering moment, before abandoning her midair to drift back down, her emerald robe billowing around her like a luxurious parachute. Eyewitness proof to most reasonable people, Mama supposed, that her cosmic collision had knocked her completely off her rocker. And they would be entitled to their opinion. But Mama knew different. Mama knew that like everything else people saw only with their eyes, how she looked was just part of the picture, and not the real important part at that.

Mama knew that maybe the entire world would look at her and see her lying there, doing nothing, apart from levitating every so often, smoke now and then blowing out of the gash lightning had slashed in her head. But what they couldn't see was the buzz of wondrous thoughts pouring through that cleft in her cranium, and racing around a mile-a-millisecond, daring her mind, which had always been so calm and peaceful and reasonable before, to suspend all disbelief, jump on the bandwagon, and take a thousand leaps of faith. What they couldn't see, of course, was that no matter what it looked like, Mama wasn't just lying there going on and off like a broken light bulb. Mama was lying there picking up signals from beyond the Milky Way.

So, of course, if anyone asked Mama how she was, she would have to admit that she was wired, Mama was. She was always wired these days. And although she was in a perpetual state of recline, how could she sleep? She could never sleep. The signals kept coming. Voices of the galaxies in her ears. Her mind split open by God. Open to everything, like a wide mouthed barrel in the rain. Just everything, music to her ears, ever since, ever since—well, there was no other way to put it—ever since the day lightning scrambled her egg.

The day lightning scrambled Mama's egg, she was taking the day off from *ma's Café*, but not from worrying about it, which had become a full-time job of its own. BJ had just come back from a construction job in Chloride, and said he'd hold down the fort, so she could take some time to sort things out. Problem was, there was nothing left to sort out. Nothing could save the place short of a miracle, and they both knew it. To Mama and BJ, *ma's* was everything. But to the rest of the world, no matter what it used to be, *ma's* was nothing now, and no amount of thinking would bring it back again. She had to face the truth: *ma's* had been hanging on by a wing and a prayer for longer than she wanted to admit, even to herself. They just couldn't do it anymore, even with BJ doing all those jobs to make up for whatever *ma's* couldn't cover. Truth was, they were stretched so thin, they were about to snap. Not the type of gal to see through a glass darkly, it took a lot to get her down. But she had come to the end of the end of her rope. There were some hard decisions to be made just around the bend. So, she was having a little around the bender of her own before she had to make them.

That's how it started. Simple as that. With a bottle of Wild Turkey, which she didn't ever drink, even in the old days, being a Scotch gal, herself. But she was trying to jumpstart a way of seeing she'd never seen from before and figured Wild Turkey just might do the trick. Hoping she'd reach a solution before she reached the bottom of the bottle, she threw on a bikini and settled into her old, dependable lounger that she'd had since forever. Her freshly washed, frizzy, copper hair was set in tight rows of metal Campbell soup cans. Her ample, voluptuous body, which she was still damned proud of, bronzed as it was from a life in the desert, toned as it was from decades of waitressing and busing her own tables, and smooth as it was from her lifelong love of lotions, was mirrored in the silver panels of her Airstream, which glittered in the high noon sun.

Protected only by the SPF 30 in her favorite suntan lotion, 'Hawaiian Promise,' and the bikini, which had been around almost as long as the lounger, but still fit—although it covered a little less of her and had to go around a lot more of her than it originally signed up for, truth be told—she took a deep, long drink, and then another. And being that she had given up drinking to excess ages ago, that did it. Liquid heat rushed through her like it was being chased by the devil, and in moments, she was ready to face that devil if that's what it took.

"Let's get this party started!" She heard herself sing into the empty desert, although she couldn't have felt less like partying. Then, taking another bracing swig of Wild Turkey, she held her sun-reflector to her face. The sun's rays raced from the Airstream to the reflector to Mama's face, infusing her with such a sizzle that the only thing she could think of was how long she could stand to fry before she'd stop thinking of all the questions and come up with a few answers.

Did she doze off, or was it the Wild Turkey kicking in? Ah, the unanswerable question. But suddenly, a Bob Dylan line popped into her head, the light inside her eyes went dead, and she was pelted by, yes, of course, "a hard rain."

"And it's a hard, and it's a hard, it's a hard, and it's a hard. And it's a hard rain's a-gonna fall," she crooned to herself, as drenched from rain as she'd just been soaked with sweat, wracking her brain for the rest of the damn song, hoping to happen upon a rosier reason than the obvious—that things were going from bad to worse—just one upbeat explanation for it to pop in like that, like a record in an old jukebox just popped in. "A hard rain" repeating in her head, she attempted to unglue her eyelids to take a look, really wishing she had a cigarette so she could think straight, though she had stopped smoking years ago.

When Mama finally pried her eyes open, the sky was black as pitch, except for the jagged bolt of lightning aimed at her like the finger of God. And the next thing she knew, that bolt from the black zapped her soup can curlers, her reflection in the Airstream lit up like the Vegas strip, and she had her first communiqué from the cosmos.

At first, she thought she was hearing a distant radio on the fritz, skidding from station to station. Then she knew what it was. Lightning had somehow struck open a channel between Mama and the Voices of the Universe. And since she had always been stuck on R&B, it came as no real surprise to her that she was being contacted in Doo Wop. Were there better harmonies in the universe? Mama didn't know of any.

Once they had a direct line into her through the brand-new blow-hole in her brain, the Doo Wop Voices of the Universe told her to hold on. She would be receiving a recipe for apple pie any time now that would save *ma's Café* and, maybe, the world. Of course, she was sure they were pulling her leg. But before she could call their bluff, they said that, by the way, an angel would be coming by in the guise of a guileless girl, and Mama should be on the look-out, because this girl, this angel in disguise, needed special protection. And to stay tuned for further instructions. They sang "Pretty Little Angel Eyes" so she knew it was true, although she sure would have liked some more specifics.

BJ found Mama on her lounger that night, awaiting further instructions. She had not moved. Didn't remove the soup can curlers from her head for fear of screwing around with the transmission. Didn't lower the reflector for the same reason. Had to keep everything the same.

BJ was worried about Mama. She looked fried. Her head was covered with melting soup cans and wisps of singed hair. Her eyes were feverish, which was understandable. Yet, she looked strangely comfortable.

"There's an angel comin' BJ," she told him, though he was too stunned by her present state of smoke blowing out of her head to respond.

"There's an angel comin' BJ," Mama repeated on the first night of her sedentary sojourn to the stars. "But the angel comin' ain't the only one," she amended.

"Oh yeah? Who else?" BJ queried, trying not to let on that he was very worried about her.

"A wounded soul," Mama confided, smoke rising in a corona from the hole in her head.

"You been hit by lightning Mama?"

"You hear what I'm sayin' BJ?"

"Yeah, Mama, I hear you: an angel and a lost soul are comin'. What do ya want me to do about it?"

"Keep a look-out."

"No problem. Wanna come in? I can just take down the door and—"

"Can't. Gotta keep listening. They're giving me a special recipe for apple pie."

BJ wondered if the angel and her plus one were coming alone, or together, or if one of them had Mama's recipe, but he just said, "No shit," as he lumbered into the Airstream to get her a cold drink, a cold compress, and something to cover her hot, hot body against the cold desert night.

Mama knew that BJ would understand. They were on the same wave length, although they sure didn't look it, due to BJ's bigness. Not that Mama was small. Oh no. Mama was curvaceous in all the right places, certainly as far as BJ was concerned. But BJ was oh so big. Like Paul Bunyan. A mountain of a man. When he wrapped his arms around her, they covered ground. The man encompassed her. He was big enough to take a nap on.

BJ was a big man with a big heart, all right, but he sure as hell looked like, and was, one tough son of a bitch. As long as he was around, nobody would ever hurt Mama.

And she was good to him, his Mama was.

And he was good to her.

Some days, or was it weeks, later, though deep into her vigil, Mama watched BJ retrieve the tray of food he'd brought her when he got home hours, or was it days, before, but she hadn't taken a bite of. She watched him look at her as if he had something to say, then not say it, because he suspected she couldn't hear him. But she could sure see him moving his marvelous carcass very slowly towards the trailer. Mama was watching, of course, from somewhere in her mind's backyard, because she had to reserve the front for new transmissions.

Fried as she was, BJ knew Mama was watching. So, he danced for her, doing a number he never showed her before, he was saving for a rainy day, which this certainly qualified as—clear skies notwithstanding. Called the "Miami Grind," it was a little something he picked up from Judie Blue Thighs, one of the strippers at "La Strippe," the strip joint—on the strip—he bounced in in Vegas. Sturdy as a tree, his body muscled from a life of never shirking manual labor, a grin on his face as wide as the great Mississippi, he raised Mama's untouched tray over his head, balanced on the palm of his hand like a waiter in a movie musical. Then he nodded to Mama over his shoulder and negotiated his Big Daddy hips up the narrow path to the trailer slow, real, real, slow.

Hoping to reach Mama under her radar, BJ began humming, although coming from the great expanse of his chest, it sounded more like a bear growling, "You're a thousand miles away."

Mama might as well have been a thousand miles away, she was concentrating so hard on the next transmission, trying to catch another glimmer of cosmic Doo Wop through her soup can antennae.

Then she heard them again.

> *"You're a thousand miles away—*
> *But I still have your love to remember you by.*
> *O my darling, dry your eyes—*
> *Daddy's coming home soon—"*

Mama's mind's eye swerved like a car going around a fast curve. They were in the vicinity of the porch harmonizing with BJ. Could it be that he was in tune with cosmic Doo Wop? He was in tune with something alright, Miami Grinding his way up the steps, taking the lead, the Doo Wop Voices of the Universe providing back up.

BJ reached the last step and bumped and grinded around to reveal a part of him so monumental that it made Mama—even in her otherwise occupied state—gasp.

"Just wanted to make sure you're alive," he winked, and closed the Airstream door. Mama watched BJ watch her through the eyelet curtained window. She wanted to let him know she was fine, which she was, though it was hard to concentrate, since her insides were lit up like a pinball machine and things were pinging in places she hadn't pinged in in years. But it wasn't just physical. Ideas she'd never had before were bursting in her head like it was a giant popcorn machine, all those perfectly popped thoughts exploding from teeny kernels that must have been secretly percolating in some unknown part of her.

Ping, ping, pop, and Mama was discussing the limitless potential of man with the Doo Wops.

"*One summer night*," they philosophized, "*we fell in love.*"

"How true, how true," Mama agreed, getting lost in the music.

BJ dumped the contents of Mama's uneaten meal down the disposer, rinsed the plate and stuck it in the dishwasher. Through the delicate eyelet curtains, she had hand-stitched just last spring, he could see her relaxing in her lounger, her chaise, her recently divinized divan, riding high with the Doo Wops, and he prayed that her faith in them, and his in her, would somehow make everything all right.

The desert chill was creeping into the air. The wind whipped up and whistled in the distance. A pack of coyotes howled their shrill response. Mama didn't move. BJ reached for the vibrant green silk kimono he'd bought her a few years back because it reminded him of Shanghai and it matched her eyes and went back out to wrap it around her and stand guard through the first of many such enchanted evenings.

The day after lightning scrambled Mama's egg, BJ had set up a giant bell for customers to ring at *ma's*, which fortunately was just up the hill from the

Airstream. Thereafter, he developed a routine of going up there whenever it rang—which in the ensuing weeks, unfortunately, but not unexpectedly, wasn't very often—and rushing back down the hill to check on Mama as soon as he could. Or else, he went up every few hours, just to check in or clean up a little. Although he kept almost constant vigilance over Mama, Mama never seemed to notice when he was gone. She seemed to be caught in some kind of magic suspension of time. And he was frankly happy she didn't have to suffer the pain of watching *ma's Café* gasping for its last breaths. So, while Mama whiled away her hours communing with the Doo Wops, believing they'd pull them through, BJ did what he could to pull them through from his end, tending to Mama and *ma's* the best he could, while keeping his feelers out for any work he could do to keep everything afloat.

When a job came up to paint the New Nebo Post Office, BJ took it because it was close and Mama seemed so content, so protected by the Doo Wops, she didn't seem to need anything else. She certainly wasn't coming to any harm, or even wasting away, although she didn't seem to be eating anything either.

The Post Office job would keep *ma's* lights shining for awhile longer. To celebrate, BJ did what he'd been doing every night since the first. He harmonized with the Doo Wops.

"Papa was a rolling stone."

The Doo Wops crooned softly in the honeyed twilight air, although this was a little out of their era, urging BJ to take the lead, so in love were they with the big man's basso profundo.

"Papa was a rolling stone. Wherever he laid his hat was his home." They all sang in perfect harmony,

Well, Mama smiled to herself, they were sure singing her song. Wherever she laid her hat was her home. Or once was, she had to face it, a long, long time ago, before *ma's Café* and way before BJ, when she and her trusty van,

SunnySide Up, were young and on the road, and there was some kind of ocean inside of her that kept pulling her in and out with the tides, moving to the rhythm of wherever it went.

Even after she settled in the desert, there was still an ocean inside her, keeping her buoyant, and because of that ocean inside, nothing really got to her. Whatever ill wind blew her way was just the brink of a storm that would blow over, or blow her overboard. It just didn't really matter. Either way, she could float it out. This was the secret Mama had learned about herself when she was just a girl. And she had lived her life in perfect harmony ever since.

Of course, it didn't occur to her—lost blissfully in the mists of Doo Wop—that for this very reason, it was no happenstance the Doo Wops were visiting her with their perfect harmonies, or that if asked, BJ would concur by saying simply, "Where else would they want to go?" Nor did Mama have a glimmer of an inkling that there was yet another thing that drew the Doo Wops to her, and that was her skin. Not just because it had an inner glow. But while it was true that in moonlight she glowed like a Chinese lantern, Mama's skin didn't merely pick up light. It picked up sound.

And that was the crux of it. The Doo Wops had traveled light years to be with Mama because they knew she was worth the trip. Their harmonies, so in tune with hers, sluiced along her curvy curves, reverberating off her refulgent and robust epidermis like the best street corner a Capella in the universe. They'd never sounded better.

"Papa was a rolling stone." The Doo Wops and BJ along with them, persisted, the big man's basso getting more and more profundo as the evening rolled on.

Oh yes, come to think of it—and Mama hadn't thought of it in quite awhile—if anybody was, her own poppa surely was. So, of course, she had inadvertently inherited, like the dust that had clung to his old fishing jacket, a fine coating of wanderlust, a need to be ready to roll, to rev up ole SunnySide and take off whenever the wind changed its tune.

Well, the wind had changed its tune every which way but Sunday, she was sure, and here she still was, being serenaded into oblivion, aware from somewhere behind the barn in her mind's backyard that BJ was gesturing to her now, to come home to him, to rise from the lounger and into his generous arms. And she wanted to. But she could not. Except for those magic moments of what she thought of as cosmic bounce, she was as stuck to her lounger as the soup cans were stuck to her head. And she was just too damned comfortable to move, listening to the Doo Wops, watching BJ, music resounding from every inch of her, while she waited for an angel and a recipe for apple pie that would make everything all right. What could make more sense?

"*Papa was a rolling stone.*" BJ took the lead, his eyes never leaving Mama.

Mama could feel his eyes on her, knew he thought she'd taken a ride to the moon on soup can wings. She wanted to tell him she'd been there all the time, suspended somewhere between the scorched earth of their predicament and the heavenly promise of Doo Wop, but she was losing her grip, slipping farther and farther away, those five words pinging her like a BB straight into the past, where her poppa was reminding her again, like he used to, at the onset of one of his "little jaunts," a twinkle in his eye, "Don't get yourself too attached to anywhere, Norma Lee."

"Oh shush!" Her momma was telling him, like she used to. "Everybody knows ladies love to stay home to take care of their man."

"You'll end up being a barnacle on the underside of somebody else's boat," her poppa went on, merely stating the obvious as far as he was concerned.

"Oh Nooorm," her momma practically cooed, like she did every time. "putting such ugly ideas into the girl's pretty head."

Her words scolded him, but it always sounded like flirting.

"Borrowing someone else's ideas is like borrowing their underwear," he dressed her down with tender eyes, reaching for his duffle, tossing it on the bed.

And back and forth it went, like a Chinese ping pong match, while she helped him pack, until none of their words seemed to matter. And in fact, nothing seemed to matter but each other.

Mama, who had been christened Norma Lee, after both her parents, Norman and Lee-Ann Walters, because she would always be the best of both of them, always listened just enough to be polite, but once she got the gist, she drifted off and left them to themselves. Because there was something she always knew. She was born self-sufficient.

She was a big girl back then, before her baby fat turned into womanly curves, a "hefty persuader," people couldn't help but observe behind her back, as if that was a terrible thing to be. But they didn't get it. She was a universe of her own.

And it wasn't anything she did. Or even thought about. It was a trait. Like her bright, split pea green eyes and copper wire hair. Like how her poppa just couldn't stay put, and her momma, well, her momma just couldn't stop making everything comfy and cozy, couldn't stop trying to make things better for her family, couldn't stop putting everyone else first.

"Whoa there!" Mama snapped herself back from her Doo Wop loop-de-loop into times gone by, thinking maybe it was time to put a halt to her runaway reminiscences, just in case they were jamming the Doo Wop highway and getting in the way of the recipe's arrival. But it was not to be.

"*Papa was a rolling stone,*" the Doo Wops insisted, letting her know that they were in this time warp together.

Mama sighed and settled in for the ride, wherever it would take her, which, apparently, was back home again.

"*Wherever he laid his hat was his home.*" BJ and the Doo Wops reminded her.

"Sounds just like my poppa," Mama thought. But, before the thought could settle in, the layers of memory fell away to reveal the other truth, that most of the time her poppa laid his hat on a shelf her momma had made out of his old road maps by the front door.

Mama had to smile, remembering how her momma could make just about everything—from coat racks to couches—from just about nothing. It was her gift, which they all took for granted.

"Oh, the riches that people toss aside!" Her momma always rhapsodized during their Treasure Quests together in the old Ford pick-up on garbage days, eying someone else's cast-offs like they were the finest works of art, seeing them not for what they were, but what they could be. And so, a thrown out, battered and broken-down old door was retrieved from someone else's trash to be sanded, stained, lacquered and reincarnated into a lovely, new dining room table.

Yard sale remnants and hem scraps were sewn together to become curtains and slip-covers, bed-spreads and seat-covers, and once, an entire sofa.

Old leaky tea pots became planters where wild flowers outdid themselves to bloom for her.

Once, when all the churches in three counties got a group discount on brand new King James Bibles with colored illustrations and had a one time only "All the Worn-Out Bibles You Can Carry for $5" sale, Mama's momma bought them all, hauled them home in the pick-up and epoxied them together for end tables and matching lamps.

"Making a home," she bubbled, "a woman's greatest joy."

And Mama, when she was still her momma's own, precious Norma Lee, took it all in, along with the timeless hours in the toasty kitchen, peeling and chopping and cutting and seasoning and broiling and roasting and baking. And when the oven was warm and the skillet was sizzling and all the delicious aromas rose up and mingled with each other like old friends, Norma Lee could have sworn she knew what paradise was. It was being in the kitchen with her momma.

"Ah, ah, ah, my darling Norma Lee, when you love what you do," her momma sighed in sweet contentment at those times, "life could be a dream, sweetheart!"

Poppa, of course, being a rolling stone, could not stay still.

Sometimes he'd be gone for days, sometimes weeks, sometimes months; sometimes he left on foot; sometimes he drove. It didn't matter. Whenever he came home, the house was spit-shined and perfect and rearranged and something wonderful was in the oven, welcoming him like one of Mama's momma's special hugs.

"I'm just a family man at heart," he'd say, tears in his eyes, hugging his two girls, who always ran to greet him at the door. Then he'd take a deep, appreciative breath, savoring all the flavors unleashed from the kitchen, and he'd whisper conspiratorially to his darling Norma Lee, "Even if I went blind, I'd never be lost, because I'd just follow the sweet aroma of your momma's cooking all the way home."

Next, he'd ask his dear Lee-Ann what she did while he was gone, looking around at the new things that she'd put in old places and clucking proudly, "I see you've been busy."

And she would, of course, demur, "Not really."

When in fact—Mama saw now, from the unique vantage point of the hole the heavens had blasted in her head—the truth about the way they lived, whether her poppa was there or gone—was that her momma was in constant, easy motion, preparing and repairing—folding and unfolding her days and nights—until time unlocked and they were just tucked inside of it in their own cycle of cooking and cleaning and redecorating and dreaming up ways to make things cozy. And so, poppa could come and go and he just always folded into Mama's momma's scheme of things.

And from the over and over again of it, Norma Lee could do it, too. Thanks to her momma, she had domestic skills. She would make a perfect wife.

But, from her poppa she got her need to leave, not because he told her to, but because she had to.

And her momma and poppa knew that they would let her go, because no matter how far away they were from each other in distance or philosophy, they believed in three things—the way they felt about each other, their out-and-out devotion to their own, precious, Norma Lee, and their unshakable belief that Norma Lee would always be all right because she had been born with an angel on her shoulder.

Mama, when she was Norma Lee, had always said yes, of course, she could feel something heavenly hovering there sometimes, to make her momma and poppa happy, when in fact, she never saw any real sign of her own, personal angel, except maybe once, in the kitchen, but it was on her momma's shoulder and may just have been the sun bursting through a cloud.

And here she was, after all these years and miles, older now than her momma was then, on the look-out again, hoping to have better luck finding this angel than the last one.

"*Poppa was a rolling stone.*"

"*And the only thing he left us was alone.*" The Doo Wops wrapped it up, calling it a night, pulling the plug on days gone by, while Mama stayed tuned for things to come, and BJ was left to worry about how to make ends meet, when both ends are the short ones.

"*Poppa was a rolling stone.*"

Miggsy was listening to music to take his mind off his thoughts. It wasn't working. He had no idea how this song got onto his playlist, but it shouldn't have been there. As far as he was concerned, the farther he kept away from his father, who was definitely not a rolling stone, from his mind, the better.

So, he returned to the ad and Cowardice.

"What's up with spelling *ma's Café* with a small *m*?" Cowardice groused. "Did she run out of capital letters and money simultaneously?"

Pleased with his pathetic pun, Cowardice spitefully pictured a rundown greasy spoon on the outskirts of some downtrodden, middle-of-nowhere town that dangled off some long-forgotten stretch of Route 66 like an arm pulled out of the socket of a corpse. And Miggsy knew at once, it could rank among the most pitiful sights he'd ever seen, the top being himself on the first day of Eighth Form, when he was still Mills Miggston the Third.

All summer, he had dreaded coming back to school.

When his parents, whom he'd recently nicknamed "the 'rents," in acknowledgment of his new relationship with them as a boarder, not a real son, pulled him from Wilde, his very own thoroughbred colt, named after Oscar Wilde, who had been all the rage in Seventh, and dragged him away from the stables and everything he loved—when they made him put on his suit and school tie to go from doctor to doctor, forced him to pee in a series of way too small plastic cups, forced him to be stripped down, and just stood by while, shivering like a sniveling idiot, he was stared at, x-rayed, measured, poked, and prodded under the magnifying glass of everyone's expectations—when they, who had never agreed about anything and never would, except that they would never be caught dead in their own kitchen— were standing side by side, right there at the sweeping marble counter with identically insipid, concerned-but-trying-not-to-be looks frozen on their faces, force feeding him vitamin concoctions and protein drinks with raw eggs in them masquerading as malteds, pretending that everything was just all right—and especially when the diagnosis came in at the end of the summer—he had never stopped dreading this day.

The Night of the Diagnosis, he couldn't stop himself, could *not* stop himself from crouching outside their bedroom door like he used to do when he was a kid watching them fight through the key hole. But this time, it wasn't about the usual betrayals, broken promises, and ultimatums. It was about whether or not to give him the dreaded pituitary hormone cocktail.

His mother, who had been losing weight all summer, rustled in and out of his keyhole view, as diaphanous as rice paper in the bedroom light.

"I'm afraid, afraid of what will happen to him, if not now, some time. We don't know, don't know, don't know, sais pas, sais pas—" she stuttered, her voice trailing off into vapor.

"Don't know what?" His father, monolithic in his black silk robe, demanded, making her say it.

"The side effects, the con-se-*kences*," she said over and over, the slight French accent of her childhood overcoming the wispy southern drawl she'd adopted over the years, but her usually lilting, girlish voice sounded like dry leaves, which his father blew away with five fatal words.

"What choice do we have?"

Frozen at the keyhole, Mills' thoughts flashed on the cow's pituitary with the human growth hormone in it, imported at great expense, of course,—the 'rents were never cheap—from somewhere impossible to pronounce, and stored, no, let's be real, *hidden* in the downstairs utility kitchen freezer in cunning glass canning jars, indistinguishable from the more edible delicacies, except *these* delicacies happened to look like shrunken cows' brains with rat tails from Frankenstein's lab, and *he* was going to be the monster.

Cut to the quick, he struggled to get up, but his body felt like jelly and he couldn't breathe. His heart was pumping so erratically in his stomach, it was sapping his strength. He staggered away from the keyhole on his knees, arms raised in bitter supplication to a God he no longer believed in.

How he got back to his room that night, or for that matter, how he did anything after that, for what was left for the summer, Mills couldn't really say, nor did he want to know. He became a waking sleepwalker. His body moved him through his life, but his withdrawal was total.

He felt cold and remote at the end of the summer, when his mother prepared him for his return to school and tried to draw him into her false excitement. He went numb to the point of not feeling his fingers the night before what should have been the jubilant drive to the esteemed Pine Cliff Academy, where five generations of Miggstons had matriculated and excelled, though none as well as Mills Miggston the Third, even at his young age. He fell mute the next morning during a painful farewell breakfast he didn't eat. He started seeing everything as if through the far end of a telescope, almost exactly when, at the last minute, instead of getting into the limo, his father, who appeared to Mills to be talking from a great distance, gravely explained that he would not be going along. An emergency with one of his valuable thoroughbreds prevented him from joining them at what had been, until now, one of his favorite family events, his annual, triumphal return to his Alma Mater with his prize-winning progeny, whose brilliance had taken the spotlight off his own more mediocre record and placed it where it belonged, on his superior genetics. Watching his father recede as the car pulled away, Mills felt nothing. The astonishing crimson and gold foliage that had never failed to thrill him during all their other drives to Pine Cliff, faded to grey with all his expectations.

Hours later, at the dorm, he sat on his bed, unmoving, while his mother unpacked for him. He was apathetic when she bid him a tearful goodbye. But, when he was finally alone, and he forced himself to look out onto the Great Lawn, everything became much too vivid.

Mills watched from the window of the room he shared with his ex-best friend, Bryce Naughton, who was already there with everyone else, while the boys of Pine Cliff Academy were lining up on the Great Lawn for their Form pictures. He wondered if they'd miss him if he didn't go down. His clenched stomach gave him the answer.

Last year, in Seventh, they would have missed him, would have called up to him to hurry up, although not by the end. In Sixth, they wouldn't even have gone down without him.

But there it was, the writing, or in this case, the pictures, on the wall.

Thanks to one of the lamer Pine Cliff traditions, every dorm room had the boys' Form pictures hung from First on up, on the north wall, under the motto, "Friends Are Our True North." And he'd believed it. Now it made him want to puke.

If growing up was a race, and to Mills everything was a race, then he had definitely been winning. He was great at everything. Everybody liked him. And he liked everybody. People were always knocking on his door. Everyone wanted to be his best friend. Things came easy, easy as pie.

He was the tallest boy in every picture, always in the middle, the others always looking up to him. In Third, he towered over everyone and dreamed of breaking the sound barrier with his sprint. In Fourth, he was the fastest runner, the captain of the basketball team. By Fifth, he wasn't head and shoulders above his pals anymore, but he was still the fastest.

By the middle of Sixth, things started slipping. That's what it felt like—slipping, slipping backwards, losing ground. His pals started sprouting like weeds all around him, outgrowing their uniforms, getting packages from home with new clothes at least once a month. But Mills' size didn't change even once. By the end of Sixth, his pals didn't have to look up to him anymore.

Then, Ellis Dunne, who had crowned himself Mills' arch rival because he'd once almost beaten him in a race—Mills, hobbling with a sprained ankle, still came in first—made his move. Dunne, the first to start shaving, formed a secret club with his personal thugs, the behemoth Thiggy Cartwright and the hormone drenched, gargantuan Forsythe twins. The club was only open to anyone who shaved, which ended up being practically everyone, except Mills, whose peach fuzz didn't count. Mills told himself that as soon as he caught up and began to shave, everything would be the way it was before. But he knew he was lying to himself.

Sometime before the end of Seventh, Shrimp Bainbridge, the only other guy on the track team as short as Mills, grew eight inches and beat Mills in the four-hundred by a millisecond. It was just a millisecond, but in that millisecond, a pain as sharp as an electric shock zapped Mills, and he knew he had not just come in second. He had lost his place.

After that, he never got his stride back.

This morning, seeing his "friends"—not one had called him all summer—for the first time since June, he hoped against hope that he wasn't really too short to fit in, that things would be like they used to be.

When he finally got up the courage to come down to the Great Lawn, all the Forms were already in those concentric clusters they always formed around the boys every other boy wanted to be with most, and who would remain *the* boys for the rest of the year. Every other year, Mills had been *the* boy of his Form. This year, it was his worst nightmare.

Ellis Dunne saw him out of the corner of his eye and smiled coldly from above a sea of fawning faces.

"Hey Mills, lose your place?" Ellis Dunne said, drawing everyone's attention to the fact that Mills was currently at the very outer edge of the circle.

"Dunne." Mills nodded, hoping to end it at that.

Fat chance.

"I see you're finally shaving. Too bad the club isn't accepting new members."

Ellis Dunne smirked, sidling up to Mills, flanked by his three personal stooges, Thiggy and the idiot twins, followed by the other boys in pecking order. As he came closer, Mills looked up at him in barely concealed horror. He'd gotten a lot taller and had obviously worked out religiously in the sun, because he was pumped up and tan and now towered over Mills who, unlike Dunne, had been diminished by his summer, having lost weight and gained a sick pallor from standing naked under all those fluorescent lights in all those windowless examining rooms. He tried to seem casual, but his tension was a black hole. It drew everybody in.

When he was sure everyone was riveted, Ellis Dunne made a big show of looking down at Mills. "How's the weather down there?" He mocked.

The three stooges guffawed uncontrollably, as if this was the funniest thing they'd ever heard. Behind them, the others held their breath.

"Your wit is equaled only by your taste in friends," Mills retorted, his voice dripping with sarcasm he didn't really feel, sounding way too much like Oscar Wilde and way too little like one of the guys.

"You're the last person in the world to point out other people's *short* comings," Ellis taunted. And that was it. He'd drawn blood. The entire crowd burst out in derisive laughter.

"Hey Mills," Thiggy said. "What happened? You shrink?"

"Yeah, Mills shrunk!" The Forsythe twins added, laughing uproariously, slapping each other on their fat rumps.

"He's shorter than a girl I dated this summer!"

Mills couldn't believe he was hearing these words coming from "Shrimp" Bainbridge.

One by one, they all went in for the kill, until everyone had put him down, everyone but Bryce, who hesitated about two seconds before caving.

"When—when we take our Form pictures, let's put Mills in a dress and, and call him *Millie!*" Bryce shrieked, using a name he knew Mills particularly despised, ending what was left of their friendship.

Mills' cheeks were burning. His stomach was turning. His mouth had frozen into a stupid half grin. He wanted to bolt, but he, the great runner, couldn't put one foot in front of the other to save his life. So, he dug in and held his ground and strictly by default, stood there, ready to take it like a man, like he'd taught himself to take it in the freezing, dehumanizing examining rooms. He closed his eyes to conjure riding Wilde into the blue mountains. But it didn't work.

Dunne nodded and his thugs seized Mills. The twins grabbed his feet and Thiggy nabbed him by the waist, pinning his arms, so he couldn't fight back. They hoisted him up easily, like a weightless battering ram, and ran him to the concrete path behind the Quad, outside the view of any nosy teachers. The others followed, shouting with unbridled glee.

Mills struggled but he was no match for Thiggy and the twins. His heart raced a mile a minute, pumping out of his chest. He heard Dunne yelling in the distance.

"One!" They swung Mills back, his feet high in the air.

"Two!" The crowd joined in with the count. The three stooges aimed him like a missile, head first toward the ground.

Dunne raised his muscled arm, ready to give the signal and stared down at Mills, daring him to plead for his life.

Mills couldn't believe it. In a matter of seconds, his head was going to collide with the hard cement and smash into a thousand pieces, like the glass jars containing the cow pituitary. He was desperate to save himself, but what could he do? Aside from begging for mercy, which he'd rather die than do, what choice did he have?

"What choice do we have?" His father had challenged his mother, the Night of the Diagnosis, before Mills tore himself away from the keyhole, but well after he should have.

"Lydia—" his father insisted, in his famous no-nonsense, Master of the Manor tone, which meant he would brook no further discussion, "—no son of mine is going to be a—a—*dwarf*."

"Don't use that word! *Never, never* use that word! Jamais!" she howled. "He's not! He's not *that* at all! The doctors specifically said he isn't *that*. He's perfectly proportioned!" She hyperventilated, winding down to a whisper. "The doctors all said it, they all said it over and over, that he'll always be perfectly proportioned, and that's exactly the words they all used. So, you just stop, you stop saying that word, because that's not what he is or will ever be. He's not that. He's just—very—short—"

"And he'll never get any taller unless we do something." He cut in, making the decision.

"Please, Donny. I beg you! We don't know the consequences! It's never been tested on humans! It could kill him."

"Be honest with yourself for once, Lydia. Don't you think he'd rather die than live his life out as a freak?" His father said with absolutely no emotion.

Whatever else they said, Mills had no idea, because his heart was beating so loudly, he couldn't even hear himself think.

But the next day, when his father went to retrieve the potentially lethal cure, the utility freezer had been upended and everything in it had shattered into thousands of pieces, the cows' pituitaries sloshing on the floor like dead fetuses.

His mother had blamed, and subsequently fired, the cleaning staff, and it was never mentioned again. Except when the news came out later about the tainted cows' pituitaries that had been smuggled into the country by some ambitious, ruthless doctors, who had apparently administered it, at great expense, to young patients, some of whom who had grown taller and some of whom had suffered terribly and died.

For one painfully honest moment, the family had stood together in silence, each contemplating whether or not Mills would have grown taller or died. Either way, Mills' fate had been sealed that night. For reasons the doctors could not explain, he was just never going to get any taller. He would remain five-foot-four forever.

Maybe this was his punishment for thinking life was so easy. He'd never know. But one thing he did know. It didn't matter that he had been nice to everybody. All the time they were dying to be his friend, slapping him on the back and congratulating him for all his accomplishments, all his successes, they secretly couldn't wait for his downfall.

"Three!" Ellis Dunne yelled, tired of waiting.

Happy to comply, his thugs heaved Mills as high as they could, then spun him around and dropped him on his ass on the pavement. To derisive laughter. He landed with a thunk that felt like every bone in his body shattering. In fact, nothing was broken but his heart, nothing damaged but his pride.

Dunne swung around and leaned over, sticking his face in Mills' face.

"You always walked around like you owned the world. But you got cut down to size, didn't you? Didn't you, freak!" Ellis Dunne demanded.

"Freak!" The other boys echoed, lining up behind Dunne.

"Fuck you, Dunne," Mills spat back, fighting tears.

Dunne recoiled. But it was too late.

It was over. His life had become a lost cause.

As the self-appointed King of Lost Causes, Miggsy knew one when he saw one. And the ad for "*ma's Café*" certainly qualified to get to the head of the list, not merely because it was so inconsequential, but especially since it had already aroused the famous Parade of Old Failures, which, once provoked, was guaranteed to repeat on him, like all those double-cheese pepperoni pizzas he'd eaten a couple of years after the accident, when he turned his back on a lifetime of discipline, and briefly contemplated suicide by clogged-arteries. For something so infinitesimal, and, therefore, irrelevant, the ad was having an enormous effect on him. Like it or not, he was about to be pepperonied back to Pine Cliff again, to where else, but Graduation Day and the ersatz Grand Reprieve.

Like everything else external about Pine Cliff, the weather was perfect. The boys were lined up in the two front rows, backs ramrod straight, in serious navy-blue caps and gowns. Their families sat behind them on the Great Lawn, their fathers in morning suits, their mothers in creamy crepe de chine dresses and elegant spring hats.

Due to the alphabet, Mills sat on the end of the second row, behind Thiggy Cartwright, so he could see nothing without leaning into the aisle, or standing on his seat, both of which would have been unseemly. And due to yet another twisted twist of fate, the 'rents were sitting directly behind him. His mother kept tapping him on the shoulder and saying how proud they were. And, in spite of himself, it felt good. He was proud of himself.

Of course, he had never told them about the Ellis Dunne incident. Instead, he toughed it out through Eighth Form, literally burying himself in his books, begging his teachers for more and more challenges to fill up his lonely days and sleepless nights. Always on the run, never stopping, taking a load of classes over the summer, he was graduating with enough advanced placement courses to by-pass high school and go directly to college, not exactly hard to accomplish, since he had zero social life or sports life or any other kind of life to keep him away from his studies, which were his only respite from the voices in his head and the silence everywhere else. So far, it had been the greatest, or, at least, the only remotely good day of his Post-Diagnosis existence. After a year of keeping the lowest profile possible, of vanishing into the woodwork or, more precisely, his school work, becoming more a shadow than a presence, he was back in the spotlight.

Aside from a whole bunch of lesser prizes for excellence in various subjects, Mills had been genuinely surprised to receive not only the coveted Distinguished Scholar Award, given only to graduating Twelfth Formers up to that point, but also the esteemed Pine Cliff Academician Award, bestowed only upon those rare students who exceeded even the exalted expectations of the Academy.

In the end, jumping up from his seat, easily leaping over the elephantine foot Cartwright clumsily stuck out to trip him, sprinting onto the stage to collect his many trophies, coming and going in such a speedy blur that it was impossible to gauge his actual height, he'd felt the same rush, the same intense exhilaration he'd once gotten from winning the hundred-yard dash.

"And now," he heard Dean Charles say, breaking into a pleasant day dream, "it's time for the Valedictory and I'm sure some of you are saying to yourselves, 'And none too soon!'"

Grateful laughter rippled across the Great Lawn.

Mills couldn't repress a smile. He'd worked very hard on his speech, which he now saw as the icing on the cake of something he thought he'd never have again. A perfect day.

"And who else, indeed, *best* exemplifies Pine Cliff's devotion to excellence?" Dean Charles' reedy voice was rising to a shaky crescendo, at the end of which, Mills would once again take center stage.

"It is with the greatest esteem," Dean Charles trilled, "that I call upon our first Valedictorian of both the eighth and twelfth grade graduating forms, a young man who has done so uncommonly well, he has been invited to attend none other than Exeter College at Oxford University, as its youngest freshman next year!"

There was no doubt about it. He'd done it. He was out in front again, beating them all in the ultimate race. He could practically feel the 'rents swell with pride behind him. From the moment the diagnosis had come in, he thought he'd never feel this way again. He could barely believe it, but his father was proud of him!

"Mills Miggston the Third! Come up here, son!" Dean Wills intoned.

He leaped from his chair and again vaulted over Cartwright's fat foot, expecting to be propelled up to the stage and across the finish line, as it were, by the applause always afforded the Valedictorian, especially since it meant the end of the long, boring ceremony was in sight. But Dean Charles hadn't quite finished.

"Mills Miggston, the Third, Pine Cliff's own shining star, who has raised our standards to new *heights*!"

In the stunned silence that followed, someone whispered too loudly, "Did he say? Did he say?? Did he say— *heights*???" And the entire audience broke into stifled, nervous laughter, chortling behind gloved hands, sniggering beneath filmy summer hats, tittering into programs, passing the word "height" around—the *"s"* permanently amputated—in a relentlessly snide game of telephone.

Instead of applause, Mills heard derision surge through the audience. His heart, which had been racing with joy, fluttered in confusion and missed a beat. But thanks to years of practice, he kept on sprinting across the stage until he reached the podium, where he suffered the added indignity of having to climb up on a make-shift box to reach the microphone, which he still had to struggle to lower.

After an eternity, when the mic was finally in position and he was ready to begin his speech, he looked out at the two people who would not be laughing because they knew what this moment meant to him.

His mother, who could not look him in the eye, appeared to be waiting for a gentle wind to blow her away. His father's face was white and locked into a strange expression, which Mills was struggling to identify, one he couldn't quite place at first, since he'd never seen anything like it on him before and hadn't thought him capable of. The arrogance, the superiority, the hauteur, even his signature air of disdain, that Mills had always thought was bone deep, had been drained away. And then, in a horrible rush of shame, he knew. His father, Mills Donald Carter Miggston the Second, was mortified.

"You'll be happy to know that this speech is going to be even shorter than I am." Mills III heard himself say, to a feeble trickle of nervous laughter and a splattering of self-conscious applause. Then, stepping down from the box, he moved in front of the podium, forcing everyone to see exactly how short he really was.

And watching them gape at him as if he were an accident on the highway that they couldn't take their eyes off, he stared them down openly and defiantly, locking eyes with each and every one of them who had treated him so harshly and dismissively all year, finally lighting on his father, the king of the intimidating, unblinking stare, until even Mills the Second had to look away.

"Will you all please stand up?" Mills said, finally, to the now catatonic audience. And, like robots, they all complied, he leaped off the stage, his navy robes billowing around him in such a way it seemed he'd just take flight. But he didn't. Instead, he landed gracefully in front of the first row of boys, all of whom towered over him, but none of whom moved a muscle or said a word as he walked among them like a tiny general reviewing his gargantuan troops

"In the long run—" Mills whispered in a silence so stunning that he could be heard clearly from the back of the Great Lawn.

"In the long run, every single one of you will have to do what I have done every day for the last three hundred twenty-three days, seven hours, twelve minutes, and thirty-two seconds. Look yourself in the eye and ask—have I measured up?"

And then he did something he hadn't done since the diagnosis. He *walked*—slowly, deliberately and calmly—up the long aisle, past his stunned parents, and across the Great Lawn.

"Summer is over," his father, Lord of the Manor, had decreed with chilly finality, on a hot and humid Kentucky evening, in the midst of a heat wave, in the middle of the summer after graduation, when the needs of Mills and the 'rents converged in a resigned synchronicity, and it was tacitly agreed that Mills III, and by implication, they, would not have to suffer the further indignity of sending him off to college. Instead, he would matriculate at home, tutored by the finest scholars money could buy. All this had been established without a word, or more accurately by a certain absence of words, intermittently punctuated by coded phrases, tossed off with brittle nonchalance, at one of their last remaining family rituals—*the formal dinner*—where hints were dropped into vast chasms of avoidance like delicate silver spoons into soufflés.

"You think so?" Lydia Aimée Charles Vanalden Miggston said desultorily.

"It is. For the boy." Mills II jabbed his fork in his son's direction without looking at him and went back to the grilled lamb.

Mills III stifled a wince and—no questions asked—the perfect family ate in perfectly uncommunicative unison.

"Dinner with the 'rents," Mills III thought, "still life, even in motion."

The room was stifling. His father cleared his throat and a servant immediately refilled his bourbon glass. His mother leaned back in her chair and languidly reached for her great grandmother Charles's Fabergé fan.

Although the doors leading to the west veranda were wide open, the room was as stuffy as the authentically over-stuffed Louis Seize chairs on which the three Miggstons sat like dignitaries on parade floats, Mills III's ochre silk brocade cushion having recently been even more overstuffed than the others, a subtle touch of his mother's, to keep him at the appropriately adult height ratio to the gilded bordered Louis Seize table. Beneath the intricate Queen Anne's Lace cloth, Mills could see their reflections in the highly polished mahogany, mother, an ethereal silhouette in pale peach chiffon at one end of the table, father, fourteen feet away at the other end, overwhelming the room as usual with his sheer presence, the cold steel of his hooded pewter eyes daring anyone to defy him, even, or perhaps, especially, when he said nothing. And in the middle, seven feet from each of them, the prodigal runt, the disgraced dauphin, propped up on his remedial throne, suffocating under his starched Royal Oxford dress collar, wanting to disappear inside his Brooks Brothers dinner jacket, awaiting word of his future. Not that he cared.

He had to laugh at himself. Once, he'd actually believed that the 'rents' demented insistence upon his dressing for dinner every night and sitting through course after uncomfortable course of blanched vegetables and parsed sentences—trying desperately to read between the lines of their cryptic conversations—meant they were grooming him for Something Big, maybe a career in diplomacy, like just about everyone on his mother's side, which meant they saw "Great Things" in him, which meant he would one day "Make A Difference" in the world, which meant everything. But instead of heralding his bright future, this stupid, asinine ritual had become yet another bitter reminder of a life once in the palm of his hand, now out of reach.

"It wasn't supposed to turn out this way!" A tinny voice screeched, like a needle skidding over a record. And then it shrieked, "the party's over!" Just in case he missed the point.

"It most certainly is *not* over! You know very well, Donny, that summer is not officially over until the stroke of midnight at the ball." His mother offered into the silence in a breathless, girlish trill.

Although she may have sounded as unbalanced as she had become, she meant the very real twentieth annual *Miggston Farms Autumn in the Bluegrass Ball*, a gala of epic proportions, she had instituted to stake out her own territory in the first year of their marriage, as coming from the east, she wanted to announce herself with a flourish and a flair.

Planned to coincide with the autumnal equinox, the official start of fall and therefore, the end of summer, a date that surprisingly hadn't been taken, Lydia's ball, in all its Old-World opulence, had immediately become a tradition for the equestrian elite, raising millions of dollars for her signature charity, The Nature Conservancy, dedicated to making the world beautiful. It was, she often reminded Mills III, one small way of "Giving Something Back."

Giving Something Back and *Making a Difference*, those two durable, guilt-producing cliché's, along with *noblesse oblige* and the Charles family adage, which appeared in petit point on silken pillows scattered throughout the maison: "*Ce n'est pas ce qu'on nous donne, mais ce qu'on nous donne qui compte en fin de compte,*" loosely translated from the French, "It's not what we are given, but what we give the counts in the end," were canons his mother had drilled into him with the fervor of a nun teaching the rosaries.

But his father was another story. His father, as his mother had so diplomatically and quaintly couched it, "never *quite* subscribed to noblesse oblige," which meant, in real words, that Mills II genuinely loathed the idea of doing anything for other people that wasn't completely self-serving. Mother's *Autumn in the Bluegrass Ball* was a prime example. Aside from the usual prestige attached to these charity shindigs, of which the 'rents now held half a dozen, over the years his mother had amassed a long and impressive list of sponsors who, by this point, under the aegis of Mills II, had footed the bills for everything that had anything remotely to do with the ball, such as re-landscaping the south meadow and the main entrance last year, and most recently, re-upholstering the Louis Seize's, although no one would actually be allowed to sit on them. They would be on view, however, behind velvet ropes.

Mills III had decided at a young age to reject his father's path and instead follow in the great Charles tradition. The term *noblesse oblige* had, at first, of course, totally repulsed him for its arrogant pretension. But then he looked it up and discovered it meant that the wealthy and privileged, and he had considered himself both at the time, of their own volition, felt obliged to help those less fortunate than they, or as translated directly, "nobility obligates."

His father felt obligated to nobody, his immediate family included.

"Come to think of it," Mills II said casually, out of the blue, as if he'd just thought of it, "considering his *considerable* academic commitments, which start next week, I sincerely doubt the boy will have the time to come to the ball."

And there it was.

Banned from his own mother's ball.

"Yes! Hide the freak in the attic!" Something malevolent hissed. "Don't let it be seen at the ball!"

"Not going to the ball?" His mother asked, stricken, not understanding and understanding all at once.

"No." Mills II said emphatically, shutting the door on further discussion. "No one will be seeing Mills III at the ball."

Later that evening, licking his newest and already deepest wound, once again alone in his room, surrounded by the bitter triumphs of his former life, he tried to, but could not, ignore the angry whispers coming from the direction of the 'rent's wing, which was odd, as ever since the diagnosis, they never argued anymore, mainly because they barely spoke. It sounded like his mother said his name and then something about the ball. Could it be she was standing up for him, that she was somehow still proud of him, and really wanted him at her gala? Not that he would be caught dead anywhere near it. But still. What if she *wanted* him there? With reckless disregard for the lessons of the past, Mills was drawn toward his mother's sitting room, a place his father rarely ventured.

Her door was slightly ajar. He peeked in, unseen. The 'rents were crammed together, side by side, on his mother's diminutive, pink satin and mahogany

Recamier, stiffly huddled over an old photo album, which was unevenly balanced on both of their laps. As tight a fit as it was, none of their body parts were touching, which was surprising, especially given how his father had taken over the teensy, ladylike couch like manifest destiny, jamming his mother, whose couch it was, against the uncomfortable, low-sloping, hard mahogany end, so the intricate carving stabbed at her bony shoulder. His mother, a stickler for good posture, especially under duress, straightened her slight back with weak resolve. She seemed even narrower than usual, narrower even, than the angry vein throbbing in his father's brutish neck. What fatal attraction had driven them together still escaped Mills since, as it turned out, his very existence proved they should never have met.

They were staring at the album's faded red velvet cover in utter, abject silence. And then his father spoke.

"You can recite the heights of every Vanalden since the Mayflower and every Charles since Versailles. It won't change anything. No Miggston has *ever* been remotely—" The next word caught in his throat. "—*sho-ort*," he drawled finally, his bourbon smooth voice turning *short* into a two-syllable death sentence. He took a long pull on the glass he held in his hand, draining the amber liquid.

"Besides," he whispered with vicious nonchalance, "he looks exactly like you."

"How can you be so cruel? How can you be so heartless?" Lydia Aimée Charles Vanalden Miggston hissed, in the soft southern accent she'd picked up over the years, recoiling farther into her side of the tiny couch.

Finally, and forever cured of listening through keyholes, Mills didn't stay around to find out who might have passed on the despised gene that spawned him. It wasn't that he didn't yearn to find out if there were someone who may have been just like him, someone who understood his torment, even someone long gone. But *if* there were someone like him, he or she would definitely have been thrown out of or erased from the family tree. Like him. Hating the 'rents with every fiber of his being, he left them to their lineage-bashing and their mutual hell.

"Fool," he cursed, in a voice dripping with self-loathing, pointedly kicking himself when he was down, not merely for the fatal faux pas of once more leaving himself open to his father's contempt, but for the far more mortal sin of believing in his mother. And even now, even now, he was still trying to forgive her, telling himself it wasn't her fault that her heart, like the rest of her, was just too thin.

But it was too late.

He was an orphan now, with an ironic twist, so perfect that it made him reel. He was dead to them, yet sadistically left alive to suffer the humiliation of living under their roof as a constant source of embarrassment and shame.

He wanted to run from the house and keep on going. He wanted to jump on Wilde and ride into the mountains, like they always did, but this time never to return. He wanted to be free of the taint of the 'rents' rejection; he wanted to cut out his own heart, so it would stop hurting. But he didn't want to die and give them the satisfaction of burying him and being done with it once and for all.

He just wanted out.

And he could do it. He could. Take nothing with him. Cut his losses and move on. There was nothing stopping him. He owned Wilde and, thanks to grandma Beryl Springs, he was rich already, and he was smart and clever. He could do it. He could. It would be sweet to leave this mausoleum and all the dreams that were buried alive here.

He reached the foyer with one purpose: to get out and start from scratch. Denounce the 'rents. Change his name. Get his life back. He grabbed the Waterford crystal door knob. And froze. After all that motion, he could not move.

He stood there while great grandmother Charles's grandfather clock ticked away, loudly counting his options down to zero until, unable to summon the courage to walk out the door and face the world as the pathetic wretch he had become, he trudged back to his room.

The next night and every night after that, Mills III didn't come down to dinner. But the 'rents never sent for him and never said a word about it, not even once.

What had saved him then, in the fall of his fall from grace after graduation, was riding Wilde.

He lived to ride. Riding was the air he breathed, his passion, his solace. It fueled him. Since he had so little weight that there was so little of him to intrude, and because of his runner's fine-tuned reflexes, he became a part of Wilde, more than just a boy on a horse, a fierce young centaur.

When he rode Wilde, he took on Wilde's breathing, his magnificent rhythm, his absolute instinct for speed, his awesome power. They were halves of the same magic whole, so close that what *he* thought, Wilde achieved. They were soul mates, one exiled from his future because he was too small, the other because he was just too big. They rode, at first, to outride each other's sorrow. Then they rode for pure joy.

They rode whenever Mills wasn't with his tutors or studying. They rode in the early mornings, in the late afternoons, over weekends and holidays, for days at a time, into the blue-dewed hills, even when the last leaves were falling and autumn turned bitter.

The idea came to Mills in mid-October when the hills froze earlier than usual. Under his tender loving care, thanks in no small part to their mutual thirst for speed, and with a nod to genetic destiny, Wilde had grown into an immense and powerful young colt with jet propelled legs. He was hardy for a thoroughbred. But still, he was a thoroughbred. Without too much thought about it, Mills broke his own unspoken rule about having anything to do with anything that had anything to do with the family and the family business, and he and Wilde began racing around the much warmer, sheltered, five-eighths mile winter training track in the late afternoons, when no one else was around.

Compared to the hills, the track was a piece of cake and Wilde just ate it up. He ate so much of it up that Mills began to time him. And was amazed.

Mills wasn't the only one.

Wilde was running so fast that Will De Longpre, Head Trainer of Miggston Farms, caught wind of it.

Will, who prided himself on knowing everything important there was to know if it had to do with his horses, his track, or his stables, had known almost from the beginning, about young Mills III and his gargantuan, highly spirited, aptly named horse. He, too, was timing them. And he came to the conclusion that Wilde, defying all odds, was clocking in faster than all the other two-year olds. But not just this year's. And not just by a nose. And to put the fizz on the beer, the dang horse kept getting faster.

Which put Will directly on the horns of a dilemma. On the one hand, he felt sorry for the lad, who had never done one thing to deserve the hand he got dealt. But it went without saying that Will's loyalty was to Miggston Farms, his home for thirty odd years, and especially to its thoroughbreds, apples of his eye, every single one, past, present and future. And this particular thoroughbred, in spite of his shaky beginnings, and for better or worse, had all the earmarks of a champion, who would bring glory to Miggston Farms.

"If ever I saw a horse on the bit, he's the one," De Longpre revealed to Mills II, in that scratchy smoker's whisper of his, that made everyone he talked to think he was telling them a personal secret, which, in this case, he was.

Mills II leaned in out of respect for the celebrated old geezer, although he really didn't want to discuss that particular horse. The vivid, *ugly* memory of that horse and its association with his son had left a very sour taste in his mouth, which he washed away with a swig of Bourbon from his ever-present hip flask.

They were in Will's domain, on their way to the training barn. They walked awhile in silence, that special Will De Longpre silence that drove Mills II crazy.

"But there's a stumblin' block," Will continued, gruffly.

"You mean, besides the fact that I would never consent to run him," Mills II said, edgily.

"Nope," Will croaked, his two-packs-a-day-too-many voice so gravelly, Mills II, big and bulky as he was, was forced to lean down even lower to continue a conversation he didn't want to have in the first place, about a horse he never wanted to think about again, for more reasons than he cared to remember. And to make matters worse, he found himself hovering there, while Will, in his usual manner, was taking his own sweet time to make his point. He knew Will's unhurried pace worked on horses. But it drove him nuts. He wished he'd just get on with it, so he could dispose of the matter and get to his horses.

"What I mean is—" Will rasped at last, "besides the fact that it's not your consent I'm lookin' for, I'm lettin' ya know he's out-and-out the fastest colt on the farm, and every time I look at him, I see a Diamond shinin' in him."

"A *Diamond*?" This stopped Mills II in his tracks. Will was well aware the Diamond Cup was his personal Holy Grail. "*The* Diamond?" Mills II demanded.

Will nodded, but said nothing.

"No, Will, not *that* horse!" Mills II roared in total disbelief, defying the great trainer to *dare* to try to convince him otherwise, even though he had learned at his father's knee, never, *ever* to cross Will De Longpre because of the one thing about him: He was never wrong about horses.

"That horse turned on me," Mills II hissed harshly, clearly putting an end to it.

Will's tight-as-a-fist body tightened. His faded blue eyes rose slowly to meet Mills II's hooded, pewter glare, and locked in.

"Watchin' that horse run makes the hairs on the back of my neck stand up. Every time," was all he said. Then, thinking about it, added, "And ya know what that means."

Mills II certainly did. It meant everything, because it was something Will would *never* say lightly and, as a matter of fact, had never said to Mills II at all. It was, however, something Will had said to Mills I exactly twice in all their years together, about two horses, and both went on to win the Diamond, therefore entering the pantheon of the greatest horses in racing history. The hairs on the back of Will De Longpre's neck were part of Miggston family lore, and Mills II had been secretly, *impatiently,* waiting for the hairs on the back of Will De Longpre's neck to stand up for him, that is, for one of his horses. Just not that one.

Still. The Diamond

He stared hard at Will, willing him to take it back.

Will's eyes turned stony. He'd had his say.

"Well, then," Mills II said, "let's get that damned horse back where it belongs."

"There's another piece to this puzzle ya know. Ya gave that horse to the boy," Will De Longpre reminded him sternly. "That means somethin.'"

"Not when the Diamond is at stake," Mills II snapped, drawing back to his full height, putting as much distance as possible between himself and any mention of his son.

"The boy is attached to the horse." Will De Longpre persisted, giving him a last chance at redemption.

"He'll get over it." Mills II closed the discussion.

The next morning, when he went to Wilde's stall, Wilde was gone.

"He's in the training barn," a stubbled voice bristled from the shadows.

"Will." Mills said dully, recognizing the great trainer's rusty growl, knowing everything.

"Ya didn't think ya could put somethin' over on me, did ya?"

"Only hoped," Mills admitted bitterly.

"Come on," Will said, gently leading him away from the empty stall towards the hub of the family business, exactly where, Mills reminded himself, he had so recently vowed never to set foot again. And look what had happened practically the minute he'd broken his own rule! He should have known better by now. But there he was, with no apparent mind of his own, putting one foot in front of the other, following Will De Longpre, as if inexorably drawn towards the seat of his rejection, the intersection of pedigree and fortune, the rarefied world of thoroughbreds, their carefully calibrated lives, their baronial barns, their heated tracks, their ever-winding trails, their never-ending pastures, and endless rolling hills. And, in the distance, on the highest hill, the brand new, ultra-modern, state-of-the-art complex, which housed his father's pride and joy, the mighty Miggston sperm vault, where, under Mills II's scrutiny, potent thoroughbred gism cocktails—the real family jewels—were concocted.

It took no brainpower to figure out that the control his father had sought and attained over all he surveyed, starting with world-champion equine procreation, made him a sort of god, which made Mills even more of an embarrassment. The man obsessed with the perfect specimen, the colossus astride his two-ton protégés, his flawless creations, his chef-d'oeuvres, his magnum opuses, had himself, thrown a dwarf.

"He's not that, not that! Don't call him that! He's perfectly proportioned. He's just very short!" His mother's voice ricocheted in Mills' head.

"Cold comfort," a pinched voice ricocheted back.

It was a still-dark, frigid morning. They were following the meandering white picket fence into the heart of his father's domain, the heart of darkness, as far as Mills was concerned.

They walked rapidly, the lithe, slender boy following the lithe, slender man. Frosty mist rose around them and the tall grass was wet with icy dew and very slippery, although neither missed a step. Will could have driven, but didn't. Mills figured that Will had decided to walk the anger out of him, or maybe the fight, or maybe the questions. He didn't know for sure, but he did know, from watching him train horses that nothing Will De Longpre did was by accident.

Will turned onto the back road that wound the long way 'round the north pasture.

"Don't you think this will piss off the old man?" Mills challenged, when they were nearing the training barn, though he wasn't sure why. He could care less what his father thought. And he wanted nothing more than to be reunited with Wilde.

"Piss him off more if anything happened to any of his million-dollar babies, includin' a certain *Wilde* one," Will De Longpre said pointedly, meaning, Mills knew, that there were already definite plans for Wilde, which reconfirmed his worst fear that he would never get him back. And it felt like losing him all over again for the second time that morning.

When they reached their destination, Will stopped as if he knew he had a question to answer. Mills was shocked to realize that they saw eye to eye.

"What am I *really* doing here, Will?" Mills asked.

"Visitin' your horse." Will De Longpre rasped dryly. "Ain't that enough?"

It wasn't. But of course, Will knew that.

"Enough!" Miggsy begged himself, back in the present and reaching for his only available lifeline, before he drowned in the past. Holding on for dear life, he reeled in the phone, and desperate to find a way out, began to dial the only number in front of him, the number on the ad. Anything to drag himself back into the present. He had learned the hard way, that the fondest memories often brought the most pain. On the other hand, painful memories certainly had their own, exquisite sting.

He followed Will into the training barn, which was heated to the exact, perfect temperature for the finely-tuned thoroughbreds, and normally would have taken the chill off, but didn't. Instead, the warm, earthy mélange of horse and hay and manure and leather and liniment opened the floodgates he'd carefully constructed from bitterness and denial, and deluged him with picture post-card visions, light-drenched snap shots of the hours he'd spent right here, in this barn, starting when he less than a year old, and first allowed to help groom some of the biggest, proudest, fastest and most wondrous creatures he'd ever seen.

"Look at the boy! A Miggston through and through! Not a bone of fear in his body!" His father had said proudly, standing where Mills was standing now, except he was a goliath, effortlessly hoisting barely year-old Mills way up onto the majestic back of the great Miggston Farms champion, Titan, where he sat with the ramrod posture expected of a Miggston.

"Tall in the saddle. Tall for his age! He's going to be a titan, too!" His father had so confidently bragged and yet so wrongly predicted, Mills thought bitterly, hating himself for still caring, which made him even more bitter, which made him hate himself even more. After all the time he'd spent trying to keep himself on an even keel, or at least afloat, here he was, drowning in remorse again. And he was about to sink deeper, when a chorus of high-pitched, high-strung, high-spirited, highly impatient whinnies burst from the stalls, nudging him out of it. The horses were ready for their morning work-outs.

Will put his arm on Mills' shoulder and guided him around, so he could see Wilde without being seen. Mills' mouth dropped, even though he should have known what to expect.

Wilde, who had been looked after only by Mills, his solitary friend, was now being attended to by a coterie of retainers. The straw in his stall was twice as thick and looked twice as soft. His stall was twice as wide.

He was being treated like a real thoroughbred.

"It's what he deserves," Will said, reading Mills' mind.

Under this roof, Wilde would be protected every minute of every hour of every day. He would have the best care imaginable.

"It's where he belongs," Will said. "He's the fastest horse on the farm, ya know."

"The fastest?" Mills repeated.

"In years," Will confirmed to his second Miggston in that many days. And, like the father, the son knew what that meant. But Will said it anyway. "He could be one of the great ones."

Mills saw it in the crystal ball of Will's eye. Like the great ones, Wilde would be meticulously trained to reach his full potential, have a short, sensational career. Then, still in his prime, he'd be put out to stud in great splendor, where his only job would be to prodigiously produce championship semen and mate with the finest fillies in the world. And all Wilde had to do for this kingly life was gallop his heart out for somebody else.

As selfish as it was, and as ashamed of himself as that made him, Mills couldn't help wishing everything could just go back to the way it was the day before, so he could have his friend back. But, thanks to his father, he didn't have that choice now, did he?

"I'd never give the go-ahead without your say-so," Will whispered in his ear, as if he never stopped reading Mills' mind. "It's up to you, ya know, lad," he said, laying it at Mills' feet.

Mills' breath caught in his throat. He couldn't believe it. He *could* turn the clock back. He *could* have Wilde back! His heart soared. But just for a beat. Because, really, there was no choice to make. From the very beginning, now that he thought of it, Wilde was destined for this.

The first time Mills had laid eyes on Wilde, he certainly didn't look like he had a prayer of qualifying to be in a race, let alone, a ghost of a chance of winning one. He was a top-heavy yearling, indignantly rearing on long, spindly legs that looked like they could barely hold up his already massive body and huge head. But they did.

Mills' father was taking him on a very special version of their frequent royal tours through his domain, because this time, for his fourteenth birthday, he would get to pick his very own thoroughbred from among the ones that had no championship or breeding potential, of course. But that didn't mean that they wouldn't be sleek and powerful and fast. Because they would be. And by the end of the afternoon, one of them would be his.

They'd come to the last and, as far as Mills II was concerned, the least of the lot. He was explaining in great detail exactly why this huge one, thanks to his numerous and painfully obvious conformation faults, would forever be lacking. The yearling, Mills II concluded, his voice dripping with that special disdain he held for the defective, wasn't worthy of his pedigree or his name; was, in fact, a mockery of everything Miggston Farms stood for, and should be rejected out of hand. And that was when Wilde, whose name at the time was Titan's Glorious Revenge, reared up on those gangly, ridiculous, Bambi legs, fixed his huge, guileless eyes on Mills II and bellowed against the outrage of being passed over, robbed of his birthright and deprived of his chance to be what he was bred to be, what he was born to be, what he apparently believed he was meant to be.

At least that's how it had appeared to father and son. The look of shock and revulsion that had crossed his father's face said it all. Mills was well aware that neither man nor beast had ever defied his father that way and gotten away with it. Needless to say, the sheer guts this had taken, even from a horse, endeared the horse to Mills, who feared for the poor creature.

"Take him away!" Mills II ordered the groom.

"No!" Mills III heard himself shouting. "He's the one I want! He's the one I want."

"He's crazy. He's ugly. And he's dangerous." Mills II bellowed.

"Please, dad, only to himself. Look, you just hurt his feelings," Mills pleaded, while walking toward the horse and carefully putting out his hand, which the horse nuzzled gently, as if they'd rehearsed it.

"Listen to me," his father said after awhile, his voice so tight, the drawl was drained out of it. "If you want him, you can have him. But you are not getting another thoroughbred, young man. You cannot trade him in when he doesn't work out and you tire of him. It's time you learned that actions have consequences." And that was that.

Mills never really understood why his father had acquiesced. But he had. He wasn't even certain at the time why he had begged his father for that particular horse, when all the others were much more athletic and graceful and certainly would be faster. But he had. And for that matter, he had absolutely no idea why the yearling had been so sure of himself, so obviously insulted to be deprived of his chance to compete. But he had been.

And now, miraculously, Wilde had a second chance, and the only thing standing in his way this time was Mills.

"I—I would never stand in his way," Mills said hoarsely, choking back tears, receding into the shadows, but not before Will saw the torment on his stricken face.

He wanted to run away before he fell apart. But Will grabbed his arm.

"Stick around," he whispered. "Stick around."

The grooms were just about ready to saddle Wilde, who was on the verge of getting worked-up, Mills could see, because a slight shiver was rippling through the fine, silky, auburn hairs up and down his long, lustrous mane. They were doing it all wrong. Well, they were doing it fine for the other thoroughbreds, who grew up with this, and so technically there was nothing really wrong with how they were doing it, nothing, really, at all. Granted, it was the very best treatment any horse on earth could wish to have. And in all fairness, Mills had to admit that as they got to know Wilde better, they'd tailor everything just for him. But still, it just wasn't what Wilde was used to. Not his ritual of prancing unencumbered before Mills saddled him and they rode off to nowhere in particular as long as they got there fast. Another shiver. No, Wilde was not comfortable. But he sensed the groomers meant him no harm. So, he stood for it.

Mills wanted to tell Will all about what Wilde needed to feel comfortable and secure. He wanted to explain to him how Wilde should be saddled and ridden—never, ever, ever with a whip, no matter what, of course—and then how he should be cooled down and cared for at night. He wanted to give Will his own private recipe for pulpy apples and ask him to pipe in a little Mozart, so Wilde wouldn't get lonely at night. But that would probably be overstepping the line with Will De Longpre in a way that no Miggston, not even his father, would dare. Even slipping Wilde's favorite blanket in his stall was out of the question. Like everything else, it might bring back too many needless memories. Mills was, plainly and simply, less than useless here, and more than anything he wanted to bolt.

But what if Wilde needed him? He had to stay. Just in case.

Then Hap Tate appeared out of nowhere to ride Wilde. This was good. Hap was a pro, but gentle. Mills stole a glance at Will, who coincidentally happened to squint his way just in time to see Mills' nod of approval.

But it didn't matter. The very second that Hap approached Wilde, Wilde went wild. Tossing his huge, proud head back and forth, ears flattened, obsidian eyes flashing, he reared up on his mighty hind legs, snorting balefully. Great gusts of air smoked from his enormous nostrils and he let out a roar that shook the foundations of the building and rang through the rafters, letting it be known, beyond a shadow of a doubt, that neither Hap Tate, nor anyone else Will De Longpre had up his sleeve, would be riding him today or any time soon.

That glorious, gargantuan, chestnut beauty of a beast knew what he was turning down by pulling that antic. It was in his blood. Of this, Will was sure. But no matter what he had to give up, Wilde wanted only one thing. To be reunited with his one, true friend. And, lo and behold, that is exactly what his friend wanted too.

Well. Who was Will De Longpre, or anyone with a lick of horse sense, for that matter, to stand in the way of fate?

"Ya look like a lad with some time on your hands," he said.

"Looks like," Mills mumbled morosely.

"Looks like I need a new exercise rider and I have a hunch you have exactly the right amount of time on your hands to be my man." Wills scratched out in his sandpaper voice.

"What?" Mills looked up, not daring to comprehend.

"What are ya waitin' for, lad? Time is money." Will semi-scolded, pointing at the highly agitated Wilde, in case Mills still couldn't wrap his mind around the idea.

But then, Mills did. To be Wilde's exercise rider meant he'd be with Wilde every single day, together, just like before. Of course, a voice in the back of his mind reminded, eventually Will would pick a real jockey to ride him in all his races. But Mills couldn't think about that now, because now all he could think about was being with his horse.

He raced towards Wilde, whose fierce, furious roar instantly turned into a whinny of such absolute elation, it was nothing short of triumphant.

Later on, and for years to come, everyone present at this reunion swore in the retelling of it that the instant that boy landed on that horse, the first rays of morning sun burst through the skylight and lit them up like they were caught in the cross-hairs of destiny. It was as if they'd rehearsed it.

"Who's the new boy?" Hap Tate asked Will, tipping his cap in the kid's direction.

"Ah, that's young Miggs—" Will started.

"Migg-**SY**!!" Mills impulsively shouted down from his horse. "Please, call me Miggsy," he grinned at Hap, giving himself something he never had before—a nickname and a new start. He wanted no special privileges, not that Will would grant him any. If anything, he and Wilde would have to work harder than everyone else. And they couldn't wait.

Although Mills had been riding, practically since birth, everything was new. They were at least a year behind, with no training under their belts, beginning with the basics. They had never been confined to a real schedule before, or raced against other horses, or tasted the chaos and commotion of the training track. They'd never broken from the claustrophobic starting gate, or tried to do the thousands of other unfamiliar things the other colts and exercise jockeys had been doing, over, and over, and over again, until it was all second nature to them.

And before any of that could happen, Mills had to learn what every exercise boy already knew—how to ride like a jockey which meant no longer sitting in the saddle, but being perched precariously over it, as if permanently crouched for a long jump, all his weight, all one hundred pounds, on his toes. The only parts of his body in contact with Wilde now were the inside of his feet and ankles. But even this slim connection, this slight nexus, was enough. Their neural connection became even stronger. From the start, riding in this strange position, which challenged all his reflexes, thrilled Mills, and before long, they were galloping just like it was second nature, just like Will had suspected they would, because, like Wilde, Mills was a natural.

And just as Mills had known he would be, Will, for his part, was much more than a brilliant trainer. He spoke a language that was to-the-bone true, sometimes without even saying a word. He had a bottomless well of patience, and something else, an intuitive, almost uncanny understanding of the boy and his horse and their silent connection to each other.

Everything came easy again. For the first time since the diagnosis, Mills couldn't wait to get up each morning, which was a good thing, since he had to be at the training track by five-thirty AM, six days a week, limbered and ready to ride. To fill up the afternoons when he wasn't with Wilde and Will, or practicing on his own, he immersed himself in his studies, which he kept up because it never occurred to him to stop, and because he secretly relished the furious debates he always got into with his exacting tutors, whom his father seemed to have picked based upon two qualifications: their great intellect and their permanent looks of disdain. Preparing for these Socratic onslaughts, while balancing his frantic new schedule, was more than a mere challenge. It kept his mind focused and alert, which in turn helped prepare him for training sessions with Will and Wilde. In his few free moments, he read everything he could get his hands on about horses and racing. By design, every corner of his day was filled. He hit the pillow each night gratefully exhausted and too tired to dream.

Three months breezed by.

"Let's take a walk," Will said, leading Mills away from the barn.

Mills thought of their first walk, the morning he lost Wilde, and felt the same dread.

"Ya know what we gotta talk about," Will said.

Mills nodded solemnly.

"It's time to pick Wilde's rider," the trainer confirmed.

Mills had been both fearing and preparing for this day. So, when Will oh-so-casually asked him to come the barn before morning work-out, he knew why. And he was ready with the names and records of those few jockeys, that less-than-a-handful of riders deft enough to ride a horse, who had up to now, gotten his directions solely through what Mills could only think of as neural transmission.

"I've, uh, taken the liberty of—only if you don't mind of course," Mills stammered.

Will threw Mills a look that meant, "Go on, but watch your step."

Mills went on, "What I mean is, I made a list of the jockeys who Wilde might be, you know, okay with."

"A list?" Will raised a grizzled eye-brow in a hint of a gesture that spoke volumes, starting with "don't waste my time."

Mills' mouth went dry, but he kept talking. "Nothing much, really. Just their stats plus an evaluation of their tactics and the pros and cons of how they'd be with Wilde, personality-wise and all." Mills felt tongue tied and parched and sweaty and pushy. But he gamely passed his three-page analysis to the great man anyway.

Will took the pristine document from Mills' clammy hands and skimmed it as they ambled down the path around the training barns in the pre-dawn light.

"Sal Fiore, Jimmy Lee Helms, Evan Garnet, Juan Rodriguez, and Lane Hamilton. All good choices. Ya did your homework, lad. But there's a name ya left out. And it's the only name on *my* list."

"Really?" Mills was stunned. He'd studied all the top stakes-winning jockeys in America, England and Europe to come up with these four names. He wracked his brain and then his stomach turned. "Will, if you mean Sam, *the Spin,* Spinosa, I thought of him, cause he's the lightest and I know he's won more races than almost anyone, but Will, he's too angry all the time. And I just don't think that Wilde—" he pleaded, afraid to over-step his bounds any further and afraid not to.

"I thought ya knew me better than that, lad," Will interrupted. "No there's only one rider for this horse, and it sure ain't Sam. Hang on a sec. I'll give ya my list."

Will jumped the low fence in front of the supply barn, pulled a tag from one of the gigantic feed bags piled on one of Miggston Farm's bat-talion of pick-ups, whipped a stubby pen from behind his ear, scribbled something on the back of the tag, and jumped the fence again.

"Here's my list." He handed the feed-bag tag to Mills.

Mills took the tag with trembling hands. The person whose name was on it would not only, at the very least, share Wilde's attention and affection with Mills, but would bond with Wilde in a way Mills never could.

"Havin' trouble readin' my writin' lad?" Will prodded. "Need some help?"

"No, thank you. I can read it. It says—" He cleared his throat and looked down. "It says— *Miggsy.*" Very funny Will, very funny. But you can't be serious."

"Funny, cause I am." Will said, not a drip of humor in his rasp.

Mills couldn't believe it. Will was offering him the chance of a lifetime. The chance to be a team and go for the Diamond and everything else to-gether. It was more than he had dared dream of. He stifled an impulse to hug Will with all his might. But he couldn't get over it. Will's trust in him was the most profound gift he'd ever gotten. It was what he had yearned for from his father, but would never get, because, unlike Will, his father saw him as he *really* was—the family abomination—an object of revulsion and derision, to be locked away from view.

"He would never let me—"

"If he wants a chance at the Diamond, he will, now, won't he?" Will winked at Mills.

"No. As a matter of fact, he won't," a pinched voice migrained in Mills' head, taunting, mocking, cruel. But correct. His father's unmitigated dread of humiliation would ultimately eclipse even his obsessive desire to achieve his life's dream. Mills would never get the golden opportunity Will was offering. His father would slap him in the face yet again. Ironically, this particular slap in the face would sting his father just as much as it would sting him. But that was no consolation because it changed nothing.

"It's a losing battle." Mills said, more to himself than to Will, hoping he didn't sound as defeated as he felt.

"Sorry to disappoint ya lad, but it ain't a battle at all. Ya see, I meant what I said just now. You are the only jockey I will train on this horse. There is no second choice. It's you or nobody."

"But that's not fair to Wilde!" Mills blurted out. "Will, it's not even like you not to give a horse every chance, especially after everything you said about his potential—"

Will turned to face Mills, focusing in on him patiently, until he had the boy's full attention.

"Don't ya see, lad? Even if he lets somebody else ride him, which he won't, he won't win without you. His heart won't be in it."

Will watched as understanding washed over Mills and something about him changed.

"Then it's up to me," Mills said finally, beginning to fathom the enormity of what Will had just told him. "I owe it to Wilde to do everything I can to get to that finish line together."

"That's how I see it," Will agreed. "But, it's a big responsibility. If ya got any doubts, lad, maybe ya better sleep on it." He turned to go.

"No! I don't have to sleep on it! Listen Will—" Mills called to him with the fevered urgency of someone abruptly but not thoroughly awakened from a nightmare. "Will, listen. I'll talk to my father. I don't care anymore what leftover piece of my soul he tries to extract this time. This is something I have to do. I will strike any bargain, make any deal. No matter what it takes, I will not let my horse down!"

"I know, lad," Will whispered, patting Mills on the back in an unusual display of emotion. "I'm countin' on it."

Mills sprinted up the hill and burst into his father's office fueled with purpose.

Mills II, bourbon glass in hand, was standing at—and dominating—the enormous, panoramic window, watching his magnificent horses on the pasture below. It did not surprise Mills that his father was so perfectly framed by the blue-grass horizon he overwhelmed, he might as well have been his own self-portrait.

"Father." The word felt unfamiliar. He hadn't said it in months and now he couldn't remember if it had ever felt right.

Mills II turned from his horses, looked down at his son. And frowned.

And Mills was face to face with his nemesis, the Grand Arbiter of Breeding, who had judged him not only wanting, but worthless. But the personification of evil in Mills' worst nightmares seemed, in the light of day, to be fraying more around the edges than in his dark visions. Something had changed in the last several months. The fine lines the sun had etched on his father's face over the years had deepened into crevasses that didn't sag like flesh, but bowed, like the heavy stone steps at Pine Cliff. His eyes were more bloodshot. He looked more tired than Mills remembered, more human.

"Mills," Mills II said dryly, glancing back at his horses, who never disappointed him, unlike his son, who had gotten older without getting taller. Although the boy had changed. His voice was deeper and he wasn't so delicate anymore, like her. Time had carved a handsome face out of the boyish softness, covered it with the beginnings of a beard. He was becoming a man, but he'd never be taller than a boy.

"Mills," he said again, maintaining a rigid nonchalance, "what can I do for you?"

Loaded question, Mills thought. So many answers. Which one to choose? You can accept me for who I am. Or, short of that, you can let me have what I want. Or, more to the point, let me ride my own horse all the way to victory in the Gem Cups and give you what you've always wanted.

"Will is convinced Wilde can make a Gem Cup Sweep and win the Diamond, and he's also convinced I'm the only one who can ride him. He really wants me to do it and that's what I want, too, to be Wilde's jockey and go for the Diamond," were the words that tumbled out first. Then, to reassure his father he understood the enormity of the undertaking, he added, "I know it's important to you who rides your horses and I—"

"That horse has been a pain in my behind since the day he turned on me," Mills II snorted. "I don't give a damn who the hell rides him. I wouldn't care if it was Will De Longpre's long lost nephew, or the gardener's brother, if he could do the job."

"But that's exactly what I'm saying," Mills interrupted. "I can do the job!"

His father's cold, hooded eyes took him in.

"You are a Miggston. Miggston men are men of standing, men of stature. Miggston men do not become jockeys. They hire them!"

"But that's just it. Will won't hire another jockey for Wilde," Mills argued.

"Then I will hire another jockey for that horse before things get even more out of hand. And you will go back to your studies where you belong."

"But—I can do both. I have been doing both! I belong with my horse!" Mills protested.

"You belong where I say you belong, boy," Mills II ordered. "And that is nowhere near that horse."

"What?" Mills stammered, while the voices in his head demanded to know how things had slid so far so fast and all he could do was keep repeating, "I don't understand. I don't understand."

"Let me make myself clear." Mills II strode across the huge room so brusquely that his steel-tipped boots set off sparks on the Aubusson rug. "Our name is our pedigree, Mills. No matter what delusion you and Will De Longpre are living under, you will not ride that horse in any of its races. I will not let you drag the Miggston name through the mud with you."

"Father, please—" Mills fought back, but it was like flailing in quicksand. "Listen—I—"

"No. You listen. I am putting an end to this right now. You will stay away from the stables," Mills II whispered through clenched teeth, advancing on Mills. "That horse is crazy enough without you making him any crazier."

"He is not crazy. Except when you're around!" Mills exploded. "You make him crazy. Like you make everyone else!"

Mills II stopped abruptly and pointed an accusing, wrath-of-God finger at his son, thundering, "You will never ride that horse again!

"Yes, I will!" The words erupted from the depths of Mills' being.

"What?" Mills II snapped, looming over Mills, everything about him demanding a recant.

"I said I will, too, ride Wilde, whether you like it or not. Because you don't own Wilde, I do. And I have the papers to prove it. So, it's up to me if I ride that horse. Not you."

"You!" Mills II laughed mirthlessly. "You, young man, are not old enough—and I think this outburst proves conclusively—you are certainly not wise enough—to make that or any other adult decision."

"I'm old enough to be an apprentice jockey and I'm smart enough to know I meet the requirements and, in case you forgot, thanks to grandma Beryl, I'm rich enough, so I don't need your money; and if you try to stop me from riding my horse for Miggston Farms, I'll take him to another farm and win for them and in the end, you will be deprived of the Diamond by your own son, the one you secretly want to hide away from sight. And the whole world will know it."

He'd said it. The truth. It was out there.

Mills II frowned, took a long pull on his drink, but said nothing. So, Mills kept talking, as if he'd worked it all out before, when actually he hadn't even put any of it together, until he heard himself saying it. It was as if something inside was guiding him, his inner tutors reminding him to line up his arguments, to think of everything. He thought of Will. And Wilde.

"The thing is," he heard himself say, "I don't want to put Will in an uncomfortable position. I'd hate to ask him to choose between us."

Something in him stopped for a breath, deliberately pausing to allow it to sink into his father's Bourbon-tinged brain, the humiliating possibility that the legendary Will De Longpre, who didn't much respect him to begin with, just might jump ship with his defective son. Or at least try to, causing a frenzy of publicity guaranteed to expose everything he wanted kept hidden.

When his frown deepened, Mills went on. "And this is Wilde's home after all. I really don't want to unsettle him. So, I'll make you a deal. I'll ride for Miggston Farms but I won't embarrass you ... and mother. I'll do it ... I'll do it ... incognito.... under a—a different name. I'll—I'll become somebody else. No one will know that one of the great and mighty Miggston men has fallen so far from genetic grace. In return, starting right now, you have no jurisdiction over me—or my horse—anymore."

Mills II looked at his son in such utter disbelief that in that thin shard of a moment, even though every demeaning word his father had just said to him was still ringing in his ears, and in spite of everything he'd just said to his father, which he could never take back, Mills still couldn't shake off the almost imperceptible, completely unwarranted, but unmistakable shiver of hope that his father, reluctantly impressed Mills had finally stood up to him, would, in new found respect, open his arms, embrace him and ask him to ride Wilde under his real name.

But of course, that did not happen.

Because in that same moment, Mills Donald Miggston the Second, caught a glimpse of something in the defiant shrug of Mills' broadening shoulders, the recalcitrant set of his newly defined jaw, that was undeniably, unmistakably Miggston, and he felt the chill of despair turning his blood to ice in the same way everything about the boy had from the moment the diagnosis had ruined their lives. He'd gone over it a million times and still couldn't figure it out. He could blame everyone else all day long, but in the one race that really counted, he had come up short. And there was nothing he could do about it.

"Don't expect special treatment. And don't barge in on me again," he said, draining his glass.

He was frozen to the bone. He couldn't bear to look at his own son. There wasn't enough bourbon in Kentucky to warm him up.

Mills' insides were spasming, but he'd done it! He was officially Wilde's rider. As of now, he had no name and no address. But he was Wilde's rider. Nothing else mattered.

Nothing.

He would not allow himself to plummet from the great heights of having his dream come true into the depths of the pity pit. He would not think of his father, who couldn't stand to look at him. He would look ahead. He had one task now, which he considered a sacred mission, and anything that dragged his attention away would be a betrayal of Wilde and Will and himself.

Sprinting across the pasture on his way back to the barns, impatient to get going, Mills went over possible new names. But none felt right, like "Miggsy" had from the start.

He had to admit it. He really liked being "Miggsy." He suspected that the close coterie of workers who were there the morning he was reunited with Wilde, had guessed who he really was. But Will had never let on. And nobody pried. It was as if they all had tacitly agreed that it was up to the new boy to say who he was, because the only thing that counted from then on, was what he did on that horse. And he must have been doing pretty well, because wherever he went around the farm, people stopped and smiled and said, "Hi Miggsy!" It felt good.

He had Will to thank for that. And for everything. Again, Mills realized, Will was looking out for him like the 'rents never had, even before, before things fell apart. Because of Will, everything he really wanted was within reach again. Even better. He already had what he wanted. An odd thought struck him. And it rang true. Will had done for him what Will did for his horses. Looked deep into him with absolute faith and complete trust and mended him.

Mills knew what he would do. With a hostile nod to his father, Mills would thank Will by riding *his* name to glory. From then on, Mills would be known as Jimmy, or Johnny, or maybe Bobby, or better still, Mickey De Longpre, Will's long-lost nephew. If it was alright with Will, of course.

It was. And Mills Miggston the Third, became Michael, "Mickey," De Longpre, "Miggsy" to his friends. The name had stuck.

At the exact time it was announced that Mills Miggston the Third was embarking upon a gap year of indeterminate length to travel and study in the Near and Far East, Miggsy De Longpre and his very few possessions, mainly books and papers, moved into the guest cottage on his "uncle" Will's property, which became his permanent address when he received his official apprentice jockey credentials.

But he spent a lot of nights in the barn with Wilde, sharing warm, pulpy apples and listening to Mozart.

Their lives revolved around the track, in every meaning of the word. Everything else was superfluous. Except wardrobe. They both needed racing gear, which meant Miggsy being fitted for his silks, a big day for any jockey, especially sweet for Mills, who had looked forward to it as a rite of passage, a true milestone. And it was made even sweeter when the tailor taking his measurements pointed out, through a mouth filled with straight pins, in the trace of a Hungarian accent that had lovingly lingered on through thirty-five years in America, how perfectly proportioned Miggsy was, how handsome he would look in his silks, what a fine jockey he would make. Mills smiled. Miggsy smiled back.

But when he tried on the jacket with the same vibrant blue *MF* appliquéd in a blaze of silver lightning on the sleeves that was emblazoned on pennants and tee shirts and banners, which had hung in every one of his rooms at Pine Crest, what he saw in the mirror, just under his smile—the pentimento of a scowl so prevalent among Miggston males that it was known in the family simply as *the Sneer*—threw him. And what he heard, instead of his own slender measurements repeated in the tailor's slight accent, was his father's bourbon drenched drawl, whispering contemptuously, "Miggston men do not become jockeys. We hire them."

To steady himself, he concentrated on the fitting. He stared at the mirror while the tailor meticulously, painstakingly, continued to take his measurements. He stared at it, not letting on that he knew, before the tailor asked, what was required of him, having had, until recently, all of his suits custom-made. He stared at it, fluidly accommodating the tailor, his calm, composed reflection belying his churning stomach. He stared at it while the tailor unfurled the resplendent Miggston silks and he felt himself resonating with the vibrant silver and vivid blue—the same blue as his eyes, which had been Miggston Farm colors for generations—the blue in his eyes and the blood flowing through his veins forcing him to remember that no matter what his name was, deep, deep, down, he was a Miggston. He stared at the mirror, and his father and grandfather and all the Mighty Miggston Men before them glared back at him, their glacial eyes staring him down, tearing him down, demanding something he could not find in himself to give them.

"Loyalty!" they demanded.

"Fealty!" they pressed.

"Quit!" they decreed, closing in on him. "Quit."

And still he held his ground. And still he stared at the mirror, until all he could see in it—all he would allow himself to see—was Miggsy, Will De Longpre's nephew, Wilde's rider. And that made him smile.

Befitting their twin destinies, Wilde was fitted too, that week, with a saddle so small, it was nicknamed "the postage stamp," and shoes so light, they weighed mere ounces. Trying them on for the first time, he leaped, pranced, reared, nickered and nuzzled Mills with such exuberance and all-out joy, that Mills shamelessly begged Will to just let them go crazy, just this once. Later, of course, they'd have to put the lead imposts into Wilde's saddle cloth pockets to meet the weight requirements, and they'd have to come down to earth, but just this once, he argued, they needed to soar.

Since any fool could tell it would be useless to say no, Will gave in. And they took off before he could change his mind.

Will watched the entity that was the boy and his horse blaze around the track in ground-eating, twenty-foot strides, like it was just a romp around the park. And, knowing they'd be doing it again, reached for his stopwatch.

Of course, they all knew that any records they might have shattered on that particular afternoon, when they were lighter than air and blowing off steam, were beside the point. The point was, despite the work-out, Wilde was barely blowing hard, which meant he had a lot left, which meant there was a good chance—and Mills had the statistics to back this up—that no other horse was faster. Or smarter. Mills had barely even used the reins, not only because of their bond, but because Wilde always knew exactly what he was doing. The way Mills saw it, barring unforeseen circumstances, only one thing could stand in his friend's way, and that was Miggsy's inexperience. So, from here on out, he had to prepare for every possible circumstance. He had to become a jockey worthy of his horse.

With a reluctant nod to study habits and personal codes hammered into him at Pine Crest, and a begrudging salute to his unforgiving tutors for drilling it into him to be thorough to the point of obsession, he began analyzing the competition, the jockeys and horses they'd be riding against, dissecting their races, breaking down their every move, crawling inside their minds, gaining more and more respect for them every day. It was daunting to realize that sooner or later, he would be facing every one of them. Some sooner. A lot sooner. At Camden Greens.

Normally, Will would have orchestrated a steady rise to the level of The Charter Stakes at the Greens, but they had started out so late that their window of opportunity to qualify for the grueling Gem Cup circuit was closing fast. So, ready or not, their first race would be against a stiff field of sixteen proven three-year olds, most of them record holders, all piloted by world class riders.

They arrived at the Greens one week before their maiden race. It was Wilde's first time away from Miggston Farms. To relax him and his young rider, Will had him in the paddock well before dawn, saddled for an early morning breeze.

It was barely light out and eerily quiet at the track. Mills felt a serenity he had never known before. Perched atop Wilde, who was galloping at a brisk, yet leisurely pace, ears pricked forward in pure enjoyment, Mills envisioned the endless rows in the now empty grandstand alive with screaming people, the track thrumming with horses, and his pulse raced. Without warning, reacting to no more than the hair-trigger of a pulse-beat quickened by a day dream, Wilde's ears pricked back and he blasted down the backstretch, almost toppling Mills.

Immediately regaining his balance, Mills put his mind back in the moment, and they swept around the far turn, cruising to the wire smoothly and easily. They were ready.

That first night away from home, Mills set himself up in the stall with Wilde, whipped up some warm, pulpy apples on a hot plate, turned on a Mozart violin concerto real low, and wasn't at all surprised when Will dropped by to see if they were settled in all right.

They spent the next six days with every nerve-ending alive, scrutinizing the competition, learning every inch of the track, until they could have ridden it blindfolded.

"Well," Will said, the night before their first race, calling it a day, after reviewing their strategy for the zillionth time, "I've been sayin' that you two can do it. And ya can."

To which he added, "Nobody's faster and the good Lord knows, nobody's smarter," the next morning at the paddock.

"And nobody's got more heart than the two of ya," right before post parade.

Rasping, "Trust your instincts!" at post-time, so it repeated in their ears under the screams from the infield.

After all the hours of preparation, their first race was a frenzy of sensations—the frisson of the Miggston silks against Mills' skin, the overwhelming swell of pride high astride Wilde, the dizzy cacophony of color in the preternaturally slow post-parade, the mind-blowing, ear-splitting clang of the bell, the feeling of Wilde's muscles tensing under him, the surge of adrenalin pulsing between them, the flash of panic, bursting from the gate smack into a roiling, teeming crush of raging, thundering, two-ton beasts in a headlong bolt for the same tiny speck of light, then the patterns emerging, angles forming shapes Wilde could slip through into the open, Wilde, instantly seeing exactly what Mills saw, sluicing right through the pack into the light, while, crouched so low, his entire body was draped over Wilde's taut, muscular neck, eyes at Wilde's eye level, pulse beating in synch with pulse, heart pounding in rhythm with heart, Mills looked out into the distance, seeing everything from Wilde's eyes. Vibrant swirls zoomed past them from around corners Mills had not seen before, while over and over and over, hind legs, springing from powerful haunches, thrust them forward, front legs pulled them up, up, through thin air, breathless, timeless, boundless and inexhaustible—breaking the track record without breaking a sweat.

They won by six lengths.

And they kept on winning. They didn't lose. Even though, under strict instructions from Will, they were careful never to win by too much again, mindful never to overwork Wilde, thus not revealing the true extent of his power, they still blistered the field. In one race after another, on their road to the Gem Cups, the jet-propelled horse and the apprentice jockey, who had so much faith in him he refused to carry a whip, streaked from wire to wire like something no one had ever quite seen anything like before.

They were written about and talked about and sought after. Suddenly, Miggsy was invited to the same galas from which the 'rents had banished Mills. Ironically, now that he was asked everywhere, he went nowhere. Though he'd longed to be invited, included, accepted before, he now chose self-imposed exile. He declined each and every invitation, politely of course, explaining that he was in training, because he was. But really, he just wanted to be with Will and Wilde, where he felt comfortable and safe and didn't have to worry about making a mistake and letting on who he really was, whoever that was. Which begged the question on everyone's mind: Who was he?

Caught somewhere between the privileged, overeducated Mills, whose vocabulary sent the best of them running for their Oxford English Dictionaries, and the undereducated Miggsy, boy of few words, most of them monosyllabic and to his horse, encouraged by Will every step of the way, he was being honed by every turn around the track into someone else. But who? If he didn't know, how could anyone else? Especially since he gave out so few clues. Even to himself.

Not that that stopped anyone. Of course, human nature being what it is, the less Miggsy said about himself, the more everybody else did. Rumors abounded about the kid with the chiseled face, who rode his horse as if they were part of each other.

Rumor had it that Will's gifted and shy nephew came from so far back in the back woods that he didn't even have a birth certificate, let alone a sixth-grade education, and that he declined invitations and avoided parties to side-step embarrassment, and that he called himself "Miggsy" in a salute the Miggston family for taking a chance on him. Rumor also had it that Will's nephew was really his illegitimate son from an uncharacteristic one-night-stand, the who, where, and when of which set off another chain reaction of rumors. And that was why Miggsy avoided parties.

But there was one special "party" that Miggsy couldn't avoid—the Winner's Circle, where Mills' and Wilde's alter egos, Miggsy De Longpre and Titan's Revenge, would be photographed with Miggston Farms trainer Will De Longpre and Miggston Farms owners, Lydia Aimeé Charles Vanalden Miggston and Mills Donald Carter Miggston the Second. It was the only eventuality Mills had not prepared himself for and Will hadn't brought up.

Mercifully, everything leading up to the first Winner's Circle photograph was lost in the blur of the first race, although there were moments of vivid pain, like seeing the 'rents for the first time. His mother, or rather the tinge of her, was, as always, an essence in chiffon, her face hidden under an extravagant straw hat. He couldn't tell if she was looking back at him through the wide brim that dipped artfully over her eyes, but he was positive the brim acted like a one-way mirror, so she could see out, but no one could see in; no one could see her face. The only parts of her showing were her peach blush lips, which were arranged in a winning but not arrogant, joyful, but not boastful, smile. She appeared to be leaning casually, lovingly against the crumbling granite mountain that was his father. But, like the smile and the hat, it was all facade, orchestrated for cameras that were capturing them as they descended from their box.

In the flush of victory, basking in the tumultuous applause celebrating the amazing upset by the two unknowns, rider and horse, Mills hadn't been paying too much attention to where they were going, until he looked around and saw that Will, who couldn't seem to suppress a shit-eating grin, had led them to the Winner's Circle, where they were about to converge upon the 'rents for the official photo.

But as they neared the 'rents, before dread could corrupt joy, something strange happened. His father got smaller, diminished by the gargantuan and extremely proud horse upon whom Mills sat beaming, his back ramrod straight, in the posture expected of a Miggston, feeling ten feet tall for good reason. He and Wilde had always been one being. Now, he claimed that height. They had come through together! Just as he'd dreamed they would! Absolutely triumphant, he jumped for joy!

In the official picture, Miggsy was leaping exultantly out of Wilde's irons and the 'rents were looking *up* at him, smiling their big Winner's Circle smiles. He'd seen those exact same poses and smiles in hundreds of pictures growing up. And what had always struck him was the way the 'rents' eyes gleamed the same vivid blue as the Miggston silks, even though, except in bright sunlight, his father's eyes, hooded as they were by his fleshy lids, had become more of a dull pewter, and in person, his mother's eyes were more of a pale green.

But unlike the other Winner's Circle pictures, this one—with his father's eyes concealed by newly acquired wrap-around, mirrored sunglasses, his mother's eyes veiled by her over-protective hat, his own eyes camouflaged by mud-splattered goggles, his true identity obscured by a different name—this one was a family portrait.

When the pictures had been taken, Mills II raised his flask in what could have been a congratulatory salute, or a coincidence. It was impossible to tell, because all Mills could see when he glanced back in spite of himself, was the reflection of the silver flask in his father's sunglasses, as he took another swig.

Shortly after the Greens, they entered the exhausting, qualifying circuit, which was the punishing run-up to the four Gem Cups. For Miggsy, although it was grueling and it felt like they'd been on the road forever, it all went by too quickly, in a blur of mud and speed. It had been nine arduous and exhilarating months of running against the greatest of the great, facing every challenge, never letting up, never letting down, making sure to pace Wilde to keep him fresh, never again releasing all of his power, just enough to break every record, including his astounding Sapphire, Emerald, and Ruby Cup wins. And now, as if in a mere heartbeat, the Diamond Cup and history awaited them, practically in his own back yard.

He'd come back "home" to Will's guest house to pick up a change of clothes, while Will took care of a few things up in the main house. He grabbed a fresh pair of jeans and his lucky tee shirt and was on his way out, to go up there and pay homage to Lettie, Will's housekeeper, who would definitely offer him some of the homemade apple strudel and sugar cookies she always kept in the oven, which always warmed him, and made him think of a home he'd never had. But then, Will's parting words sank in, and he sank down onto the unforgiving saddle leather couch to catch up with himself.

His father had summoned him! Well, not *him*, Miggsy, and not summoned, exactly, just told Will he wanted to see "the boy" before the race tomorrow. Will had divulged this little chestnut just before they reached the cottage Mills had been calling home for almost a year but had probably spent less than a month in all told, due to their non-stop schedule.

"Ya don't have to go," Will assured him, when Mills recoiled, "but it's not out of the blue. I guess he thinks it's a sort of a good luck tradition to have a little pow-wow breakfast before the big race, because your grand-daddy did it—twice—ya know, with his jockey."

"You mean *you* and *grandpa* started this whole stupid breakfast thing?" Mills blurted, emphasizing the word, "you."

"Fraid so," Will nodded, clearly uncomfortable. He really didn't like to talk about himself. And he certainly didn't like carrying loaded messages from Mills II to his son.

"You and grandpa were friends. You liked each other's company. So, you had breakfast together. So big deal. Two breakfasts do not a tradition make," Mills reasoned out loud, relieved this would get him off the hook.

"Point is, lad," Will rasped, "they do. Ya see, I never, ever ate before a race back in my jockey days, and your granddaddy, well he never did either. But for some reason I sure can't remember now, if ya don't count nerves and a sleepless night, we decided to get an early bite together before the Pearl, in our first run for the Diamond with the great Titan, and when we won, we started jokin' that catchin' that bite together did it, ya know, brought us luck. So, of course, sure as shootin', we did it again the next time we had the chance, and don't ya know if that beauty, Titan's Glory, didn't bring that Diamond right back to Miggston Farms, like his magnificent daddy did. We grabbed two bites together and we grabbed two Diamonds. Ate the same thing both times, too. Like it or not, that's how traditions start, lad. All it takes. And now Miggston Farms has another chance at it, and Mills II doesn't want to be the one to jinx it. He just wants to wish his jockey luck over breakfast like his daddy did."

But just who did his father think that jockey was? Just who did he think would show up? Wasn't he in the least bit concerned about what would happen to his little charade when it was just the two of them? Or was that begging the question that his father was thinking of anything at all besides winning and luck and tradition and not jinxing things, all of which, admittedly, were not to be taken lightly. This, of course, begged the equally charged question of how Mills could look Will, his savior, in the eye, and say he didn't have the guts to honor the very tradition that Will had started. It would be setting himself up for very, very bad luck to say the least, not to mention the height of ingratitude.

"Ya really don't have to go," Will had made a point of repeating, anticipating Mills would be having this conversation with himself. "But if ya decide to, remember, you're not the wet-behind-the-ears lad ya used to be when ya moved into this place. Not by a long shot. Ya've earned your spurs lad. And ya've made your mark. Ya've *already* pulled off what no one else could—though the best have tried—for, what is it now, the last eleven years? Ya don't have to prove yourself to *any* man. Not that ya ever did. Believe me, as God is my witness, I'm tellin' ya the truth."

Mills wanted to believe him. He really did. But the catch was that he had been brought up by both 'rents—for totally separate but equally selfish reasons—to believe that he could never, ever stop proving himself. And he certainly couldn't stop now, when it only meant everything.

Especially to his father, who had craved the Diamond with the same thirst he had for his beloved bourbon. It was a well-known secret Mills II wanted out of his father's shadow and a Gem Cups Sweep was his only ticket. The well-kept secret—that he was completely dependent upon the son he had exiled and the horse he had reviled and wanted to shoot, to do it—was as irrelevant as it was ironic.

What was relevant was that the renowned Miggston Farms trophy room now displayed, together again for the first time in a decade, the priceless Sapphire, Emerald and Ruby encrusted cups that led up to the longest and most rigorous race of all, the Champions' Stakes. And so, what was relevant was that their destiny was waiting less than forty miles away at the fabled Newland Park, where, if they could just pull it off, they'd be awarded the prize of all prizes, the Newland Cup, featuring four rows of flawless diamonds for four flawless rides, a feat so monumentally difficult, it was achieved only nine times in its one hundred and eighty-two year history, the last, thirty-five years ago, when Will De Longpre and Titan's Glory, The Great Titan's celebrated son, astoundingly did what Will and The Great Titan had done thirty-five years earlier, and seized all four. Now that rare chance was awaiting another Titan and another De Longpre, the storied stallion's direct descendant and his rider, the legendary jockey-turned-trainer's "long lost nephew," rumored to be his illegitimate son, but secretly the banished scion of Miggston Farms, grandson of Mills I and legitimate owner of Titan's Revenge, son of Titan's Glory, grandson of The Great Titan.

Bloodlines were aligned like planets. The countdown had begun. Their defining moment was less than twelve hours away.

But first, should he choose to, and signs were unfortunately pointing to yes, Mills had to endure a breakfast he would not eat, with the last man on earth he wanted to see. Thinking of his father was like remembering the sound of chalk on a blackboard—practically as bad as being there. He cringed. But he shook it off, hoping that maybe, just maybe, that's all his father was by now, just a cranky noise in his head, that maybe Will was right. He had moved on without knowing it, maybe that slightly queasy feeling he was feeling, was just a case of phantom heartburn. Maybe, in the light of day, his father had lost his hold on him.

About to go, he passed the neatly stacked piles of Winner's Circle pictures he hadn't had a chance to go through and maybe never would, when it struck him that he'd forgotten something. He ran to the bedroom and grabbed the only photograph in a frame, the only one he kept by his bedside, a snapshot, taken by Hap Tate, right after the Wyndham Stakes, of Wilde, Will, and himself—Will's arm around his shoulder, his arm around Wilde's neck—laughing, as Will liked to say, like there was no tomorrow, which was exactly how it had felt.

Now, tomorrow had come. Mills took the picture from its frame and slipped it inside his jacket.

"I was wrong," his father had said the next morning.

He had arranged a very down-home breakfast in his far from down-home private suite high above the track, overlooking both the starting and finish lines for the coming mile-and-a-half race. The menu, offering exactly what Mills I and Will ate before their wins—courtesy of their favorite greasy spoon—featured only foods that people with any sense just didn't eat anymore: hash browns grilled in lard, thick slabs of bacon and eggs fried in bacon grease, a pile of country biscuits and a stack of toasted white bread, both slathered in butter, all to be washed down by acrid, over-percolated coffee. Mills marveled at Will's metabolism, that he could have eaten any of it and not become a dead weight on his horse, or so deathly ill, he fell off; because, personally, those bilious, greasy smells colliding against each other were making him nauseous and head-achy.

Of course, he never ate before his races, because he wanted to put as little weight as possible on Wilde, not to mention that it made him queasy to even think of having a bite, which his father should have known, but probably didn't. The best Mills could say of their relationship at this point, was that they hardly knew each other. He hadn't been alone with his father since being abruptly dismissed from his office during their final blow-up almost a year ago. Yet, thanks to Wilde's amazing winning streak, he'd certainly been in his father's presence a lot, albeit always on horseback, which gave him an edge and took his mind off the fact that the 'rents never once— even when he won the Ruby—invited him to the grandstand with them, for the simple reason that they couldn't stand to stand next to him. Still, he had become remarkably adept at benignly tuning his father out, exactly what he thought he was doing now, nodding amiably every now and then, not actually listening. But one word slipped through.

"Wrong?" Mills repeated in disbelief. His father never, ever admitted he was wrong.

"Yes. And you were right."

A second stunning admission.

"About that horse of yours," his father went on, with no sign of his usual holier-than-thou-ness, "—that horse has made me—well, it's made me proud."

"Really?" Mills said, warily.

His father took out his omnipresent flask. It was six o'clock in the morning.

"You and your horse have brought glory to Miggston Farms. Thanks to the two of you, and Will, of course, we've been on an un-*pre*-ce-dented winning streak. For that, your mother and I are extremely *appreciative,*" he said, his re-lubricated voice lingering over every syllable. "I—*we*—want you to know that." He held his flask up to his lips, blocking eye contact.

Mills nodded, unable to talk

"And, son—"

He'd just called him son. His father had just called him son. What was he trying to pull? Mills looked directly at him for the first time. His father's eyes, reflecting the new morning light, had turned Miggston blue, like his own, but they were bloodshot and ringed with dark, bruised circles. He did not look like a man on a winning streak.

"I also want to commend you on your—your dis-*cre*-tion," his father said slowly, gazing away from Mills, out onto the track, emphasizing the second syllable as though it held the key to everything. He paused to take a deep drink. "Never letting it go to your head. Keeping to yourself. Your mother is especially proud of you for that."

Yeah. Right. Proud of him for not letting on he was their son. Thanks, mom, he thought bitterly, for your vote of confidence.

They were sitting across from each other and thanks to a certain reupholstered Louis Seize cushion discretely placed on his seat for everyone's comfort, they were pretty much on eye level. He waited for his father to go on, trying to ignore the massive, stomach-turning, pile of food congealing between them.

Mills II took another long draft and using the flask as a shield, forced himself to steal a glance at "the boy," his son, who had come through every ordeal, taken on every challenge, broken every record, driven his horse through every finish line with the irresistible force of a Miggston, his son, who was honored, sought after, called strikingly handsome by strangers, his son, whom he still could barely bring himself to look at. And yet, he'd been there at every race, watching the boy's daring, high-speed, wire-to-wire act through binoculars, knowing more about him from afar than he ever had when they were living under the same roof.

He'd known, of course, that Mills would not eat the repulsive breakfast he was offering because, like most jockeys, he never ate before his races and, with his delicate stomach, he'd never eat this. Yet, he put out this ridiculous spread because that is what his father had done twice and twice his horses had clinched the Pearl and claimed the Diamond. Now, he finally had his own chance at immortality, of standing a little taller in his father's long shadow, but not with a horse he had nurtured since birth and a best friend for a jockey, like his daddy did. No, he would be forever linked in history with a horse he'd secretly wanted to put down, ridden by a jockey, who thanks to him, no one knew was his only son, banished for the unfor-givable sin of being too short.

Mills II took another drink. Then another. And another. He had done it all wrong. And now he could put it right. He could put it right, right now. His son was waiting.

"Now, this afternoon—" he began slowly, "after you win the big one—and I *am* confident that you *will* win it—when your mother and I come down into the grandstand, son, I want you—well, I want you to—"

Mills was frantically casting about for another way to look at it. But he couldn't find one. He was head-achy and his stomach was queasy, true, but there was no other way to see it. His father was about to ask him—not just to meet up in the Winner's Circle—but to, at last, join his family on the grandstand, where they would reclaim the Diamond and their son, in a moment of complete and exquisite public and personal victory. He didn't want to care, but his heart, which hadn't gotten the message, was beating in his throat.

Feeling good about himself for the first time in a very, very long time, Mills II sat back against the plush leather banquette, closed his eyes and allowed himself to imagine the ecstatic crowd on its feet, screaming, shrieking, cheering wildly, thirty-five years of bottled-up expectations exploding into a pandemonium of acclaim, adoration and, yes, respect, all aimed in his direction, while he stood on the grandstand, victoriously hoisting the Diamond Cup, *his* Diamond Cup, high overhead, his son at his side. And he cringed.

Gripping the flask with a suddenly shaking hand, Mills II took a quick nip to shake off the abject shame that overtook him every time he remem-bered how short the boy really was. But, in spite of himself, he shuddered again. So, he took another, while his son hung onto the silence.

"Now, in the commotion that follows—which will be like nothing you have ever experienced before, believe me—" Mills II finally went on, while the potent liquid slowly coated his nerve-endings, "when your mother and I come down into the grandstand, I want you—I want you to remember to—" the words began to flow as fluidly as the bourbon loosening them, because, really, he'd known all along it could only come to this— "stay on your horse for the ceremonies, like you've been doing. The crowds love it."

'What?" the word fell from Mills' lips in a croak.

"Things are going to get very crazy and it would be easier all around if you stayed on your horse, when we get the Diamond—" Mills II whispered a little too harshly.

Mills glared at him. "What?" he repeated, gripping the table to stop the room from spinning.

"I want to know that we understand each other," Mills II pressed, unable to stop, wondering if he could hate himself more. The boy deserved better than this after all he'd been through, all he'd risen above, all he'd accomplished. But that didn't change anything. Unless he was on his horse, or propped up on his Louis booster seat, Mills II not only couldn't bear to look at him, he couldn't bear to be seen with him. And there was nothing he could do about it, except drink.

"Remember, discretion is the better part of valor," Mills II urged, apropos of something he knew nothing about.

Mills tried to say something, but his throat had turned to sandpaper.

"I know Titan's Revenge and Miggsy will bring the greatest trophy of them all back to Miggston Farms where it belongs, and that for the good of Miggston Farms, our little secret will remain just that, our little secret." Mills II said tightly.

Gathering himself back together to the full height of his hauteur, he stood up, putting an end to it, obliterating Mills' panoramic view of the track behind him, casting a shadow over him.

Mills wanted to spit something really horrible at his father, something that would devastate him as much as he had been devastated, something that would bring him to his knees for once. But everything was reeling, and before sinking to his own knees, all he could come up with was a feeble, peevish, "Yeah, right, our *little* secret—*me!*"

"This is not about you or me, but what is best for Miggston Farms. Don't you ever forget that!" Mills II bellowed self-righteously. But he had no moral high ground. He knew it. And he knew Mills knew it.

"I hate you!" Mills yelled, bolting from the table.

"Mills!—"

"My name is *Miggsy!*" Mills screamed, lurching for the door and slamming it behind him.

In the ringing echo of his son's departure, Mills II told himself he hadn't really done any damage, that on the contrary, he'd gotten his son's adrenalin pumping for the race, that the boy would turn his rage into a hunger to prove himself even further, and he'd urge his horse to do the same, so they'd win by a few more furlongs, and break a few more records, which was the point, wasn't it? So, he couldn't be the person he'd just proven himself to be. He hadn't just lied his way through his moment of truth. He lifted his flask to amnesia, but it was empty.

Blind with fury, Mills didn't know who to blame first, his father, who had never missed an opportunity to destroy him, or himself, for giving his father so many of them. What about Will, who should have prevented this disastrous breakfast, but didn't. He had trusted Will like, well, like the father he wanted so desperately. But a real father would have protected him, no matter what—

"Whoa! Slow down!"

Somehow, he was outside Wilde's barn and Will had him by the shoulders. How he'd gotten here, he didn't know.

"Leave me alone." He wrenched away from the trainer.

Will immediately let him go and tried to get Mills to look at him, but Mills refused to make eye contact.

"Can I help?" Will said gently.

"You could have but you didn't!" Mills said, his fury mounting. "And now it's too late."

Mills tore away from Will, grabbed the snapshot of Will, Wilde and himself from his jacket pocket, ripped it apart, threw Will's ragged third to the ground and crushed it with his heel, grinding Will's face into the dirt.

Inside the barn, Wilde whinnied edgily. Will went to calm him.

"Now you go on and calm yourself down, lad," he ordered, closing the door, his rasp—pitched perfectly between impatience and sympathy—lingering behind in rebuke.

Mills locked the door to his room at the barn and tried to compose himself. He made tea, he meditated, he prayed, he cursed, he did sit-ups, chin ups, push ups, but he couldn't escape it—the queasy throb in the pit of his stomach that was threatening to churn its way through him like battery acid and convulse into a migraine. He tried to clear his mind, to focus on the race, something he never had trouble with before, no matter what. But the throb had already reached his temple.

Then it was time.

He went through everything on automatic pilot, putting on his silks, posing for pictures, weighing in. He was there but not there. When it came time to listen to Will's last words of advice, all he heard over the pulsating roar, was his own frenzied litany of his father's iniquities. He was sick to his stomach.

Will grimly boosted him onto Wilde.

He made it through the post parade half blinded by the biliously vibrant waves of color bouncing off the other jockeys' silks.

Lining up at the gate, his pulse was racing furiously, its stuttering tattoo sending tremors through Wilde, who snorted and whinnied.

Mills patted him with clammy, shaking hands.

Terrible shockwaves surged through Wilde's body. He blew hard, shook his head and absorbed them all.

Mills got into his crouch, lifted the reins. His hands were no longer shaking, but it felt like they were. His teeth ached like they were biting down on a bit. His mouth tasted metallic. His skin was on fire. But he was freezing, and his head was so heavy, he could barely hold it up.

The bell rang, jangling him to his core.

The doors clanged open.

Wilde exploded from the pack, blasted down the lane to the inside.

The horrific image of a boot heel—his own boot heel—crushing Will's face into the dirt, blasted through Mills' mind, detonating a minefield of remorse. If only he could take it all back. If only they could go fast enough to turn back time. He urged Wilde on.

Wilde screamed past the grandstand and ripped around the first turn in a blur of speed and mud, clocking suicidal fractions.

In their private aerie high above it all, Lydia Aimée Charles Vanalden Miggston hid under the organza cloud that was her hat, clutching her champagne glass like a lifeline. Beside her, Mills Donald Miggston the Second reached for his bourbon.

"What the hell does he think he's doing?" he cursed. But he, of all people, knew.

He'd show his father. He'd win the Diamond; he and Wilde would do it. And when they charged through the wire, he'd find Will and get down on his knees and beg his forgiveness.

The Miggstons, along with everyone else in the boxes around them, and the crowds in the grandstand, and the masses pushing up against the infield fence, watched in fascinated dread, as Wilde, eerily, continued to accelerate.

Thunder rumbled in the distance. Or was it thundering hooves reverberating in his aching head? Either way, they had to go faster, faster, to outrun the past.

Breathing hard, Wilde dropped flat and ripped around the Clubhouse turn, surpassing unsurpassable speeds, obliterating the legendary track's mile record—probably forever.

Were they moving at all? Were they even moving? The sun throbbed against his face. His pulse throbbed against his throat. The finish line throbbed against the sky less than a half-mile away, where his father waited in the throbbing heat, behemoth hand outstretched, demanding that they shake on it, that Mills would *never* be good enough to be a Miggston. But he would never shake on it. He wrenched his hand away.

He didn't feel his right-hand recoil, didn't feel the hot gusts of wind thrashing at him, or his silks stuck to his sweat-drenched skin, didn't feel Wilde swerve in frantic confusion, careening around the last turn, and he didn't hear the blood-curdling screams warning them they heading towards the rail.

Blinking sweat away like tears, Mills saw it through fogged goggles. Just beyond them, less than a furlong away, glistening like a spider's web—the wire!

"The rail!" a hundred thousand voices howled in absolute panic. "They're going to hit the outside rail!" They hurtled toward it—a thousand pounds of iron muscle stamping out the boy's unbearable memories with great, sweeping strides—dark visions pressing them irresistibly toward that single point, the competition, fortunately, more than forty lengths behind.

Oblivious to everything now, but the need to leave everything behind, they tore down the track, slamming into currents of blistering, sweltering air, leaving everyone else in their wake.

Grown men wailed. Women who would have comforted them were shrieking in terror.

Lydia Aimée Vanalden Miggston sank into the banquette, the color draining from her already pallid cheeks, her glass falling, shattering.

Mills Donald Miggston drained his glass, silently begging God to forgive him.

Mills could feel his father's eyes burning through him, demanding the prize he had waited his whole life for but didn't deserve: a cup made out of brilliant, light refracting diamonds. How fitting for a man who sucked the light out of everything, who never, ever gave, but only took. But he wasn't going to take *this* away!

Lightning flashed across the highly charged sky.

"*N'est pas il ce que nous sommes donnés—*" His mother's wispy voice, or was it the wind, whispered in his ear, reminding him, like she always did, before he had to hate her, of the Charles way. "*It's not what we've been given but what we give back that counts.*"

Thunder exploded behind them, propelling them toward the shimmering sliver of light.

"Stop!! Please stop!!!" The crowd pleaded, although it was inevitable now. They were so close to careening into the rail—so close!

So close! They were so close to the finish line now, so close to coming full circle, amazed he hadn't seen it before, all his times around the track, the end being the beginning. Because wasn't that what he always came back to, what he'd always wanted. To go back, unwind time, start again. And this was the way, the Charles way back. If he gave his father this last prize, expecting nothing in return, time would unwind, everything would go back to the way it was before, and his father—and his mother—would love him again.

"Don't bet on it Bucko!" a tinny voice blared from somewhere inside Mills' pounding head, snapping it back to a nightmarish reality where the hysterical, horror-stricken crowd was on its feet screaming, shrieking, sobbing, praying, because they were moments from impact.

"Oh my God! No!!" Mills choked, jerking sharply on Wilde's reins.

But before the words rushed from his mouth, before his stomach finished its lurch to his feet, Wilde skidded backwards, rearing up on exhausted legs, flinging Mills into the air like a rag doll.

Lydia Vanalden Miggston's screams pierced the swollen sky. Mills Donald Miggston, reached for her hand, gripped it tightly.

At the height of his trajectory, in the split-second before he plummeted to the ground, Mills thrust out his arms and threw himself back onto Wilde's neck, now so slick with sweat, he began to slide, pulling them both further backwards.

The crowd held its breath in stunned silence while they teetered there, Mills sliding down Wilde's neck, fingers slipping through Wilde's slick mane, right thigh vainly trying to anchor itself to Wilde's slippery back, left leg frantically kicking, thrusting, finally finding the dislodged and twisted stirrup, jamming his boot into it.

Wilde staggered back, rear hooves clawing dirt, front legs flailing, thrashing, slashing at thin air.

The pack thundered around the bend, destroying the silence.

They would not, would not, take this prize away.

Ears pricked, eyes flashing, snorting defiantly, Wilde rallied whatever reserves he had left and, fighting for balance, braced himself—steeled himself—to take advantage of his competitors' momentum. Feeling their force, their speed, their will, their hunger to win, their hot breath closing in, he ignored the tremendous pressure on his own fragile ankles, the added burden of his friend's weight on his tired neck, and, flexing burned-out thigh muscles, kicking off from spent back legs, he lunged forward onto his aching front legs, towards the real finish line, which shimmered in the blazing sun like a mirage.

Whispering, "I'm so sorry, so sorry," over and over, into Wilde's ear, Mills pulled himself together enough to appear to be in control, while fierce jolts of pain shot through his foot and up his leg, because he couldn't seem to get his boot out of the twisted irons, couldn't think straight, couldn't truly gain control of the ride.

But it didn't matter because, beneath him, wheezing raggedly, doing what he was born to do, keeping the promise they made to each other on their very first day, when the boy had saved his life, Wilde dug in, unaware that every hard-won stride was firing missiles of raw agony through his friend's wracked body, and, mustering the last ounce of strength he had in him, valiant heart hammering, weary neck, with Mills clinging to it, Wilde carried them both across the finish line—in one great soaring leap—and once on the other side and out of the way of the oncoming hooves, collapsed.

Stuck. Miggsy was stuck; didn't know what, what to do, couldn't figure it out. Trying to wrench his leg out he twisted it tighter, pain was excruciating. Wilde so close, so close, struggling for breath too, someone crying, my friend, my friend, it's all my fault. What I've done is unforgivable, getting harder to breathe, head buried in Wilde's wet, warm hide, Wilde's heart pounding wildly in his chest, and coming at them, coming at them, pounding the turf, erupting the ground under them, exploding around them—a stampede.

Will would have prayed if he were a praying man. Had been once. But any belief in God he might have had, couldn't hold up under the weight of what fate had done to the lad, casting so much pain and despair in the boy's path that anyone with half a brain would have given up on God long ago. But it wasn't God to blame today. He alone had let the boy down. Let the horse down. Let himself down. Should have seen it coming but was blind-sided, not a real good trait for a trainer, not at all. Whatever went on during breakfast, he could only guess. But it never crossed his mind that the man would sink *this* low, not only to destroy his own son, who never did him a minute's worth of harm, but to demolish his one chance of getting the one thing he wanted more than anything. But, no way around it, that's exactly what he did. And Will didn't see it coming, didn't see it coming at all. Saw the opposite instead, because the man had started talking about "the boy," out-and-out pride bursting out of his voice. By the time they clinched the Ruby, the man couldn't seem to stop talking about "the boy's" many feats of "derring-do".

Will saw how desperately he wanted to be reunited with his son, all right, but didn't reckon with the strength of the weakness beneath. He had misconstrued the father and betrayed the son, who could have been his own son, at least, that's how he'd come to think of him. And yet he had let *this* happen.

He ran to them, watching the other horses speed across the line, while the sound of ambulances shrieked above the shrieks of the crowd.

They were crushed together in sweat, exhaustion and sorrow, the boy and his horse. The boy's eyes were closed, but he opened them and, before Will could apologize, he said, in a small, but determined voice, "Promise me Will! Promise me! You won't let Wilde die! Promise!"

Will grabbed Mills' hand and promised. Then the boy closed his eyes, his arms, still around his horse's neck.

While the horse and the boy lingered on the edge of life, the Racing Authority reviewed the race and, in a unanimous decision, declared that since Titan's Revenge's valiant last leap before collapsing carried them far enough ahead and out of the way of the onrushing field to avoid further catastrophe, he would remain the winner of the Diamond, thus achieving a rare Gem sweep, securing the elusive, priceless Diamond Cup for Miggston Farms—parenthetically giving Mills Donald Miggston the Second, his Holy Grail.

Mills drifted in and out of consciousness for the better part of a week. Will did not leave his side, except to tend to Wilde, whom he dedicated himself to bringing back from the brink of death. It was touch and go, and would be for a long time, but he had promised the boy, no ifs, ands, or buts. And this time he would not let him down.

Fever spiking, the acute viral infection doctors blamed for causing hallucinations and, therefore, the accident, coursing through his bruised body, Mills tossed and turned restively, locked in a nightmare, awake or asleep, wanting to die. His mother was there, in the corner of a dream, in a flurry of chiffon and nervousness, his father, granite and resolute; there was the flutter of her hand on his cheek, the faint hint of his Bourbon, her perfume. And there was Will, holding his hand, putting ice on his dry lips, trying to apologize for letting him down. But Mills knew it was all his own fault and although he loved and trusted Will more now than he ever had before, he couldn't stand the mixture of guilt and pity in Will's eyes every time Will looked at him—and something else, something worse—self-doubt—the one thing a trainer just could not have. Thanks to him, Will was a broken man.

He awakened reluctantly to the ebullient news that he'd gotten his wish. Wilde had officially won. Their astonishing record remained unblemished by defeat. His stomach turned at this pyrrhic victory, this coup de grace, this uber irony. He'd won the Diamond and lost everything.

He barely paid attention to the doctor's somber prognosis that—due to the way his bones had been crushed because he'd lodged his boot backwards in the stirrup, then fallen on it—his recovery would be long and painful.

He fought to hold back tears, when he was told, sometime later, as if it were good news, that there was a *slight* chance, but a chance nonetheless, he might, in time, after a lot of physical therapy and more than a little luck, regain enough viable partial use of his crushed left leg to graduate to crutches and maybe a cane, but for the time being, he would be confined to a wheelchair.

In keeping with Miggston Farms policy towards injured jockeys, the 'rents paid for a top-of-the-line, state-of the-art wheelchair, and twenty-four hour a day private nurses. Mills, of course, had been admitted to the hospital as Miggsy De Longpre. But the 'rents never disabused anyone of the mistake, never revealed his real name, never reclaimed him as their son, even during his darkest hour. And for that, he would never forgive them.

When he was strong enough, he gave Will De Longpre Power of Attorney for Wilde's safe-keeping, to keep his horse away from his father's authority or control, in case anything happened to him. Wilde was still not out of the woods, Will said honestly, and promised again that he would be. He would be. But his voice sounded shaky.

Four months later, a few weeks after his sixteenth birthday, with the help of a sympathetic orderly and the wheelchair bankrolled by the 'rents, Mills snuck out of the hospital in the middle of the night. He had made remarkable progress, everyone said, pushing himself beyond human endurance in rehab. But they didn't know that driving himself to exhaustion was second nature to him, and much better than letting his mind wander, that just to keep himself from becoming suicidal, he had driven himself to the point that he was able to walk on his own, albeit, with great difficulty. But the looks of pity and revulsion on everyone's faces as he gamely tried to take just one step were too excruciating. Seeing no need to hang around for more, he left, taking with him only one thing, his grandmother Beryl's Bentwood rocker, which she had left him along with the bulk of her vast estate, and had been his only comfort during the long days and nights when he could not walk, but couldn't stand to lie down a moment longer.

He also left with enough pain killers to kill whatever pain he might ever have, and enough guilt to kill the pain killers. Thanks to him, the family he so desperately wanted was as shattered as his bones. The crippling limp, which the doctors said he would have to live with, would be his mark of Cain, his constant reminder that he had failed his friends, betrayed their faith in him and ruined their lives, and for that he deserved to suffer every moment of every day of his life.

He wrote a note to Will and Wilde that said, "I will always love you. I will miss you every day of my life. Please don't try to find me. I promise not to do anything rash." Pathetic. But, if he had tried to write what was in his heart, he would have been there forever and could never leave. He had rearranged those four sentences dozens of times until he settled on that order, which he still wasn't happy with. But he put it into an envelope addressed to Will anyway and deposited it in a mailbox he passed outside the hospital, when he wheeled into the night and onto the ramp of the waiting, fully equipped, chauffeured van, which, unlike happiness, or peace of mind, or a chance to take it all back, was something his money—which now included his enormous purses from the Emerald, Ruby, and Diamond—could buy.

He drove out of Kentucky and away from any reminders of blue grass and horses, and stopped, finally, at a tiny apartment in a nondescript city, somewhere in America.

He could barely hobble. It took him forty minutes just to get across his small living room, and he knew it might never get better. He missed his friends so much he couldn't breathe, blamed himself so harshly, he could barely stand to be alive.

He welcomed the shrill voices of rebuke that tormented him when he was alone, augmented his misery with torturous trips outside, expressly to endure the covert glances, the "thank God that's not me!" looks burning holes through him, as he slowly dragged himself down the street. Instead of sleeping, he shuffled around the small apartment, punishing himself by ceaselessly reliving the last race. He allowed himself only one diversion, reading. He read until his eyes were bloodshot, devouring everything he could get his hand on, everything, of course, except anything that might remind him, or give him any news of his old life. With one exception: a short, terse, uneasy phone call to Will, a month into his sojourn, to ask about Wilde and let Will know that he had not done anything rash. Fighting tears, Miggsy ended the call as abruptly as he had started it, after Will said Wilde was hanging on and Will would never give up on him.

Time passed with the dogged slowness of his laggardly limp. In numbing monotony, days became years. But nothing lessened the ache in his soul.

"Hello?? Hello??"

Over a line so staticy it sounded like it was coming through an old-time short-wave radio, a voice rumbled in Miggsy's ear demanding his attention, disorienting him. Then reorienting him.

He was apparently still in the living room of the latest in a series of apartments he'd escaped to over the years, and it was pretty much like all the others, only much, much bigger because he was much, much faster. Now, instead of taking forty minutes to cross a tiny living room, he could limp-sprint from one huge room to another and back in less than forty seconds, even executing ragged, lopsided leaps over the mountains of books he'd read over the years, then piled on the floor, in ever more labyrinthine obstacle courses that seemed to challenge the laws of physics. Oh yes. His time in solitude had not been wasted.

"Hello?" The gravelly voice repeated, on the verge of losing patience.

"Hello?" Miggsy ventured, tearing himself away from all things remorseful, noticing the ad still clutched in his hand and the absence of Cowardice.

"*Ma's Café,*" the voice growled. "Can I help you?"

"I—uh—read your ad in the uh, Daggett Gazette," Miggsy said, dully alarmed that he'd apparently initiated this call without knowing it and was now oddly unable to hang up.

Static. Deep breath. Extremely deep. Grand Canyon deep. Then, "I'm not sure—" More static. "—still—" and finally "—for sale."

"Not still for sale? You have another offer?" Miggsy gasped, truly shocked.

More static. Another deep, deep breath. More static. Then, "*Ssss—*"

"Yes? Someone *else* wants it?" Miggsy's pulse was racing. Suddenly he *had* to have it.

"Well, wait a minute, before you commit to them, you should know that I, that I, that I can, uh, be there in a few days," he extemporized, possessed.

"You got a name?" The growl demanded through the static.

"Mills Miggston the Third," Miggsy heard himself say with uncalled for pomposity, to put the voice in its place, wherever that could be—and immediately regretted it. If he'd had a spare leg to stand on, he would have kicked himself for dredging up and then pretentiously spitting out the name he hadn't called himself, or even uttered, for almost a decade, just because it might impress and hopefully intimidate a bunch of static on the other end of the line. That name had never done him any good. And it certainly wasn't going to start now. After everything he'd been through, all the aliases he'd assumed in all the cities he'd lived in, he was still just Miggsy. And he would always be.

"Well, Mr. Mills Miggston the Third, that's some serious name you got there," the growl growled through their poor connection. "But I won't hold it against you. Now you tell me where you're coming from and I'll tell you where you're going."

"If only you could," Miggsy thought, "if only you could."

"Big" John Nash, or "BJ" to his friends, rattled off the appropriate information to the guy with the long name and short attention span. He'd been doing everything he could to keep *ma's Café* going for so long, that even now, when he was in the middle of giving directions to a potential buyer, he was still wracking his brain to come up with something else he could do besides sell. But nothing came to mind that he hadn't already tried, to no avail. There was nothing else he could do to save Mama but sell *ma's*.

"Don't forget to follow the arrow all the way around—" he heard himself shouting into the more and more unstable connection, which suddenly clicked off of its own accord, leaving his voice trapped somewhere in the void, but exactly where, he didn't have a clue. So, he put the phone back and stared at it, hoping for the best.

"What? What did you just say?" Miggsy kept shouting to dead air, dumbly wondering who this *"ma"* person *really* was, and if she existed, what she was doing right now to prepare for the sucker with the cash (that would be he) that the gruff voice (which he hoped to God wasn't *"ma,"* or worse, her hit man) had just reeled in.

Day after day, week after week, BJ had wracked his brain to figure out something to save *ma's* just in case that apple pie recipe that would be salvation didn't get there on time. All this while, Mama had stayed tuned, day and night for that recipe, but she was constantly interrupted by news flashes from the time/space continuum, so it was slow-going, although, thanks to the Doo Wop serenades, she hardly noticed time going by at all.

For BJ, however, time was whizzing by so relentlessly, the first of the month was coming at him like whiplash.

Mama, for her part, was doing her part, shifting her soup cans to boost her chances of getting that recipe as pronto as possible, when one starry night, a day, or maybe a week or two, or maybe just an hour into her vigil, something in her hiccupped. Without warning, Mama felt herself and her cherished chaise dislodged from gravity and sucked into a whirring vacuum with everything around them, the yard, BJ, the Doo Wops, the desert, the plains, the mountains and valleys, the oceans, the continents, the planet, the solar system, the galaxy, time and even space, everything sucked in with her, every star in the sky, the sky itself, everything, zooming billions of miles and years backwards through the time/space continuum, which, itself, was becoming compressed ever smaller along with them, until nothing existed at all, but an infinitesimal atomic ball of everything, inside of which was Mama herself, or at least the essence and the promise of her and BJ and the Doo Wops and everyone she knew or ever would know or meet, or never know, along with everyone and everything that had ever been and would ever be in every galaxy everywhere—before there was an anywhere—all those capricious possibilities crammed together in a teeming micro-cosmic tenement in the absolute middle of nowhere, the que seras of infinity jostling restlessly against each other, compacted into a dense, molten, microscopic speck of hot-blooded primordial potential, suspended in the nowhere, waiting to blow.

Another hiccup and Mama was riding the time/space continuum back to the present and down to earth, to her own backyard, pondering fate, luck, happenstance, and apple pie.

"Blue Moon," the Doo Wops offered by way of welcome.

"You didn't happen to catch drift of that recipe while I was gone?" Mama wondered aloud. But alas, they had not.

By the time Mama had been on her apple pie watch going on two and half months, BJ had done a half-dozen odd jobs around what was left of the anemic town to fill in for what *ma's* was not bringing in. Sadly, they added up to not all that much money, when all was said and done, since almost everybody in the forgotten place was in the same position as BJ and Mama (though no one could be in exactly the same position as Mama). Unable to refuse a neighbor in need, he kindheartedly did his usual meticulous work and accepted whatever they felt comfortable paying. And, though they could offer him only a fraction of what the jobs were worth, once they asked, he could not turn them down. It was how he was brought up: to help others. Sometimes, when he was painting, or repairing, or restoring, or lifting objects no one else could, like pianos and appliances, he overheard people speculating about Mama. Even though everything was whispered, it was hard to escape the rumors about her. The general consensus was pretty simple, that the lightning bolt had more or less shorted out her brain, and now she was either talking to herself, or listening to imaginary voices, or both. BJ never let on that he heard anything, and he never answered their unasked questions. What could he say? That the voices they all were sure were in Mama's head, were so loud, not to mention irresistible and infectious, that he found himself singing along with them whenever he could? That was probably easier to swallow than the whole truth—that not only were they as real to him as they were to Mama, but he couldn't help but assume that such a heavenly chorus could only come directly from, well, where else but heaven. And so, therefore, how could he not believe in them?

Thing was, believing in the Doo Wops was the easy part. Their soul-soothing melodies, which captivated him daily, were more than enough to make any man trust that everything would turn out all right. But, when he was out of their thrall, unable to escape the gossip, or the numbers on the bottom line, it kept getting harder and harder not to worry. Not having a direct line to the heavens like Mama, BJ wasn't in on the actual game plan. The only thing he knew for sure was that even with his outside work, bills were piling up faster than they could get paid, with less than nothing left to put aside to pay the back taxes. To make matters worse, with the locals keeping away out of some alleged deference to their privacy, the only customers left at *ma's* were the inconsiderate ones who came to gawk and often left without ordering anything, when they couldn't "take a gander at the lightning lady" even after offering BJ "good money."

Hoping the Doo Wops were planning a touchdown before the clock ran out, BJ had kept everything going as best he could, sometimes feeling like he was juggling tractors. Organizing every day around the well-being of Mama and her beloved café, he did all of his jobs at night, after the end of the dinner shift, just in case someone showed up at *ma's* wanting a burger and a little company. He stayed with Mama all day, when he wasn't needed at *ma's,* which was most of the time. Whenever he worked, no matter where he was, he always checked in on Mama and *ma's* during his breaks. Neither ever needed him. But, as it turned out, the one thing he didn't think of, did.

The night BJ did an emergency roof-repair on the First Baptist Church, he came back to find that Ole SunnySide Up, Mama's cherished VW van, was missing, stolen from behind *ma's* when he was helping out the little church. Instead of sleeping that night, he searched everywhere he could think of, putting up signs, offering a reward for the van's safe return, no questions asked. All the while, of course, he was cursing the thieves' luck that the key was permanently stuck in the ignition and that ole SunnySide had decided to start for them, considering she'd more or less given up the ghost since Mama had turned the channel and left the station. Praying the van wasn't already broken down for parts, he held onto a hunch he couldn't shake—which he would have considered ridiculous, if he wasn't already singing along with imaginary voices—that if only Mama was more herself—not that this part of Mama wasn't a big chunk of who she always was too, communing with the universe, and all— but if she was just a little more in the day-to-day, if she could just, maybe, whistle, so SunnySide knew to hold on, the old van would come puttering up the hill again. Or maybe, a sober part of him suggested, this was just another kind of a prayer, a step beyond hope, into the only thing left: faith. Maybe, that's what this was all about, trusting that the universe, which brought the Doo Wops, would deliver Ole SunnySide of her own accord, along with the angel and the apple pie recipe that would save *ma's*. Or maybe, all this hoping and praying and trusting was just a smokescreen to keep him from facing Mama with further heartbreak. He just couldn't bear to tell her that—along with everything else they were about to lose—her oldest companion was gone. It would break her heart, which would surely break transmission with the heavens. It was simple, if he did anything to break either her heart or her transmission, he'd never forgive himself. But a part of him knew that the time would come when he wouldn't have the choice.

BJ's breaking point came the day someone he thought was a customer, who looked like he could sure use one of Mama's famous bottomless cuppa coffees on the house, served him with the Final Thirty-Day Notice from the government about the delinquent property taxes on *ma's Café,* which had been inflated by interest and penalty fees into such a grotesque num-ber, BJ choked when he saw it. It might as well have been an eviction notice. After more than thirty years in business, *ma's Café* had thirty days to exist.

BJ tried to understand how the same universe that sent the Doo Wops could also deliver the Thirty-Day Notice. The only answer he could come up with was that the best the universe could do these days was send the Doo Wops for diversion, so Mama wouldn't have to witness the end of her dream.

BJ had read and reread the Notice for possible ways to get another ex-tension, stall for time, postpone the inevitable, but there were none. They'd run out of loopholes. It had been a Catch-22 of the worst type for years because the worse business got, the higher the taxes became. Tried as they might, he and Mama couldn't come up with enough money in the last few years to pay off the property and other taxes on the café, or they would have to begin with. And now, even though they had made partial payments of what seemed like a lot of money at the time, with the assessments, penalties, interests and other fines that made no sense to him, adding up to a figure he couldn't make if he worked twenty-four hours a day, seven days a week, for the rest of his life, BJ felt trapped for only the second time in his life.

From the instant BJ had first laid eyes on Mama, he knew he would throw himself in front of a Mack truck coming at her at two hundred miles per hour without blinking an eye, to keep her from harm, and that, from that day forward, he would do whatever it took to keep her safe and sound, not, of course, that Mama would ever consider herself the type that needed being kept safe and sound. But what BJ's big, oversized heart knew was that Mama's big, oversized heart was just as breakable as anybody's.

And now, all the bigness of their enormous love for each other had whittled down to this. The only thing he could think of doing to keep Mama from harm's way and save the little they still had left, was to do the unthinkable—sell *ma's* and the land under it, which was surely worth something to somebody—so he and Mama could to pay off the taxes and all *ma's* other debts and have enough left to hightail it out of whatever was left of town, before the government took back *ma's* and the desert took the rest. And though it broke his heart to even think of separating Mama from *ma's*, he had to believe he could find a better place for her, on higher ground, where he could get as much work as he could handle, which meant a whole lot, and Mama could commune with the Doo Wops, free from worry and strife.

Since selling *ma's* was not something he had ever dreamed of doing, BJ certainly had no intention of doing it without Mama's approval. Unfortunately, however, Mama being in her current condition, was in no condition to have any kind of sit down. Well, maybe that was a bad choice of words, being that all Mama could do was basically sit down, stuck as she was to her lounger.

BJ knew where the deed was, of course. Mama had made him her partner and back-up person in case something happened to her. And there was no doubt about it, something *had* happened to Mama. Thing was, in their whole time together, BJ had never taken one penny from her he didn't earn. Never even had a sandwich he hadn't accounted for. It was how he was. Besides, *ma's* was not BJ's. It wasn't his to sell out from under her. But if he didn't do something quick, when he could, others would come and take it away from both of them. At least that's what the Notice said. It said they had thirty days. Thirty days before they lost everything.

BJ had always counted on himself to take care of Mama. And he had, no matter whatever came up, because he had the size and strength and, thanks to his daddy, the know-how and desire to do things no one else could.

He was a big man, with big capabilities, brought up to believe that there was nothing so broken it couldn't be fixed, if you put your mind and muscle to it. It was one of his daddy's many pointers about the responsibility of being big. And he guessed it made sense that on the day he was facing the biggest crossroad of his life, he could hear his daddy's voice in his head, reminding him, never letting him forget, who he was and what was expected of him.

"Never pick a fight!" His daddy had drilled into him, as if bigness was their religion and this was his catechism.

"Because if you do, you'll have to account to me," he emphasized in his "take no prisoners" whisper, when BJ was still Little [Big] J and his daddy was Big J, the biggest man that town had ever seen, still bigger than BJ, still able to put the fear of God into him.

"The tale of your whole future," his daddy told him a lot more than once, "will be told in your first fight."

Then, after thinking about it, he would always add, as if he'd just thought of it, "Will you end up a bully, a coward, or a really big man? Yessiree, Little J, your fate will be sealed by your first fight."

All that seemed a long way away to Little J, but he knew his daddy was just passing on what his daddy had told him, and his daddy's daddy, and all the way down the line, echoing generations of Nash's, because their bigness was a responsibility, which, his daddy cautioned, could turn into a heavy burden and lead him down a lonely road.

"No one's ever gonna believe you got a brain in your head," his daddy said, in his most serious growl. "The bigger you are, the stupider people will think you are. So, ya gotta outsmart 'em—by knowing more than they think you know—being a good listener—making yourself useful—never letting on ya know what ya know—so no one ever really knows."

Instead of lullabies, instead of prayers at night, instead of small talk, his daddy's words of wisdom filled every room they were in, bouncing off the walls in endless ricochets of advice. And BJ, no matter how young he was, could feel the truth of it, even if he wasn't sure exactly what it all meant and why.

Little J adored his daddy, who had been mom and dad to him for so long, it always felt natural that there were just the two of them. Big J was the town's handyman because he could fix anything. Something else he taught his son.

Looking back on it, from the time he was very young, he never had an idle moment. His days were filled with his dad teaching him by word and deed what it meant to be who he was.

BJ's daddy prepared him for school by teaching him the final two things he needed to know before he got there: how to read—because he was so big his teachers would sit him in the back of the room and pretend to forget him, and how to fight—because the bullies wouldn't be able to stop thinking about how to get him.

"Now, like I told you, never, ever start a fight," his daddy said, when Little J turned four. "But believe me, Little J, you won't have to look for one, because it'll be waiting for you. So, here's what ya gotta do. Ya gotta have one fight that ends all fights. And the way to do it is to make it public and make it fast. Let everybody see that with very little effort you can do a whole lot of damage. Now, the hard part, the part that will say everything about you, is that with the things I'm about to teach you, it will be real easy for you to hurt people real bad. But you can't. You have to promise me you will never harm anybody—unless your life is in danger.

Then BJ's daddy swore him to secrecy and initiated him into the secrets of what he called "The Art of the Wise Warrior," which he had picked up when he was stationed in the South Pacific doing things he refused to talk about.

Like all his other life lessons, BJ's daddy drilled the Art of the Wise Warrior into him, so it would be second nature.

He spent the first three months just learning how to breathe.

"It's got to be over one, two, three." His daddy said months later, when he decided Little J was ready.

"One: Use your opponent's attack to bring him down by using his own force against him. Two: when he gets right about here," he demonstrated on a giant cousin, who was spending the week-end, "step out of the way like this, grabbing his arm like this, which will bring him to his knees, like this. Then three: go for the pressure points here and here, or here and here, or here and here. It'll knock the wind outta him and keep him down. And Johnny boy, when you do this, don't forget rule number one: never, ever lose your temper, no matter what anybody says or tries to do to you. Or no matter who wins, you will lose."

And his daddy had been right, as usual, because even on the first day of kindergarten, he was already bigger than a lot of the sixth graders, which made everyone uncomfortable in a way he never could have understood if it wasn't for his dad. Just like he had warned, some kind of alarm went off the minute the older boys saw him—especially the bullies—that made them want to beat him up just because he was big. Which he couldn't let them do. He had to stop them short, starting right there, in the playground. So, he could spend the rest of his school days in peace.

"Remember," his daddy had said before his first day of school, "the instant you feel trapped, that means you have to look in a different direction.

Just like you can't see stars in the daytime, there's all sorts of possibilities you can't or maybe even won't see at first, but when you do, the way will be clear."

"Big oaf!" the biggest, toughest and ugliest of the sixth-grade boys shouted across the yard at recess, when the teachers were off, sneaking a smoke.

"Tommy Logan's on the warpath!" The other kids screamed, running for cover.

BJ's daddy had warned him about Tommy Logan, who had already been in teenage detention camp for beating up a high school kid when he was twelve. But BJ wasn't prepared for the pockmocked bulldog coming at him with hate in his beady eyes and spittle coming out of his twisted mouth.

"Hey, I'm talking to you, you big oaf! 'Fraid to look me in the eye?" He sneered, catching up.

BJ stopped and looked him in the eye, which was easy, since they were the same height. And he got it. Tommy Logan knew he had to knock the new kid down while he still could, before BJ got any bigger, which BJ wasn't going to let him do. He turned around.

"Coward!" Tommy Logan taunted, following BJ, who was striding away, head held high, like his daddy told him to.

"Monster!" Tommy Logan yelled when BJ didn't take the bait, running after him, the other kids running to catch up, gathering behind him, but not too close.

"Everybody knows your momma died because you were born so big you tore her in half!" Tommy Logan shouted maliciously, repeating what the whole town had been talking about for years, coming at him, hands clenched into fists.

BJ whirled around, cheeks burning, heart shattering, breaking the first rule of never getting mad, feeling trapped, because even though his daddy had prepared him for something awful, this was too much. Something horrible he never felt before was burning him up like a fever, taking him over.

"You killed your own mother!" His tormentor jeered.

"Liar!" BJ screamed, his hands clenching into fists, too, ready to strike back, to wipe the smile off Tommy Logan's smug, puggy face. But then his daddy's voice came back to him.

"No matter what they say, it will be lies," it reassured him, "lies aimed at making you lose your temper. So, don't you listen to them! And don't you believe them."

BJ slowly unclenched his fists, turning quickly, ducking his head just slightly, like he'd done so many times it was second nature to him. Tommy Logan lunged past him, losing his balance, his fat fist thrust out in a missed punch.

BJ reached out, grabbed Tommy Logan's arm and brought him to his knees.

"Take it back about my mother!" BJ demanded, twisting Tommy Logan's muscled arm, knowing he could break it like a twig.

"Ow! Cut it out!" Tommy Logan pleaded, trying to sound tough.

"Take it back!" BJ demanded again, twisting Tommy Logan's arm a little more, feeling the thrill of burgeoning power surge through him for the first time. If he broke Tommy Logan's arm, no one would blame him, they might even thank him. One thing was sure, no one would ever bother him again. Plus, it would serve Tommy Logan right. Picking on a little kid, even if he didn't look little. Saying bad things that could never be taken back. Tommy Logan deserved to suffer.

"Remember, Little J, you're not the judge and jury," his daddy's voice cut in, warning him for the zillionth time that this first fight would be the cross-roads of his life.

"It's your Rubicon, Johnny, boy. Once you cross it, you can't cross back. You'll know what I mean when you get there."

He was six years old, and he was already there. And even though he sure didn't know much, he knew enough to know that some people had to act their age. But he, he would always have to act his height.

He looked down on Tommy Logan who was so stupid and ugly, even a kindergartner could tell he would always be miserable. Tommy's nose was running. His eyes were dull red dots, and his entire bulldog face was squeezed together, trying not cry, though tears were spilling out every-where. His life as a bully was over and he had no fall-back position. BJ couldn't help pitying him.

"Promise you won't pick on anybody else—ever—and I'll let you go." BJ said in a voice that threatened pain he knew he would not deliver.

"Okay! I promise!" Tommy Logan surrendered, giving up the fight in front of everyone, including the teachers who had come back from the teacher's lounge just in time to see, through a cloud of residual smoke, something they had never seen before, Tommy Logan going down.

They gave Tommy Logan a month's detention for starting the fight.

They gave BJ a one day suspension, and the day he came back, they put him on the wrestling team, where, taking his daddy's advice like he always did, he proved so useful in winning the State Championship, and was such a solid team player, he was made Co-Captain in the third grade.

Of course, he became the school hero for cutting Tommy Logan down like a poison tree, but he never thought about it much, except that it felt good to have friends, and be a part of something bigger than himself.

"Make yourself useful, Little J. Be part of the team," his daddy had advised him, "and no one will wanna pick a fight. And you know what else? You'll feel great. And when you feel great, people will feel great being with you."

BJ always made sure he was able to do things that came in handy. Like his daddy promised, he always felt good about it, and he never wanted for friends. Naturally, when he and Mama got together, their universe just opened up and so much love came pouring in and out, that even his big-ness seemed small in comparison to what he felt for her, what they felt for each other, and what they felt for whatever part of the world passed through their doors.

"They say when you're born big, God has big plans for you." BJ's daddy had told him when he reached high school, mainly, BJ thought at the time, to keep him out of trouble by keeping him focused on something bigger than himself. And he had never really believed it until Mama.

All the time he'd been with Mama, during and after the hey-days of *ma's Café,* he knew his daddy had been right about that too, because for the first time he'd felt like a part of God's big plan.

But now there were no bullies to bring down, no real jobs to be had, no matter how dangerous or rough, nothing being big and strong could do to save the day.

Now, he was at a loss about God's plan again.

All he could do was what his daddy always told him to do when things were looking glum. Hope for the best, have a little more faith than usual, and oh yes, prepare for the worst.

BJ took the deep, focusing breath of the Wise Warrior, sat within the calm it created, then reached for a pen, to compose an ad to put in the classifieds about selling *ma's Café,* all the while, wondering how insane someone would have to be to answer it. Less than a week later he found out: someone exactly as insane as a certain Mr. Mills Miggston the Third.

It was too bad about the Testarosa. Ultimately, it would have made the wrong financial statement. Miggsy knew it the minute the idea popped into his head: To drive! Get the speed back! Live again! Rush to his destination, his destiny, still in the driver's seat. But showing up in that kind of car, along with cash or its equivalent, was asking for it and even though he might have been suicidal, he was no longer into pain and suffering. Besides, he knew what would happen if he got his vintage Ferrari, purchased during his idiotic *Speed At All Costs* phase, out of storage, or wherever he'd left it during his dismal *Failure to OD* phase (during which he nearly puked to death, twice, but lamentably didn't), and floored it cross-country. He wouldn't be able to stop himself. Once on the road, he'd have to open it up, drive it like a demon, just to feel alive. But, eventually, just like before, the despair would return and he'd start taking every chance he could that wouldn't endanger others, hoping to end it all even before arriving, challenging the sadistic God that was keeping him alive at every hairpin turn, on every has-been highway, to end it for him then and there. He didn't have to remind himself that although he might get his wish and find himself careening, skidding, swerving, even plunging to certain death, something would go wrong and, like a demented, inverted Super Hero, Miggsy, A.K.A. *GimpMan*, he would not die. He'd merely be crippled in another ingeniously self-destructive way. And if there was anything he definitely didn't want, it was to be even more crippled than he currently and permanently was. Of course, he could have saved himself the brutal fantasy, since the Testarosa was out before it was in, and he knew that from the beginning too. Even if he abandoned the Deadman's Curve option and everything went smoothly, it would still have taken too long to drive. There *was* some sense of urgency to the venture. Apparently, there was another self-defeating masochist out there, waiting to beat him to the punch.

He begged himself to abandon the plan altogether for all the obvious reasons, including the most obvious, that it was insane. But he just couldn't. Instead, compelled by a need so overwhelming, it was simply beyond his capacity to brush off, to be the very first in line to buy an entirely useless, not to mention inevitably filthy diner in a town whose only claim to fame was that it had once been an exit off Route 66, he decided to fly. After all, while he dawdled, time was running out.

Time was running out.

BJ had to tell Mama there was a fifty-fifty chance someone with the oddball name of Mr. Mills Miggston the Third, sane or otherwise, might be on his way at this very moment, to save and evict them. He'd been holding off, still hoping the recipe would get there first. But even if the recipe got there now, it would probably be too late, unless there was a million dollars baked into it. He had to tell her.

"Mama, darlin' we gotta talk about *ma's*," he offered tentatively. "We're running out of time."

"Time is on our side." She giddily offered, apparently channeling Mick Jagger.

"Not anymore, Mama—"

"Trust me BJ, the one thing we sure as hellfire won't run out of, if we keep going in this direction, is time," she assured him, considering herself somewhat of an expert, having just been there and back.

"Of course, I trust you, Mama, but—"

But before he could say another word, she was gone again, fathoming for the first time, the uncanny way energy she didn't even know existed before, ricocheted inside atoms, and how those microscopic masterpieces mirrored the very cosmos she'd just toured.

"Every atom is a universe, BJ, a universe of endless possibilities!" She enthused, while the electric pop of excitement accompanying this discovery launched her and her lounger from the laws of gravity.

Hovering in midair, eye-to-eye with BJ, her green robe billowed around her lounger like it was a magic carpet, while smoke rings encircled her soup can curls and the secrets of the universe slipped through the nick in her noggin.

"Did I mention that our potential is as vast and limitless as the universe?" She whispered in his ear, before the lounger with Mama on-board, floated down again.

BJ couldn't help but wonder why, if that was true, their own personal universe seemed to be crashing in on them so relentlessly.

"But Mama, darlin' I gotta tell you that I made a big decision about *ma's*—" he tried again.

"I'm sure it was a dandy one, so have a little faith," Mama interrupted again, swinging her attention away from the subject at hand and towards the singed cactus behind BJ, where she was picking up the strains of "Angel Baby."

She looked like a little girl to BJ, her face filled with wonder, and he was perplexed at how Mama, who always had her two feet planted firmly on the ground, could possibly be wrong about this. After all, he had just seen saw her levitate. He heard the Doo Wops, too. And it certainly didn't matter to him that people, however few there were left to notice, thought Mama was so loony, she was beyond the bin. Lying there, smoke blowing out of her head, moving to the groove of the universe, BJ knew that Mama had never felt so sane.

But still, there was no word about the promised recipe for apple pie.

And still, no angel.

Except from the Doo Wops, who were now back in full force, crooning, "*It's just like heaven / Being here with you—*" as unconcerned about the shakiness of the situation as Mama.

"Ah BJ," Mama popped in again, in one of her suddenly frequent pop-in, pop-up, pop-out pop-back-in episodes, "listen to my lovely Doo Wops, popping up around your head like harmonizing hummingbirds."

"*You're like an angel / Too good to be true—*" the Doo Wops serenaded Mama, and BJ's heart strings resonated with their harmonies.

"No, no, no," Mama amended, "more like a halo."

"One thing's for sure Mama," BJ smiled, pleased to have her back, for however long, "halo or not, I'm no angel."

Then, swept up in their irresistible rhythms, as the Doo Wops segued into their quintessential rendition of "That's My Desire," BJ proved it.

On the off-chance that maybe, just maybe, if he took Mama's mind off looking for the recipe, it would find her before either Mr. Miggston the Third or government agents showed up, and that would be enough to save the day, he brought out the heavy artillery. Adding his bass into the balance, BJ bumped and grinded his way through the Top Two of the All Time Top Ten Best Stripteases he'd had the amazing luck to behold during his vagabond years, working his way up and down Route 66, as host, maitre d' and bouncer, ending the countdown by joining the Doo Wops in a grand finale of "Earth Angel," while executing the tantalizing routine taught to him personally by Krystal Night, in appreciation of him beating the shit out of her full of shit boyfriend, who'd given her a black eye.

"Why those girls took that abuse, I'll never know," he told Mama, wondering if she could still hear him, rotating his hips in the slowest motion he could muster, in case she could still see him.

"They're mainly sweethearts. Older and younger than you'd think. You, of all people would see it too, Mama. You'd see it in their eyes. I know, I know, I've told ya this before. Krystal Night and Judy Blue Thighs. *Those* gals are your angels, all right, your *earth* angels. If that's what you're lookin' for," he said to her general direction.

But Mama was rotating her soup cans in search of a wave length for a miracle to surf in on.

"Right now, what I'm lookin' for is that recipe, BJ. It's gonna save the café and then some," she said, turning her head south-southwest before disappearing into wherever it was she went, again.

"Ya reckon?" It wasn't a question so much as a hope for a last-minute miracle, a prayer for a reprieve.

BJ looked at Mama in her state of divine neglect and his heart just melted right into hers. He breathed deeply, relieved, though he wasn't proud of it, that she didn't want to hear what he didn't want to say.

"Keep a look-out for that angel, BJ," Mama said, with an urgency she'd never had before.

"Trouble is," he whispered, sending a hoarse rumble in her direction that vibrated along the roasted cow grass under her chaise and shimmied right up her root chakra, "if you look around these days, there's nothin' left but fallen angels."

"You're lookin' in the wrong direction," Mama chided. "The angel's not fallin', she's runnin'."

Jane Angelina was on the run.

"Twenty-six thousand, three hundred ninety-five, ninety-six, seven, eight, nine—"

She ran the numbers together in her head to match her pace, coasting by the phantom junction where the now defunct Route 66 once had a brief rendezvous with the road she was taking, the long ago deserted New Hope Highway, which, thanks to the fact that it was no longer anything more than a dirt road going pretty much nowhere, should have been called No Hope Highway. It certainly had no hope of ever being a highway or real road of any kind ever again. But there was something about its very forsakenness that drew her back; something about its solitude and anonymity that called to her. That, of course, and the knowledge that it was the shortest way from home to work and back again, when it was vital to be on time, at an even five miles. And she had counted every one of No Hope's miles, every one of its eight thousand, eight hundred yards, every one of its eight thousand, forty-five meters, every single one of its twenty-six thousand, four hundred feet. She even multiplied them by the number of times she'd gone back and forth: twelve times a week times the fourteen weeks she'd been working at Crisp-EEE-Burger, which was one hundred sixty-eight times she'd traveled this five-mile road, mostly in the dark, since she left before sunrise and came home at nine or ten. So, she knew New Hope Highway like the back of her hand, could run it blindfolded, could feel when it was time to veer left into Leisurama Acres, the immobile mobile home park she currently was calling home.

"Four hundred!"

She'd made it in record time tonight without meaning to. Did the whole thing in less than twenty-five minutes in spite of the overloaded grocery bags clenched in each hand. And in the perfect poetry, had anyone been around to see it, although no one ever was, the sheer lyricism of her stride silhouetted in starlight, those grocery bags appeared as weightless as a relay runner's baton, even though in one, sixteen economy sized cans of chicken noodle soup were slam dancing and in the other, two half gallon bottles of Wild Turkey were clinking in an endless round of precarious toasts to a future Jane Angelina couldn't face.

No, she would not think of it. She would concentrate on the numbers. There was comfort in counting and covering ground, she told herself, gliding past forlorn remnants of what New Hope Highway once was, shards of gas station signs spiking up from the dirty sand, glistening in stolen starlight.

Her impossibly long legs barely touched down, making her appear to the casual observer, had there been one, to be flying.

"Okay," she said out loud, reminding herself to slow down at the entrance to the park, which, of course, wasn't a park at all, but a field of alternating dirt and cement slabs that had seventy-four—or more specifically seventy-three, as of Thursday—old, beaten down, beached mobile homes that weren't mobile at all, that never would or could go anywhere ever again, if they'd ever gone anywhere before. They looked like gigantic, rusting cigar tubes with gerry-rigged porches and old cars scattered around them like neglected lawn furniture.

She had to laugh. Trailers that were going nowhere planted in a "park" that looked more like a parking lot. And, of course, the cruelest joke of all. Its cheerily misleading name, Leisurama Acres, made it sound like everybody was sitting around playing cards. This, of course, couldn't have been farther from the truth, even during the hey-day of the stogie-shaped "Leisurama" trailers the park was named after, which, paradoxically, she was sure no member of the real leisure class would ever set foot in. But she didn't want to think about paradoxes tonight and she especially didn't want to dwell on the biggest paradox of all, why, for some reason yet unknown to her, even though she could barely keep her feet on the ground, she was grounded here, with the rusted-out doublewides under a sky full of stars.

She decided not to take the short-cut through the tract with the recently quitclaimed trailer, where the stray dogs roamed for scraps, which could be dicey, except the dogs hadn't been around lately. These days, it seemed that no one had a scrap of anything to spare.

It would have been perfectly safe tonight, but she wasn't in a rush to get home. Instead, to keep her mind busy counting mindless things, so it wouldn't start enumerating the innumerable ways she had failed, she took the long way around the outer edges of the grassless, treeless park, counting car parts.

She reached the back of the Farrell's trailer. Right behind it there was a big stretch of broken concrete and dry, straw grass, where there used to be hook-ups, abandoned long ago, for reasons everybody ruminated on but nobody knew for sure.

And then there was nothing left to count but her footsteps and her thoughts. One thing she wasn't going to count up were the jobs she had counted on since leaving Chloride. As if she didn't know it was five and a half, the half being the one she got at that Frostee Freeze in East Cadiz that mysteriously closed the day she started. She was beginning to feel like the Typhoid Mary of the fast-food industry, because every time she started working somewhere, the whole town ended up closing up around her, pushing her west, from Amboy to Ludlow to Newberry Springs. But she was running out of towns.

Slowing down, Jane Angelina climbed the two rickety steps onto her front porch. In the dim and flickering porch light, had there ever been anyone to look, she would have appeared to be no more than a slice of luminescence, a sliver of moonlight, a refugee from the evening sky, lighter than air, kept from floating away only by the grocery bags.

She collapsed onto the old swing her father had made out of a cut down door, especially for her, that she had taken down and put up again and again, always using the original rope he had rigged, every time she moved, which, as it turned out, was more and more these days, five times in the last three years, just to find work in a town that wasn't drying up under her feet and blowing away before her eyes.

Carefully balancing the bags on the uneven, slatted wood floor, so the Wild Turkey wouldn't knock over the chicken noodle, she settled into the seat her dad had long ago sanded to her slight contours and years of use had polished to a bony shine. Stretching to her full length, long, slender legs dangling way off the porch, she tilted the swing back a little, arched her slim neck and shoulders to release dog-tired muscles, tore off the net that was holding her wild, gossamer curls hostage, and shook her head to give them their freedom back.

The rope under her fingers was so badly frayed, it was barely hanging on by a thread. But she couldn't bring herself to replace it as long as it still held somewhere inside of it, no matter how faint, the echo of her dad's pulse, from all the time his fingers wrapped around it to push her.

She straightened her leggy legs and pumped, hoping to swing away the feeling of failure that was bouncing around her insides like pepper pie.

Because, like her beloved swing, she was at the end of her rope.

When she first got the job as the drive-thru-window order-taker slash cashier at Crisp-EEE-Burgers in East Yermo, all signs had pointed to it being the one that could last. When they told her she had job security, it sounded so official, so permanent, that she believed them because at the time it all made sense, especially since they were the only drive-through burger place in East Yermo. And from the very beginning, everyone said she had a "real knack" for the job.

To make things worse, things just kept getting better. After being at Crisp-EEE-Burger for a couple of weeks, Jane Angelina couldn't help concluding that they were consistently throwing away between two and a half and three and a quarter heads of lettuce daily. Then she couldn't help computing backwards to figure out the optimum number of lettuce leafs (seven hundred fifty-two to be exact) per average number of burgers sold daily. From there, it was a hop, skip and a jump to help out with the rest of the stock, and within a month, in the words of Earl and Esme Elps, the triple EEE's of Crisp-EEE-Burgers themselves, she had saved them "a bundle in lettuce leaves, ground round, paper goods and plasticware alone," which was what led to the offhand "job security" remark that she mistook for a promise.

And, in the hiss of fresh onions being tossed on the skillet, in the sizzle and fry of deliciously greasy burgers being slapped on the grill, in the fizz of the soda, and the slurp of the Slurpee machine, in the hubbub of caterwauling radios and the rasping sputter of idling cars, and in the electronic ka-ching of the cash register, Jane Angelina was riding high, turning over burgers, fries and change at a breakneck pace, right up there with the cashier pros who had dedicated decades to the skill, or so she was told. And the busier they got, the faster she got at it, until she hit her stride, it felt like flying and she knew she had found her calling.

But no one could have predicted that a famous four-town chain like Burger Boy with all its bells and whistles and giveaways and come-on-backs would open up across the street, to drive Crisp-EEE-Burger right out of business. And Jane Angelina right out of a job.

The porch swing creaked reliably on every third sweep, as she swung to its familiar rhythm, feeling the weight of the world on her delicate but determined shoulders. As of today, she had no job. Out of all the numbers she had counted in her life, she was down to zero. And she didn't know what to do.

"When you don't know what to do, my little angel," her dad had told her time and again on this very swing, "start counting the stars in heaven. Before you can finish, something will come to you."

Jane Angelina looked up for the first time at the star freckled sky, wondered if maybe one of those stars was her dad, trying to point her in the right direction, and began counting.

Picking up speed, propelled by the rhythm in the numbers, the cadence of her counting, she aimed that swing right up toward the heavens, and then, at the very crest of the arc, suspended by a thread somewhere between earth and sky, she looked down through a worm hole in time and saw herself a thousand years ago, when she was four.

"A thousand fifty-seven, a thousand fifty-eight ..." Jane Angelina was counting the stars in heaven, had already counted the freckles on her arms, but she kept forgetting the number of freckles, and trying to hold freckles and stars in their separate places was harder than it seemed.

She had been practicing counting every day, even though she could already count higher than Billy Willbur, who was in kindergarten, and she still had years to go to get there, because she knew that everything in the whole world depended on counting. Like when her momma said, "How many times have I told you, Jane Angelina, to make up your bed and clean up your room!" She could say, "three times today; seven times yesterday; that's ten times in two days." And that would always make her momma go real quiet, and that was a good thing.

Numbers were so reliable. They were always the same. Not like when someone said, "How are you, Jane Angelina?" And she had to think about what to say back. There were just too many answers you could get all tangled in. But numbers could be counted on.

Once she tried only giving number answers to *how are you* questions.

"How are you, Jane Angelina?"

"Seven and a half out of ten."

That seemed to make people nervous, so she stopped talking in numbers.

But it didn't stop her from knowing that whatever kind of a day she might be having, however shaky the ground felt underneath her, there were *always* twenty-three daddy and fifty-seven Jane Angelina footsteps from the front gate to the kitchen, where there were always three place settings on the table, though only two people ever ate there, and her momma always took one last swig directly from the bottle when she heard Jane Angelina's dad coming, and then popped three Chicklets—one-two-three—into her mouth and chewed like crazy, way too fast to count, to kiss him hello. Everything in life, happy or sad, was accounted for with numbers.

One afternoon, *this* afternoon, the voices coming from inside the bedroom were so ugly that Jane Angelina grabbed her mom's dog, Rummy, and buried her head in his prickly fur to drown them out.

"How many, how many times have I . . . ?"

Jane Angelina hugged Rummy so tight, all his fleas began to pop off of him like even the fleas couldn't stand it. She began counting them.

"How many times have I told—have I *begged* you?" Her dad's soft voice scolded and pleaded at the same time.

"One—two—three—four—fleas about to hit the floor," Jane Angelina sang to herself in a nursery rhyme rhythm.

"Leave me alone!" Her momma wailed in that tinny voice of hers which meant business.

"Twenty-four, twenty-five, twenty-six, twenty-seven dirty old fleas not goin' to heaven." Jane Angelina chanted, squishing fleas between her fingers.

"Maybe if you'd just try!" Her dad spit out.

"All I do is try!" Her momma's voice sounded like breaking glass.

"This isn't good, Lily, isn't good for our daughter," he reasoned with her.

"Don't use her against me! She's not even your—"

"Don't, don't don't!" Her father's voice, exploded unexpectedly and un-characteristically, shutting her mother up for the first time. "Don't you go there, Lily! She is my precious Jane Angelina and I will do anything I can do to protect her, even from you!"

Jane Angelina gave up on fleas and ran around to the very back of the backyard to the private place she'd found in the bushes last summer where the garbage cans were. But her momma's voice raced after her like a speeding bullet. So, she ducked.

There must have been a thousand ants around the largest can due to a nearby popsicle stick with lots of strawberry ices still left on it.

"I try and try." Her momma's wails pierced through the bushes and bounced off the garbage cans, sending shivers through the line of ants headed for the ices.

"Try harder!" Her dad sounded all cramped up.

Jane Angelina decided to concentrate only on ants that reached the popsicle stick.

"Fifty-nine, sixty, sixty-one—"

"You promised, Lily. You promised."

Jane Angelina rocked back and forth on her haunches studying the ants, wondering if they had ears that could hear what she heard.

"No, *you* promised! You promised you'd *never*—" Her momma's voice got smaller and smaller, and still, Jane Angelina could hear it clearly, even when it was barely quivering, "*ever judge me.*"

"One hundred seventeen, one hundred eighteen, one hundred nineteen—"

"That was a promise destined to be broken!"

The words burst from her dad as if they'd been cooped up inside him for way too long.

There were one hundred thirty-two ants covering the popsicle stick at the very moment when the silence started. Jane Angelina and the ants held their breath and waited in the stillness for all hell to break loose.

"I live in a world of broken promises!" Her mother finally howled, scattering the ants, messing up Jane Angelina's final count of ants on a popsicle stick. Now she didn't know what number to tell Sally Watson, who depended upon her to be exact, which was one of the things she loved about Sally.

"But *I'm* not the one who deceived you!" Her dad whispered. But Jane Angelina heard every bitter word and although she wasn't exactly sure what it all meant, besides trouble, it made her stomach turn.

"No, but you were the one who said you would be my one true friend!"

Besides Sally Watson, Jane Angelina had seven friends, including Jacky Jessup and Billy Willbur. Her parents had none. Sometimes of the two parents she had, zero were really there.

Every day every thing had a number. Deep in her heart of hearts, she had one wish and it had to do with numbers. She wished that at least one night, three people would sit around the dinner table together and be a family.

"For God's sake, Lily! I'm trying to help you! Why can't you see that?" Her dad pleaded.

"You promised I could always count on you. But it turns out I can't count on you at all!" Her momma shrilled as if she hadn't heard him.

Counting the stars in God's heavenly sky was another matter from these things on earth, however, because they kept blinking in and out all the time. And then there were the shooting stars that if you missed them, your whole count would be off, and your luck would be even more iffy than usual.

And counting freckles wasn't any easier. Especially now.

Because thanks to swimming in Doc Mobry's pond all day, millions of freckles kept coming out on Jane Angelina's arms, a lot like when the stars came out on summer nights. And the minute she saw the freckles twinkling in the firmament of her arm skin, she thought of that church song about the stars in God's firmament on high and that was it. She just had to find out exactly how many of each, because she just knew that this was the night that when she counted up the stars in the sky and the freckles on her arms, they would add up to exactly the same number. And her wish would come true.

But the yelling just got louder and louder, until it drowned out all the numbers and she just couldn't hold freckles and stars straight, no matter how hard she tried.

After that, things got silent for so many days that it hurt to count them, and then good luck struck in a bad way, when her dad got steady job five towns over and had to leave real early in the morning before everyone got up and didn't get home till way after everyone was asleep. And he all but disappeared from her life, haunting her like a ghost whose scent she caught in hallways and around corners. And nothing ever really added up right again, except on Saturdays, when he came home just after dinner, as soon as the stars came out, just in time to push her on her swing.

Jane Angelina held on to the swing and shut her eyes tight to ward off one more second of remembering. But those pesky memories just grabbed her with their sticky little fingers and pulled her into the darkness behind her lids.

It was time to leave. Jane Angelina, the head Queen Bee in the gala, end of the year, fourth grade insect play, feeling glamorous in padded yellow felt, glittery black antennae, and sparkly, gauzy wings, went to fetch her mother, who didn't want to be called momma anymore, now that Jane Angelina was a big girl and in school, and had to "show some respect."

Jane Angelina envisioned her mother, who had promised to get dressed up for this momentous occasion, looking like she did in the photograph, when she was "Lily Preston, Miss Paradise of the Hotel Eden," her eyes, spotlights of love shining on something just beyond the camera. But tonight, sitting in the audience, her eyes would be spotlights of love shining just on Jane Angelina

Not able to wait another second to see her mother in the navy-blue silk suit she got the time she won the modeling contest at the Hotel Eden, the "proudest moment" of her life, impatient to start their magic evening together, Jane Angelina raced towards the tiny, closed-in back porch that her mother called her "day room." Her padded Queen Bee feet flew across the hallway, doing all twenty-seven and three-quarters steps in a split-second, but what she saw through the half open door made her stop short.

Her mother was still in her slip, on the Salvation Army fold-a-way cot she made everyone call her "chaise," propped up on two pillows, looking into her Scotch glass like she always did, trying to read the washed out letters that used to spell out "Lily **P**reston **M**iss **P**aradise of the **H**otel **E**den!" although only the **L**, the **H**, the **E**, the two **P**'s and the exclamation point were really left, so when her mother turned it around and around in her hand, it spelled out, "**H E ! L P P**."

Jane Angelina slipped into the edge of the tiny room.

Lily Preston Murphy, the former Lily Preston, Miss Paradise of the Hotel Eden in the old Palm Springs, didn't look up but just stared at her glass, the last of a set of six, her own personal crystal ball.

"Are you almost ready?" Jane Angelina's voice, embarrassed as it was to have hope, came from so far inside her Queen Bee's costume that it slipped out in a whisper, but it got through.

Lily Preston Murphy's attention snapped from the glass to the door. "That was the time," she said, forcing herself back from the somewhere over the rainbow that the whisky always took her. "That was the time," she rhapsodized.

Trying to focus on her daughter, she cranked herself up on the mattress, which was worn down to a thin strip of used-to-be padded cloth barely covering rusted out springs that groaned with so much vexation every time she moved, they were like disagreeable, meddlesome spinster aunts always putting in their two cents.

"You promised you wouldn't break your promise." Jane Angelina's wispy voice caught on a snag in her throat and disappeared back into her costume.

Even through the sweet whisky haze, Lily Preston Murphy could see in her daughter's eyes that whipped dog look, like Rummy, who was that way when they got him off the street, still begging for a crumb of kindness, no matter how many times he got kicked around. Once a stray always a stray. There was no way around it. And Jane Angelina, God bless her, had the soul of a stray. Her eyes were just too deep to travel to. Every time Lily looked into them, she drowned. But not today. Today she would get up. Today she would go see her daughter in a play. How hard could it be?

She raised her glass to Jane Angelina, but in the glistening amber blur she saw the blade of a man who went down as smooth as Scotch, holding out his hand for her.

Trying not to believe the promise in his smile, Lily Preston put her free hand down and leaned back on her arm to ever so gracefully propel herself up. But her arm could not support her weight.

Jane Angelina saw her mother's match stick arm buckle under the strain of holding up her puny body and raced across the tiny room on a collision course with the cot. Skidding to a halt not a second too soon, Queen Bee stomach crushed against the metal frame, gossamer wings fluttering furiously, balanced precariously on one bean pole leg, not knowing whether to move forward or backward, suddenly hearing voices she didn't understand buzzing inside her ears, Jane Angelina thrust her skinny arm out of the Queen Bee's ovoid body for her mother to grab onto. But her mother would not let go of her terrible grip on the glass, the last of a set of six.

Jane Angelina wanted to shout, "put the drink down, momma! Please put it down!" But that would be to say the words no one was allowed to say. So, she just fluttered there in an awkward arabesque, holding out her hand, thinking about the other words she was never allowed to say, words like scotch, like bourbon, like whiskey, like, like ... She held her breath to keep it all locked in, feeling a little woozy from the murmuring in her head.

"Ya gonna make me do all the work pretty lady? Or are ya gonna get off your high horse and dance with me?"

"Oh? Are you asking me to dance?" Lily Preston purred, extending her lily-white hand.

His hand reached out to take hers. They leaned into each other and were dancing before they started to dance.

"Momma. It's time to go. Take my hand," Jane Angelina whispered a little too loudly, to drown out the voices. But whose voices, she could not begin to say.

Lily Preston Murphy, awash in voices now, took a long, resolute pull on her drink, willing herself, over the noisy protests of the rusted-out springs, to be galvanized into action by the harsh jolt of cheap whiskey tearing a path through her gut on its way to her ulcer. But instead of rising effortlessly, as she had done so many times in her dreams, she lurched forward.

To Jane Angelina's horror, in the split second before her mother could steady herself, her frail arm slammed against the cot dislodging the last glass from the Hotel Eden, which exploded from her hand and crashed into a thousand pieces, not because it hit so hard but because like almost everything else in the room, it was threadbare.

Lily Preston Murphy sat at the edge of the bed in a daze, while bourbon and fractured glass rained all over her and the pillows and the almost-new Chenille bedspread and the sheets.

And on Jane Angelina, ruining her beautiful costume and the rest of her whole life! She couldn't show up at school reeking of the family secret.

No one would ever talk to her again. She would have zero friends. She smelled like the one word she was not allowed even to let herself think. She tried so hard to hold it in, but she just couldn't.

"I smell like a—a—a—drunk!" she blurted out, wanting to die on the spot.

Lily Preston Murphy flinched, like someone slapped in the face in a movie.

"Look at me! My costume is ruined!" Jane Angelina sobbed.

Lily Preston Murphy's gaze hovered for a moment somewhere in the vicinity of the Queen Bee's soggy wings, before it fell upon the whisky-doused splinters of glass, which sparkled like golden stars in the scuffed linoleum sky around her feet.

"The Hotel Eden is gone and I'll never get it back," she gasped, sliding from the cot, her voice as shattered as her glass.

Jane Angelina could not take her eyes off the curious constellation on the floor. In her seen-better-days white satin slip and her sad disarray, covered from head to toe with twinkling, jagged shards, her mother looked like some kind of fallen angel. And Jane Angelina's heart broke for her.

Maybe it was the scent of whisky loosed in the cooped-up room. Or maybe Jane Angelina was still reeling from the voices which kept fading in and out like a far away radio station she really didn't want to tune into. But what really veered her off her tracks, were the ghosts shimmering in the splintered glass, reflected in every glistening sliver, etched by her mother's longing. Jane Angelina saw it all, the girl her mother had been and the magic that had bewitched her—the outstretched hand, the crooked smile, the man and the dance that lasted all night but ended too soon.

"That was the time, that was the time," she heard her mother say, but if in the here and now, or there and then, Jane Angelina would never be sure. The only thing she could be sure of was that her mother was small and broken and she needed someone to put her back together and help her find her way back home, which is what you had to do for fallen angels.

And, as Jane Angelina was standing there contemplating remedies for her mother, all thoughts of herself just slipped away through the break in her own heart, and vanished into the whisky mist.

"But I never meant, never meant to—" Lily Preston Murphy stammered, to explain the unexplainable.

Again, Jane Angelina reached out for her. "I forgive you, momma," she said, tears welling in her eyes.

Lily Preston Murphy pulled herself onto her knees, looked up into Jane Angelina's eyes, and saw Jesus.

Looking into her daughter's eyes and seeing Jesus would be enough to drive *any* mother to drink. But, since Lily Preston Murphy had experienced this phenomenon *while* drinking, and since she was down on her knees anyway, she decided to pray. She prayed for strength. She prayed for salvation. She made promises she had never before been able to keep.

She thanked Jesus for lifting up her soul, though it was Jane Angelina who lifted her body and carefully carried her into the bathroom, and bathed her, and tucked her in bed in a clean flannel gown, and brought her soup. And nursed her back to health. And it was Jane Angelina who forgave her and who looked after her, keeping vigil during the long nights of her slow recuperation. But it was Jesus who Lily Preston Murphy only had eyes for now. And it was in His name, that in the bloom of her miraculous recovery, she vowed to become *a better mother.*

And when her strength finally returned, she kept that vow.

In her first act as *a better mother*, she shed her maiden name and all its ties to the past, joined the church, padlocked her day room, officially renounced drinking, except on religious occasions when it would be sacrilege not to, and plopped Jane Angelina into Sunday School and Bible Studies Class.

On the day of her Baptism, washed clean of, and freed at last from, original sin and all those other dirty little sins that it attracted, she dedicated her life, and Jane Angelina's, to Jesus, whose Gospel, especially as interpreted by Pastor William, would surely keep her daughter on the straight and narrow and so far away from temptation that Jane Angelina would *never* fall from grace as she had done.

By the sixth month of her conversion, Lily Murphy had read and re-read the New Testament so often, she could recite most of her favorite parts by heart, and did, whenever she was around her daughter, which was often, since now that she was stronger, she took it upon herself to follow Jane Angelina around the house as the girl did her chores, devoutly, somberly, resolutely quoting Matthew, Luke, John, and countless others who were all very concerned about keeping Jane Angelina away from the forbidden fruit and on the path to deliverance. Whether Jane Angelina was making her mother's special soup, or cleaning up, or doing the laundry, or even her homework, Lily Murphy always went this extra mile to save her daughter's soul.

In the eighth month of her conversion, Lily Murphy hit a snag on the road to redemption. Taking to heart, Pastor William's pointed papal advice that it would be easier to get to heaven on the family plan, Lily Murphy made a personal plea to Jesus to save her marriage.

Steeped as she was in His teachings now, striving as she was to become the perfect Christian mother, struggling to raise the perfect Christian daughter, took so much out of her, she explained to Jesus, she hadn't had time to even think of being the perfect Christian—or really any kind of—wife. And it wasn't really her fault that she hadn't begun work on saving her husband's soul, because his soul wasn't around to be saved. Truth be known—and after all, who can hide the truth from God—she couldn't remember the last time they actually spoke or even crossed paths. She did recollect looking up from her evening meditation on the Book of Revelations and seeing him outside on the swing with Jane Angelina. But exactly when that was, was hard to know.

At that point in time, in fact, Jane Angelina's father was working five towns over and only came home every other weekend, during which he mostly slept from exhaustion, except for sitting under the stars with her, trying to fit into the arc of those moments everything that was the best in him that he had to give.

And when on her mission from God, Lily Murphy drew him back home, she knew it was not with the brave, helpless smile he had fallen for so long ago, that she could no longer try to muster. What drew him back, she decided between Communion and Confession, what drew him back in, well it certainly wasn't the girl inside her, who so far, even Jesus couldn't resurrect. No, what drew him back was the hold her daughter had on his heart.

And so, in the ninth month of her mother's conversion, Jane Angelina's father miraculously found work closer to home for the first time in years. And although he left very early and worked very late, for a whisper of a moment every day, they were a family.

Settling into this strange routine, life went on, with the three of them residing under one roof again, not for hours or even weeks or months, but years.

They made it to their fifth Christmas together, exchanging modest gifts around a flocked plastic tree trimmed with a hodgepodge of crucifixes and saints, and topped with a cross formed by a choir of cherubs that sang, "Oh come all ye faithful, joyful and triumphant." While her mother skittishly trilled along in a voice tinnier than the thrift store angels, restively rearranging the tinsel, Jane Angelina who could by now quote the New Testament, chapter and verse, held her breath and decided not to count how many hours of not drinking five years took up, although of course she knew it was forty-three thousand, eight hundred.

Exactly eight thousand seven hundred sixty hours of not drinking later, Lily Murphy celebrated the sixth Christmas of her conversion by finishing off Holy Communion with "just a few more sips of Holy Wine" than usual, "to put me ever more in touch with my Maker."

But she could never get close enough. Lamentably, after her initial, illuminating glimpse of Jesus, things kept getting darker and salvation seemed to be slipping farther and farther away. Deprived re-entry to her own personal Eden once before, the former Miss Paradise came to a solemn decision. No longer taking her title just as a sin of the past anymore, but also as a sign—and perhaps even a promise—of future redemption, she resolved not to lose her way this time. Instead, she prayed even harder, pacing the house, clutching her Bible, furiously reciting the Scriptures. Until, one feverish night, Lily Murphy got what she was praying for, a special delivery directly from Jesus that to get back on that fast track to salvation, she had to pull herself away from earthly concerns, which she translated into not doing the laundry.

She observed Easter that year rededicating herself to the body, the blood, and the resurrection, by setting up a makeshift communion altar in her former day room, which she un-padlocked with the solemnity of the Apostles opening Jesus's tomb, and cleaned up. Once again on her hands and knees in an act of contrition, she confessed, while she scrubbed, to sins committed so long ago that if there were pictures taken of them, they would surely have faded.

When her former day room was spotless, she re-anointed it, "My Little Chapel of Jesus of the Gospels," sometimes praying there all night, since she wasn't sleeping all that well anymore anyway, taking her own Holy Sacrament of vanilla wafers and Gallo wine in the deep, ecclesiastical hush-hush.

Those were the nights that Jane Angelina and her father sat on her swing under the stars to count into eternity together. And it was there that they said good-bye.

"Come with me, Angel," he had pleaded in the weeks before he was set to leave for a better job in another state. But of course, he knew she could no more go than he could stay.

Wishing things had worked out differently, he held her high in the swing like he had when she was a little girl, to give her enough velocity so, when he let go, she could touch the stars. She was sixteen, and long and lanky, like he was, and still lighter than air.

Watching the moon glow on her radiant skin, he whispered in her ear. "Reach for the stars. You're already an angel, so you won't have far to go." And released the swing.

As Jane Angelina sailed heavenward, balanced so perfectly on the swing she looked like she was flying, he walked away.

By the time Jane Angelina graduated from high school, her mother had reached just the right balance of piety and self-righteousness, with of course, just the proper tinge of self-pity, to justify her more and more frequent need for Holy Communion.

Ever vigilant and attentive, Jane Angelina had concocted just the right balance of ingredients to put in her special soup to modify, at least in her own, homemade way, some of the effects of too much holy wine, even though she knew that nothing, no amount of Holy Wine, not even Jesus Christ, Himself, could ever satisfy her mother's deep, abiding thirst.

"Janey! Janey Angelina! Is that you? I need my soup! I've been waiting for my soup!" Lily Preston Murphy, the former Miss Eden from the Paradise hotel, called from her day room.

Jane Angelina's stomach clenched from the swing's sudden descent.

BJ turned down Front Street, which he had long ago made a point of never doing anymore. Tumbleweeds the size of watermelons were blowing right through what used to be Lem Johnston's, Young Widow Heaney's, Babe and Sam Gundry's, and even the Olsen family's houses.

That's when his memory woke up, swigged down a fast espresso, turned around and bit him in the rear. Time slowed down, the wind blew, and in the dusty haze of swirling sand and dust, the entire Olsen brood, all eleven of them, marched out like they used to every Sunday for church, in size places, neat-as-a-pin, from their clean-as-a-whistle house, where he and Mama had dinner so many times, it was like a second home, but he saw now, was hardly more than a shack.

In his beloved pick-up, Lucille, BJ drove aimlessly up and down streets he used to know, but weren't even streets anymore. He counted without meaning to, the people who just pulled up stakes and blew away. Seemed like the whole town had rusted out and was turning back into sand, along with the dream Mama dreamed in "the halcyon days," as Mama called them, of *ma's Café*, when this town was more than a bunch of junk cluttering up the desert.

He drove for several more forsaken miles, mindlessly turned right, and there it was, what was left of the exit he'd taken off Route 66 on that fateful day his life had changed forever. And although it was almost too hard to bear that everything associated with this town, even the highway that led him here and the exit that delivered him to Mama, had turned to sand, it wasn't really a surprise to end up back here where it all began.

He was coming off his post-bouncer career high of being named Industrial Awning, Porch Furniture and Canopy Covering Salesman of the Year for the Southwest Region, Barstow to Needles, which he'd achieved by a solid year of dropping by every factory, building, hotel, restaurant, café, diner, and dive in twenty-seven counties, seven days a week, fifty-two weeks a year, and he was getting mighty tired of the road. Well, everything about the road except Lucille, the finest pick-up that ever rolled off a Detroit assembly line.

Thanks to his windfall year, due to the good people of the Southwest Region, he had just treated himself to Lucille, who was brand spankin' new, full of herself, bright and shiny, and as loaded with piss and vinegar as he was. Add to that a suspension that was too smooth to be true, and naturally, they just couldn't help struttin' their stuff, cruising the back roads on and off Route 66, BJ reminiscing about his footloose days and ruminating about his future, because, after all was said and done, once he became Salesman of the Year, the challenge had drained right out of Industrial Awnings, Porch Furniture and Canopy Covering. He was thinking of all that as he drove up that hill and approached the brand newest and certainly the shiniest of his potential customers, *ma's Café*, at high noon.

And there she was. Strutting down the freshly welded aluminum steps, which were shimmering in the noon-day sun in front of *ma's Café*.

She had flaming copper hair, the color of forest fires, that frizzed and coiled out from her head like rusty bed springs, and clashed perfectly with her bright, robin's egg blue, crisply starched, tight, one hundred percent cotton, at least two hundred ply waitress uniform, which was cinched at her plump and generous waist and took his eyes for a wild ride right into her luxuriant cleavage. And what's more, every fine, oh so fine, inch of her was reflected over and over and over in the diner's shiny aluminum panels, endless, never-ending Mamas radiating from the original Mama like she was the entire chorus line from Harrah's coming down to greet him personally.

She descended those steps like the Queen of Rhumba and he knew that whatever she was dancing to, they were playing his song.

She was just going to check out the owner of the brand new, fully loaded, oversized pick up, when she saw Paul Bunyan loping to the café, carrying a sample case the size of a steamer trunk like it was an empty sack.

He was whistling. Not just with his lips, but with his whole body and soul. He was filled with music whistling through him. Something she couldn't resist in a man. Plus, there was so much of him to whistle through. Something else she couldn't resist.

He crossed the street in two strides and by the time he took her Pond's cold-creamed, soft-as-butter hand in his big ham hock mitt to help her down the steps, not that she needed any help, their fates were sealed.

"And what's a tall drink of water like you doing in this neck of the woods?" she offered by way of hello.

"I'm here to interest you in patio awnings. Canopies to shelter your beautiful café from the harsh desert sun. Ya know, a good awning can add ten years to the life of your exterior wall," he said, with unabashed appreciation of Mama's exterior construction.

"Well," Mama said, eyeing his sample case, "no sense discussing this in the hot sun. Come inside and show me what ya got."

Over the most ambrosial lemonade he'd ever had the good fortune to savor, he did.

With the aid of his mammoth sample case and all the vivid solid, striped, and patterned wonders within it, which he called to the fore in a tour de force of color and hue, a dazzling display of Dacron and vinyl, BJ took Mama on a dizzying journey through the world of world-class canopies and awnings, giving her the ins-and-outs, the ups-and-downs, the nitty and the gritty, the general low down, and the what's-what. And when he was through extolling the virtues of the 99% UVA protection, confirmed by two independent laboratories, having already pointed out the finer points of adding aircraft grade aluminum to industrial strength Dacron, not to mention the genius of applying at least four coats of urethane for maximum strength, fade resistance and protection, and when Mama was still aahing, having already oohed over his amazing demonstration, utilizing a scaled down, "accurate to the last lug nut" replica awning (which appeared in his prodigious digits as if from thin air) to prove beyond a shadow of a doubt that the best awnings, such as his, could lower indoor temperatures in rooms, such as hers, by up to twenty degrees Fahrenheit, without the use of air-conditioning or even fans, and when he had reached the crescendo, unveiling a brand-new line of light reflecting awnings, in colors so vibrant—thanks to the magic of modern science and a top-secret, newly patented process called "fliridescence"—they could be seen for miles, day or night, as far out as Route 66, when he at last revealed the very last sample, the very top of the top of the line, the ne plus ultra, the brilliantly "flirescent" *Silverado Awning* from the cornucopia of his case, and it was all laid out for Mama, Mama laid it all out for him. Pure and simple, Mama had plans for New Nebo. She was going to put New Nebo on the map!

She was a knockout, Mama was, on that first thirst-quenching after-noon, the billowing pillows of her saucy bosom pouring out of her delicious décolletage like a Niagara Falls of honey every time she leaned over to pour lemonade into what had turned out to be one frosty glass after another.

"Believe you, me," BJ told Mama when he had talked himself dry, clear-ing his samples from the table in an eye-blink, watching her work *her* magic on another pitcherful, "I've sampled lemonade from Teaneck to Topeka to Tehachapi and back again. I am no lemonade tenderfoot by any stretch. In fact, some have even called me a lemonade aficionado. So, you know, I've had my thirst quenched and my whistle wetted by the best of them. But it's still hard to believe that something so—" he paused here, searching for the right words and smiled the Grand Canyon of smiles when he found them "—something so deeply *stirring* could come out of a little lemon juice, water and sugar."

"Well, I just make it the way I like it," Mama demurred, fanning herself with a menu.

"Well," BJ rumbled, draining another glass, "I sure do like it the way you make it."

His voice, having run out of juice somewhere along the way, was now reduced to a soft, velvety growl that rose up from the core of him and re-verberated through the café.

"Guess we're just birds of a feather," Mama cooed, pouring another round while the earth moved under her feet.

In the end, when Mama special-ordered the spectacular silver and white striped top of the line *Silverado,* BJ promised to come back and in-stall it personally.

The day the awning arrived and BJ with it, Mama offered free lemonade to all her customers, neighbors, and friends to celebrate. Everyone was still buzzing about the great sleight of hand, prestidigitation, abracadabra, hocus-pocus, and all-around legerdemain that Mama had already pulled off, convincing the post office, in coordination with nothing less than the United States Marines, to move the entire town of Nebo, or at least its name and post-mark, by creating a New Nebo and giving it its own exit off Route 66. Of course, after taking a gander at the silver extravaganza that had materialized over *ma's Café*, just like the beacon for weary travelers and other potential customers BJ had promised it would be, every other store owner on New Main Street ordered reflecting awnings in all the newest "flirescent" colors, created from the process of "fliridescence," extracting the promise that BJ would come back to install them personally. Naturally, when BJ did the math, he realized he'd be spending a lot of time in New Nebo, which is exactly what he wanted.

When the sun had long ago set on the Awning Welcoming Celebration, Mama and BJ sat in Mama's newly paved patio kicking back, winding down, looking up at BJ's handiwork. Above them, an enormous canopy of shimmering "flirescent" silver and white stripes illumined the darkening desert. And, if that wasn't enough, BJ's special surprise gift for Mama, his personal piece de resistance, *ma's Café,* spelled in letters so luminous that to anyone traveling on Route 66 for miles in every direction, it looked like *ma's Café* was written across the sky.

And if even *that* wasn't enough, on this wondrous night it was BJ who offered the liquid refreshment, twelve-year-old scotch he'd won off of some pretty big high rollers in a Poker game outside of Reno, that he'd been saving for a special occasion. And, from the moment he laid eyes on her, he knew that if Mama didn't qualify as a special occasion, nothing ever would.

For her part, Mama's normally big-hearted heart, not to mention every other working part of her, was just about bursting to forgo her own blathering and hitch a ride up and down every one of the thousands of miles of memories she figured BJ had up his stupendous sleeves. But there was something about BJ and the way he listened like he whistled, with every part of him, that unhinged *her* memories, and no matter how hard she tried to head them off at the pass, and herd them back in, they kept making a break for it, giggling like school girls at recess. She couldn't help it. She was bursting with stories to share with this man.

"Well, putting the blind preacher and the nun-masseuse on hold for a second," Mama heard herself say, trying to put a stopper on another story before it popped out.

"Let's just say, me and SunnySide Up," she went on, meaning the bright yellow VW bus parked under its own personal, fliridescent canopy, that had been her only traveling companion and confidante for years, "me and SunnySide," she repeated, because it bore repeating, "we sure put on a lot of miles together, most of them off the beaten path."

Mama took a long, ruminative pull on her drink, savoring the aged scotch. Then, she lifted the bottle in a silent toast to all the dusty towns she'd been drawn to.

"And, if there's one thing I've learned," she said, summing up her life on the road, knowing without asking that BJ would say the same, "you don't choose the desert. The desert chooses you."

It was true, Mama confided, her eyes sparkling in the flirescent light, she had never really *chosen* the desert, and she had never exactly *meant* to settle down. It was just that having left home when she was barely sixteen, and after being on the road non-stop ever since, she had rolled her tired and weary bones up to that strange intersection, that Bermuda triangle junction of Daggett and Nebo, in the same twinkling of an eye that Irma of

"Irma's Café" put out her *For Sale* sign. And after years of going nowhere in particular, settling down somewhere for awhile didn't seem like a half bad idea.

She had looked up from the sign, and there was Irma herself, nodding through the glass and waving her in like a long-lost friend. Irma, who looked to be on the retread side of forty, was skinnier than spaghetti and wiry as a terrier. Irma's wiriness trampolined up and down her body and right out of her head in wisps of hair that escaped from her high shellac, high performance, perfect beehive. She looked to Mama like she could read the future.

"So, y'interested in real estate?" she tossed off over her shoulder, opening the door and heading back towards the kitchen. "Or do ya consider yourself more like, say, a rolling stone?"

Now, Mama's poppa was a rolling stone, but if there was one thing he loved, besides his family and the road, it was real estate. At least he said that's why he covered so much ground. Mama, who was still Norma Lee at the time, loved her poppa. But, when all was said and done, she was left driving in his tire tracks, up and down phantom highways through towns she'd only heard of from postmarks on post cards, trying to divine his philosophy of life on the road from streams of words that trickled through him and then dried out before the post cards did.

"I know you gotta follow in my footsteps," he told her once, when they were fishing.

"It's in your blood," he offered later, then fell back into his fishing stillness.

And on the way back, after complimenting her for her catch in that way of his with, "the trout were swimming to you, like they always do, Norma Lee," he lapsed into silence again, then said, completing a thought he hadn't started out loud, "But when all is said and done, it ain't right for someone else to own the land under your bed, now is it?"

Of course, SunnySide Up had solved that problem in a sort-of, sort of way. Since she owned SunnySide, wherever they went, they were home. But she was seeing holes in her thinking big enough to drive SunnySide right through. Problem was, her poppa was a rolling stone, all right, but there was only one place he ever called home. And it was on solid ground, not wheels.

"Can ya cook?" Irma asked, beckoning her away from her ruminations, and to the counter with a fresh pot of coffee.

In fact, Norma Lee loved to cook. Cooking, to her was like meditating was to people who meditated. Besides traveling, which at that moment was the farthest thing from her heart's desire, and sinking into a good man who, so far, was hard to find, cooking up a storm was her all-time favorite thing to do, and truth be known, it was getting a bit cramped in ole SunnySide.

"Love it." Norma Lee said, saying it all.

"Well then, sweetie," Irma said, tucking Norma Lee under the wing of her confidence, like the sister they both never had, slowing her seventy-eight RPM voice to thirty-three and a third, "you'll make a friggin' fortune here!"

"Well," Norma Lee admitted, shyly, a shadow of doubt momentarily clouding her zeal, "I sure love do love to cook, and I do adore baking hams, casseroles of all kinds, and potatoes in all their glories, but I'm just not one for baking pies, cakes or cookies, without help from my friend Betty Crocker. Never had the knack. Not that I don't love eating them, of course. But pastry's never been my thing, Irma. Ya think it'll matter?"

"Oh pahleeze," Irma smiled, hugging Norma Lee. "Just as long as whatever you serve is fresh and served with a smile, no one will even notice who baked it, you, Betty, or Sara Lee. Me, for example, I burn the toast half the time. I'm a crappy cook. Hate it, as a matter of fact, but I'm doing a helluva business. Ya know why? Two reasons. Location and Charm."

Irma leaned across the counter to pour the proffered coffee and filled Norma Lee in about the history of the ever-expanding military base, and its never-ending supply of customers, hungry for some home cooking and a little flattery.

"That's where the charm kicks in sweetie—" she winked, displaying hers. Her Revlon's Fire & Ice lips broke into a smile that made Norma Lee feel like she was being let in on a really delicious secret, which as it turned out, indeed, she was. No doubt about it, Irma, albeit a little ragged around the edges, was definitely in a class of her own.

She reminded Norma Lee of the gypsy fortune teller who stopped her on the street just outside of Kingman and said, "Trust your instincts."

"So," Irma asked, leaning in real close for some girl talk, pointing out the window to SunnySide Up. "Been on the road long?"

"Feels like it." Norma Lee thought out loud. "Seen lots of gas stations."

"Where've ya been?"

"Everywhere I could think of going that was hot and dry." Norma Lee said, feeling every mile for the first time.

But weary as she was, Norma Lee assured Irma that she'd do it all again, because every place she and SunnySide had set foot in and every person they met had their own, special stories they were just spilling over to tell, and their stories intertwined with each other and with the history of the Mojave, itself. And all she had to do was sit down and take it all in. Sometimes she'd have a palaver in a local bar, sometimes a chit chat in a neighborhood diner. She'd just sit a spell, with her ham and eggs or bourbon straight up, and listen with her open heart, and the stories flowed.

And they kept coming, like all the coffee she could drink for a quarter, up, down and around the parched back roads of the Mojave, as a student of history, until SunnySide's tires were as bald as cue balls and they rolled her right into Irma's Café.

"I can tell you're a people person." Irma ventured. "And if you're as good a cook as I suspect you are, sweetie, the world's gonna beat a path to your door!" A few more determined wisps of high gloss hair sprung themselves from her shellacked beehive to help emphasize the point.

"You ever travel?" Norma Lee asked, knowing the answer.

"Sure did, once."

"Where'd you go?"

"Where *didn't* I?" Irma stage whispered. "If ya catch my drift, sweetie."

Norma Lee nodded, filling in the dots of the Irma picture.

"This place has been very good to me," Irma smiled. "But now it's time to move on."

"I know what you mean," Norma Lee said, because even though she seemed to be suffering from a temporary loss of wanderlust, she really did.

"I know you do," Irma winked. And Norma Lee and Irma saw in each other kindred spirits.

"It's a steady business, guaranteed, and it's about to get even better," Irma assured her new-found protégée, after sharing a pot of coffee, a shot or two of her favorite sherry, and war stories about the sorry state of manhood these days. And somewhere in the middle of it, striking a deal.

"I gotta admit it, Irma," Norma Lee confessed, holding out her hand to shake on it. "I don't have one more mile in me. But what I do have is at least fourteen ways of making pot-roast, a repertoire of hams I've been itching to try out, a God given talent for omelets and hash browns, and a nest egg I've been waiting to crack open."

With the timing of jewel thieves, Irma reached down to the safe, opened it and extracted the deed, while Norma Lee reached down into her brassiere and extracted a compressed roll of bills from which she quickly counted out the agreed upon down payment.

"I'm tellin' ya Norma Lee, sweetie," Irma trilled, pocketing her new capital, "you'll recoup your investment in no time. The place is already a gold mine, what with the military base down the block, and now with that new TV show rousing the whole country to head for Route 66 again, honey, with *real* home cookin', well, folks'll be flocking to that Nebo exit and right to your door like bees to honey! But I'm off to pursue my life long dream of being a Vegas showgirl, while I still got my looks. The way I see it, it's now or never!"

And with that, she put her John Hancock on the deed, tossed the keys to Norma Lee, threw off her apron, high-stepped it out from behind the counter, and headed to Vegas.

And Norma Lee had herself a café, on a piece of land all her own.

"Send me a post-card. You know the address!" Norma Lee shouted after Irma, fully believing that no matter what side of forty Irma was pushing, it didn't matter. She was a force of nature. "Las Vegas watch out!" Norma Lee remarked to no one in particular. And she meant it.

The first thing she did was remove the "*Ir*" from the "*Irma's Café*" sign and rename the place "*ma's Café*" The next thing she did was cook up a storm and throw open the windows and doors to let the sweet aromas of her labors escape into the desert air. By the end of dinner time, the word was out, *ma's Café* was a hit.

And though she was barely twenty herself at the time, when all those fresh-faced boys from the base, some still wet behind the ears and away from home for the first time, came pouring in, looking for some real home cooking, with, let's face it, a little mothering on the side, well, what was Norma Lee to do, but open her arms and become the very "*ma*" after whom she had coincidentally, perhaps even serendipitously, christened her new café.

Watching Mama admire his handiwork on Awning Celebration night, BJ knew what heaven was. It was making Mama happy.

Maybe it was the exhilaration, not to mention down-right exhaustion from a job well-done, or maybe it was just the very essence of Mama, herself, but she was coming through on a wavelength BJ had never heard from before. How else could he account for the fact that his teeth were ecstatically sinking into a tender morsel of succulent pot roast, while his taste buds tangoed to a saucy medley of the most tantalizing spices that had ever graced a braised beef; and that he was lapping up the whole melt-in-your-mouth mélange, as if he were really and truly there, on that very first night at *ma's Café.*

But before he could settle into *ma's* then soon to be famous, "bottomless cuppa and dessert along-with," Mama was off and running, getting all wound up around Irma. So, he took another swig of the Scotch at hand and tagged along. He already could tell Mama would be the last one to consider herself the sentimental type, but her eyes sure misted up talking about Irma. He watched her bat away some pesky tears, which were loitering in her glorious split pea green peepers, turning them, in the awning's flirescent light, into spellbinding, clear-as-glass-grass-green emeralds, which dazzled in his direction.

Though not one taken to flights of fancy, BJ sure knew a take-off when he took one. Lost and loving it in her lush and luscious hot pink lip gloss lips, "bewitched, bothered and bewildered" by the exact scent of jasmine that seemed to follow wherever Mama went, and lingered on long after she was gone, BJ was a goner and glad to be. She was an ocean of a woman, the reason for his journey across the desert.

"Believe you me, BJ," Mama went on, not entirely oblivious to the effect she was having on the big guy, who had certainly coiled her springs. "Believe you me," she repeated, a twinkle illuminating her currently emerald tears, "ole Irma had a lot more going on under that beehive than bobby pins and hair spray, if you catch my drift."

Which, of course, he knew she knew he did.

"That Irma," Mama laughed softly. "What I owe her!"

Mama leaned into BJ and began to whisper, though there was no one near, because, the thing was, no non-military personnel besides Mama ever really knew for sure how a forgotten, no name, one block town, with the bad luck of not being right off Route 66, went from languishing on a hillside in the middle of nowhere, somewhere behind the base, to thriving as the town of New Nebo, with an exit of its own.

BJ handed her the bottle and watched her throw her head back with such gusto, it took his breath away, which, considering his lung power, was saying a lot.

Again, the Irmaness of Irma had overcome Mama, and she had the most uncontrollable desire to spill the beans, all of them, to this giant man with the behemoth heart, who had built her a canopy that rivaled the stars.

So, she did.

"Ya see," Mama picked up where she usually left off, "when Irma handed me the deed, she let me in on a secret, strictly on the QT, just between us gals, about the café, and the base, and Nebo, and the thing was, that Irma actually could see into the future. Sure, she laughed it off by saying she could only see a 'few feet' into it, 'just a peek.' But it was enough."

Mama leaned back in that way of hers, took another swig, and aglow with scotch and recollection, revealed to BJ what Irma had told her on that other fortuitous afternoon.

It had whizzed by in fast-forward, but Irma had caught it the minute she caught sight of the girl through the window: the whirl of tires crisscrossing the country in search of that one place that felt more like home than home, that old fashioned apple pie of a Norman Rockwell Saturday Evening Post cover dream that lingered on like a phantom limb, that Holiest of Holy Grails: the loving arms of unconditional love. And believe it or not, finding it served up in hearty portions by a girl with the warmest smile Irma had ever seen, in a cozy diner right off the Nebo exit, at the tip of the Marine Corps base, that magic sector, that blessed triangle of land that, due to a clerical error in the long-forgotten past, a real SNAFU, if the truth be known, the U.S. Military had fortuitously forgotten to acquire.

And that was the gist of Irma's big secret.

That *Irma's Café* was in the very unique, rather extraordinary and extremely lucrative position of being, due to the military's providential real-estate blunder, the only retail establishment off the Nebo exit, so close to the base, it was surrounded by it. And considering her well-known, non-existent cooking skills, Irma had sure made the most of it, loving every minute. But if there was one thing her own mother had impressed upon her, it was that a gal's only got so many good years, and hers were zipping by faster than a run up a silk stocking.

So, envisioning her glorious gams up there where they belonged, with the best of them, on a Vegas chorus line, she had put herself in the hands of fate and placed that For Sale sign in the window, smiling at the boundless possibilities such a tiny act conjured. And when she looked up, there was destiny smiling right back at her.

From the first moment Irma saw her on the other side of the glass, she saw it clear as day. It was written all over every generous inch of Norma Lee. There was something about the girl, young as she was, that made her just feel comfortable. Some people generated heat, but Norma Lee radiated warmth, something's-baking-in-the-oven warmth that draws you to it, and makes you feel sit-right-down-at-the-table-and-have-a-cup-of-home-made-cocoa-with-fresh-whipped-cream-on-top comfortable. Or maybe it was her hair, a rowdy tangle of tightly coiled, copper filaments that seemed to set off sparks every time she laughed or even shook her head. Irma couldn't be for sure, but she suspected that *that* very something that was lighting Norma Lee up from the inside out, would lead people to her door. Plus, when they got there, it would be worth the trip, because unlike herself, the kid could cook. She was sure of it. Irma, who was nothing if not a hit-the-nail-on-the-header, just knew from the way Norma Lee's future pirouetted up and down her beehive, that the kid was destined for greatness.

And she was right.

By the time BJ had been drawn to it, *ma's* had exceeded even *Irma's* success, and as Irma had predicted to everyone who would listen, became a destination, not just another stop along the way. Mama had long ago paid off her debt to Irma, who sent her, along with the official, certified, notarized, fully executed Transfer of Ownership, a glossy picture post-card of her new life, featuring the chorus line of Olive Oyls at "Popeye's-On-the-Strip," with, believe it or not, Irma herself, right there in the middle, kicking up a storm.

BJ knew this to be true, having noticed the post-card framed in a place of honor behind the gleaming soda fountain on his first visit. He wasn't surprised when Mama confided that long after she had paid her debt, she continued to send Irma a little extra something every month just to say thanks for believing in her, because everything was going her way, as Irma had so confidently predicted. It was the beginning of the hey-days of *ma's Café* and thanks to the base and the constant stream of traffic flowing to her from Route 66, things just kept getting better and better.

Until some clerk, in some forgotten back room of the base, on some other assignment, happened to stumble upon the original map at the same time that, in a moment of disastrous synchronicity, the new Administrative Assistant of the new base commander, decided to "tie up loose-ends." And all hell burst loose.

Was the base thinking of expanding again, as it had before, when it absorbed all of Nebo, except, unbeknownst to them, that certain quirky piece of land? Was the military just getting a little testy, times being what they were? Or was the new base commander's new AA merely overreaching? Who knew? Whatever the reason, the order bounced down from on high with the speed of a fastball. They wanted *ma's Café* off their property pronto, even though, whether they knew it or not, technically, it wasn't *on* their property.

Of course, at this point, *ma's Café* was so popular, everybody up and down Route 66 knew it was in Nebo. It was even on a bunch of maps as a *must-stop*, and Mama, understandably, did not want to give up her exit. Besides, Nebo wasn't just where she had settled down. It was where she belonged. And she knew it from the get-go, when Irma told her that Nebo was Biblical for "little shepherd." It just felt right, after all her days and nights on the road, sometimes feeling like a lost lamb, herself, that she would be the one giving other lost sheep a little taste of home, if only for the time it took to have a cup of coffee.

So, when Mama was summoned to the base by a very official and slightly threatening letter, signed by Major General Vince Alan Murdoch's

Administrative Assistant, Mama was prepared to respond. Because Mama had no intention of leaving Nebo.

The day Mama arrived at the base for her big eviction meeting, she brought two things: the deed, which proved she did, in fact, own the land in question. And, more important, her famous herb-crusted, Coca-Cola basted ham, with apple currant glaze, studded with cloves and drizzled with honey.

Mama had a reputation as a real head-turner back then, and she had turned more than a few heads on her way in, not only because she was carrying a large crockpot wrapped up in a vibrant red cloth. But, more to the point, because she had foregone her usual waitress uniform for the only thing she owned that seemed appropriately military—white toreador pants that fit her like a glove and a navy bolero jacket adorned with a complete set of antique brass officers' buttons she once got as a tip. Her hot-wired hair set off sparks from one end of the corridor to the other, as she clicked down spotless linoleum floors to her own special rhythm, in a pair of red high-heeled mules that Irma had left behind just for this occasion, along with the sage advice, "Honey, when the time comes, use *all* your ammunition. *They* will."

In a rhumba of red, white and blue, Mama followed a baby-faced private in starched khakis, who barely looked old enough to be a hall monitor, to a small conference room.

Inside, a somber officer stood at rigid attention at one end of an oversized conference table, which dwarfed the room.

"I'm Major General Vince Alan Murdoch's Administrative Assistant." The AA introduced himself, without actually mentioning his own name. "I'm here to present the military's position. It won't take long."

New to the base and the assignment, the AA, who had just recently been made Captain, and prided himself on putting out fires before they started, was trying to get all of the pesky paperwork out of the way before it crossed Major General Murdoch's desk, so his transition would be as smooth as possible, which of course would reflect well on the AA, and bring him one step closer to getting the Golden Oakleaf of a USMC Major well ahead of schedule.

This was his last meeting of the day. He had calculated it would take fourteen point seven minutes tops, to lead her to the conclusion that it would be in her best interest to relocate voluntarily, willingly, and with great dispatch. He fully anticipated he would dispose of the *ma's Café* affair before it became a blunder of larger proportions. But he had to act fast, due to the irrational loyalty to the place expressed by the few other officers who knew of this meeting. He, of course, had no such attachment and never would. How she had been allowed to stay there all these years, no matter how great her hash browns were purported to be, was a case of rampant recklessness that could have jeopardized national security and would not be repeated under Major General Vince Alan Murdoch's watch while he was AA. To insure this, he'd already put into motion, his plan to close the Route 66 Nebo exit to all but military personnel.

"Now, Miss Walters—" he began, his smile cold and dismissive.

"You can call me Mama," she said, her smile dismissing his dismissal. "Everybody else does."

"Please sit down, Miss Walters." He gestured to a chair at the far end of the too-big-for-the-room table, his focus fixed somewhere above her forehead, covertly taking her all in.

So, this was the "ma" of *ma's Café*. She certainly didn't look like anybody's mother to the AA. But being anybody's mother obviously wasn't her appeal. Nor, he surmised, was her cooking. Irregardless of what some horny Marines thought.

Mama sat down as instructed, and settled in with her usual equanimity. Say what he might, for however long or short it took him, and no matter if he looked over, under, or even through her, she knew the outcome. She had it in the palm of her hand in the form of a notarized deed with that magic word, "inalienable," right there in black and white.

"You and I both know you have no legal right, whatsoever, to the property in question," the AA rolled on, getting down to the business of getting her to vacate without a fight. As he was sure she knew, he tersely explained, she was operating a business on U.S. Government soil, and would have to cease-and-desist. This was the potential trigger point, the cease-and-desist part, where someone like the curvaceous Miss Walters, someone, that is, who was no more than a squatter on government property, her formidable assets notwithstanding, was likely to go ballistic; so, he built in sixty-three extra seconds to deal with that contingency, and paused, as planned. But she didn't go ballistic.

Instead, she stood and began to unwrap the cloth from around the pot.

Choosing to ignore whatever disruption was happening at the other end of the table, the AA soldiered, or more accurately, marined on. When he unfurled a map of the area, the visual aid he was using to illustrate, incontestably, that the U. S. government owned the land under, over, up, down, around, and across *ma's Café,* Mama unfurled the cloth to its full length. It fanned out all the way across the table towards the AA in endless ripples of red, or more precisely, relentlessly undulating radiant energy wavelengths, which made him slightly dizzy and not amused.

Of course, having long ago disposed of the clutter of wonder in his life, it didn't cross the AA's mind to inquire about the odd but splendid cloth, or even look at it terribly closely. Therefore, he could not see and would probably never know that it was made up of hundreds of oddly shaped pieces of damask, seamlessly stitched together by Mama's momma, or that it had special meaning to Mama, since her momma had given it to her the day she left home, with the very nest egg she had used to buy the café from Irma, secretly sewn into it.

When the AA, keeping his eyes glued to the map, reiterated, on behalf of the Government of the United States of America, that it was time for Miss Walters to stop playing games and vacate USMC property ASAP, which he pronounced "aysap" to emphasize the urgency, she stood up, sashayed to the middle of the table, placed the pot, with the herb-crusted, Coca-Cola basted ham bubbling in it, on the cloth between them and opened the lid.

A whoosh of clove and honey-spiked steam swirled through the room, heating it faster than a Santa Ana wind in a sauna.

While the AA willed himself not to sweat, Mama walked towards him, fanning herself with the deed, sending some much-needed air, along with the redolent steam in the AA's direction, and while the ham crackled, and the AA willed himself to stop thinking of home, she calmly presented *her* position that she was, in fact, the *inalienable* owner of the property in question. When, at last Mama reached the AA, she stopped fanning and handed him the deed. He glanced down at it stiffly, took a closer look, and gasped without moving a muscle.

He'd expected something much less official, like no deed at all. Seeing her in the flesh, so to speak, he'd naturally assumed she'd try, in vain of course, to flirt her way out of it. But she hadn't. Plus, the document sure looked like the real thing, which would drive the irksome quotient of this matter right into the discomfort zone. Still, he had the trump card, which he fully intended to play as soon as his mouth stopped watering.

Trying not to inhale any more of the savory aromas than he had to, the AA waved the deed up and down in advance of making his final point, which only made matters worse. Before he could get his mind off the ham and back on track again, and seriously advise her that regardless of her civilian rights, if she didn't move voluntarily, he would, on behalf of base commander, Major General Vince Alan A.K.A. *Bulldog* Murdoch, be forced to evict her, the very imposing, barrel chested Major General Murdoch himself, appeared in the door-way, inadvertently sealing it like a cork, locking in all the savory flavors that Mama's ham had to offer.

"What is going on in here?" the Major General demanded, his voice booming down the conference table like a fifty-pound bowling ball.

Mama watched the AA snap to attention, an amazing feat, she reflected, as he had never been in any way at ease.

"I'm sorry sir, I, I know this is highly irregular, but I can explain, I'm sure. She *does* have a ham, sir, but it's more of a nuisance than a problem."

"A ham?" Major General Murdoch bellowed to the AA, who was looking back through the eyes of his own, swiftly sinking career.

"I mean deed, sir," the AA began to stammer, still at attention yet coming apart at the seams. "But as you can see, sir, she also brought a—uh—honey baked ham."

"If I may step in here," Mama volunteered, removing a carving knife, a serving fork, a tray, and a trio of plates, knives, forks and damask napkins in various shades of burgundy, ruby and claret that didn't match at all and so matched perfectly, from her end of the cloth, "it's actually an herb-crusted, Coca-Cola basted ham, with apple currant glaze, studded with cloves and drizzled with honey. And it's for you."

She lifted the glistening ham from the crock-pot and placed it on the tray, where it sizzled as she sliced.

"Welcome to the base, general." Mama beamed, inviting Major General Murdoch and his uncharacteristically confused and disoriented AA to the table, where she was now placing the wine-hued napkins on the vivid red cloth alongside plates piled high with thick slices of tender, crispy ham and rosemary-kissed, pot-roasted potatoes.

Major General Murdoch had been told more than once since he'd gotten here, that it took more self-control than even a Marine could muster to pass up one of Mama's home-cooked meals. And here was one in front of him, already, he had to admit, living up to its hype.

"As inviting as that Coca-Cola basted ham you've got there might be, it will not change the outcome of this meeting," the general barked. But there was no bite in it, as the bite in his bark had other things on its plate.

"Now that we've cleared the air of any hint of quid pro quo, I, for one, have worked up an appetite, and I hate to dine alone. So, you fine gentlemen might as well sit yourselves down and have a bite to eat with me before it gets cold." Mama took the deed from the AA's hand, and gestured with it, for her hosts to take their proffered seats and become her guests.

"Well, as a Marine officer *and* a gentleman, I wouldn't want to let a lady down." Major General Murdoch pulled out her chair for her, then sat down, delight lighting up his bulldog face. There was something about the confusion of reds on the table cloth and napkins that put a warm, holiday glow around everything.

And while the general and the AA, following his lead, cut into their tender repast, Mama cut to the chase.

"Major General Murdoch, as you can plainly see, this deed was originally given to Irma Ludley's family by the Mojave Indians themselves, and it passed right on through the generations directly to Irma, who sold it to me fair and square. Now, I understand that even though *your* base actually grew up around *my* property, and technically, I am not on your base, you still want me to move. And I'm sure you've got your reasons. Believe you me, I'm a big fan of the Marines. I've loved every one of your boys I've fed over the years; never was a one impolite or ungrateful. So, I'll make you a deal, or if you'd like to see it that way, a very reasonable request."

But the Marines weren't exactly listening, or more accurately, they weren't *only* listening to Mama. They were also immersed in their own, extremely non-military thoughts. The AA was thinking about why he hadn't noticed the amazing tablecloth before, marveling at how cleverly the oddly shaped pieces were sewn together to form a pattern that was not at all haphazard, and how much the caramelized red currant glaze reminded him of stained glass. And the Major General, well, he was thinking about how he hadn't had Coca-Cola ham since he was a boy, and that *this* ham was even more delicious than he remembered, if that was even possible. And he sighed, remembering how much simpler life used to be.

Mama watched the general and his AA lose themselves in their meal, and it warmed her heart. So far, in her life, she hadn't met anyone, man, woman or child, who wasn't hungry for that special something that a good meal had to offer. Clearly, these fine Marines were no exception. And neither was she. Mama served herself some ham and potatoes and joined them.

In the end, it was arranged that Mama would exchange her property "on" the Nebo base for real estate she had already picked out parallel to the base, on top of a forgotten hill, on a no name street, to be called New Main, accessed, according to special signs that would state simply, "New Nebo—Home of *ma's Café*—via a new off-ramp, which would by-pass the base entirely.

That was Mama's deal. A New Nebo with an exit of its own. Take it or leave it.

Why they took it, nobody knew for sure. Not even Mama. And that was why she had never talked about that meeting with anyone before, that and her deal with the general that it would be their little secret; since even he wasn't sure what exactly had transpired.

When Mama moved herself into New Nebo, of course, she immediately shared the wealth, inviting friends to open up stores rent free on the street leading to *ma's Café*.

"Ah, BJ," Mama sighed, on that first night, feeling the effects of scotch and moonlight, "the traffic's been streaming to our doors ever since. Just like I promised everyone. And now, with our new awnings! Well! They'll be able to find us from Lord knows where! Pure and simple, New Nebo is a charmed place. These are our halcyon days. Yes, they are!"

They'd held on for a long, long time, longer even, than the town held on. Thanks to *ma's* reputation, new people kept coming with old maps, even after the highway began to change. But that was before the I-40 completely bypassed the Nebo exit altogether, before all the fast-food chains bypassed the need for home cooking, before the need to keep going bypassed the need to slow down and enjoy the ride.

And although, looking back on it, everything, including their luck, had been running out on them ever since the last exit in the last town was decommissioned and Route 66 all but vanished from the landscape, it just never got to Mama before, the way it got to BJ, because Mama always believed that the Mother Road and *ma's Café* and everything they stood for, could not fade away. But, as it turned out, for the first time, Mama had been wrong.

It didn't matter that in all the years he'd known Mama and been part of *ma's Café*, with all those thousands of strangers who walked through her doors and became friends, Mama had never served one bad meal, poured one burnt cup of coffee, or turned one soul away, paying customer or not.

It didn't matter that Mama had a knack for cooking and a heart of gold. Nothing else mattered but this: the government letter was a time bomb and ever since it arrived, BJ could hear it ticking down the days in the background. But now, it was getting so loud that it was about to drown out everything, even the Doo Wops' voices. One way or another, something drastic was about to happen. Mr. Mills Miggston the Third had called again; this time to say he was actually on his way and would be there in several hours, to be exact.

All this was boomeranging around inside of BJ as he turned Lucille around and, with a lump in his throat the size of St. Louis, headed back to *ma's Café*, to wait for fate to come knocking.

The guaranteed "no-brainer" flight with a convenient connection out of Albuquerque, that the bright-voiced, cliché-spouting travel agent promised Miggsy would be a "piece of cake, no worries, just a hop, skip and a jump," was turning into an endless, brain-numbing nightmare, thanks to a very late take-off on the first leg.

He couldn't believe he'd told himself that hiring a private jet was entirely out of the question, because it would cost more than double the amount he was prepared to pay for *ma's Café,* which was throwing good money after bad, when really, he saw clearly now, through the sweat misting his eyes, it was mainly to spite Cowardice, who had repeatedly suggested it.

"Surely, you're not going to attempt this on your own? Surely, you'll hire a jet, so you don't get us lost somewhere in the middle of some wretched airport," he had said, in that nasty way of his that sounded too much like Mills II letting him know he couldn't handle the trip the "normal way" like "normal people". How could he succumb to that insult? He could not, of course. Erego, here he was.

Limping frantically around the Albuquerque airport in search of the gate, hoping to reach it before the plane took-off, Miggsy tried to ignore the pitying stares he'd gone into seclusion to avoid, by reminding himself that he was almost there. He was about to embark on the last leg of his journey. Within an hour he'd be in the town of New Nebo.

Nebo! The minute Miggsy had finally deciphered the name on the ad, he sensed this could be the capper on the story of his life. The more he thought about it, the more convinced he became it was a masterful solution, so much more subtle than accidentally crashing into a tree, so much more civilized than smashing up a classic Ferrari in the process. Such a brilliant centerpiece for his resume of ruin. Not giving up! *Never* giving up! Instead, taking over a losing proposition, a completely lost cause, in a loser town, named after the very mountain range on which one of antiquity's biggest losers, Moses himself, stood, at the exact moment he lost everything.

How could Moses, the spokesman with the lamentable speech impediment, not remind him of himself, the jockey with the pitiable, gimp leg? Each born—*called*—by Fate or God to a task he was then rendered pathetically incapable of performing.

It was on Nebo, of course, that Moses recognized his utter failure, in that defining moment when God wagged an Almighty finger and intoned, "Everybody who's going to the Promised Land take one step forward. Not so fast, Moses," simultaneously humiliating Moses and keeping it light.

That's what Miggsy had been trying to do. Keep it light. And he had. All the way to Albuquerque, a nice enough airport, unless, he thought ruefully, you're looking for a gate ominously labeled "Freight—All Other Airliners" and you're not sending a package. By the time he finally found it, at the farthest, deadest end of the terminal, the plane was about to take off. In a frenetic burst of speed, he limp-sprinted to the gate. Drenched with sweat and out of breath, he handed his ticket to some burly guy who looked more like a baggage handler than a flight attendant, who then rushed him onto the only plane that flew locally, which, the perky travel agent described as, "practically a private jet," but to Miggsy's horror, turned out to be a two engine, combo passenger-freight dune-hopper, unloading in Daggett, just a few towns over from New Nebo.

Miggsy tried to act nonchalant, while the baggage handler-flight attendant, whose name he now saw was Bruno, according to the stitching on his uniform, showed him to one of the few seats that had not been torn out to make room for cargo.

"Heads up!" Bruno warned, turning from him, grabbing a carton, then tossing it into what Miggsy suddenly realized was the last remaining seat on the plane. To his utter horror, he was the only human passenger onboard.

He wasn't ready for this! He wanted to jump from his seat, screaming.

Instead, he looked up into Bruno's big bear face and asked, in a voice dripping with an insouciance he certainly didn't feel, but assumed was fall-out from his upbringing, "Will there be a movie on this flight, Bruno?"

"Name's not Bruno," the big man rumbled, fastening Miggsy's seat belt. "They just got a deal on the uniforms."

Miggsy waited for further explanation. But the engines began revving and the faux Bruno went back to work securing him into what he saw too late, was not a regular seat belt, but a thick, leather harness. To his horror, he was not so much being strapped in as trapped.

"What the hell was I thinking?" He frantically reproached himself at the top of his lungs, but he couldn't hear himself over the motor's furious thrum.

"My *arms*—are—stuck!!" He screamed, struggling against the strap.

"Ya better stay put there. We're about to take off!" The man who would—or wouldn't—be Bruno roared, apparently not getting the gist of Miggsy's actual dilemma.

"Get me out of here! I'm pinioned, for God's sake!" Miggsy shrieked.

"What?" The Bruno imposter shouted into the escalating drone, deftly heaving boxes that weighed a lot more than Miggsy onto the shelves surrounding him, strapping them in.

"What?" Miggsy shouted back.

"I said," Bruno boomed, "tighten your seat belt. It's gonna be a bumpy ride!"

And, to Miggsy's amazement, the big guy mimed ashing a cigarette, a la Bette Davis, with one beefy, languid hand, while yanking on Miggsy's harness again with the other, constricting his vital organs, further disorienting him.

"Stay put! For your own good! It could get awful messy out there!" Bruno warned, grabbing a parachute pack and vanishing into the cockpit.

"Don't leave me like this!" Miggsy demanded, but it was too late.

Less than fifteen minutes out, they crashed into a storm.

Lightning glanced off the wing outside Miggsy's window. The plane lurched and plunged three hundred feet, wind screaming like a siren. Instantly, that old, familiar adrenalin-laced thrill spiked through him, jarring him to action. He shimmied down in the seat, extending his arm so far it almost snapped. His fingers reached out and shakily grasped at the clasp. But the plane was shuddering wildly, he couldn't undo it.

Everything was in violent motion. Rows of heavy cartons struggled against their restraints. Boxes unleashed from surrounding seats crashed around him. The plane took another dive.

He thrashed and flailed, desperate to escape.

"But why?" Noel Cowardice popped up uninvited again, sounding more than ever like an upsetting blend of all Mills' most tedious, patronizing and punishing tutors, with a hint of his perpetually condescending Aunt Aida, thrown in.

"What's the fuss about, really?" Cowardice's voice coolly went on, when the plane failed to fully recover. "You're finally going to crash into oblivion. You should be thrilled."

The storm tossed the dune-hopper around the sky like a paper plane.

"The thrill," Miggsy screamed into the storm, struggling vainly to break free, "is gone!"

And it came to him like a second wind. He didn't want to cash in his chips. He wanted to live.

"I will not," he shrieked at the top of his lungs, "die like freight!"

And he didn't.

The weather cleared, but not before diverting Miggsy and the other cargo from the Daggett Airport to a landing strip over fifty miles south of their destination.

When the boxes shutting him in had been removed and Bruno unharnessed him, every bone in his body was in pain. His left arm was hanging limply at his side, looking longer than his right. His leg ached in a way he didn't like.

He hobbled down the aisle toward the blast of light from the open door.

Squinting into the sun, Miggsy disembarked from the plane onto his bad leg, which buckled under him. Barely regaining his balance, he limped unsteadily down the ramp, while two new Brunos began hurling packages out the door, over his head, to another new Bruno, who hauled them into the back of a pick-up.

"Great. Starting out on the wrong foot," Miggsy muttered to a passing parcel, when he mercifully reached the ground, on an ersatz landing field on the end of which stood a gigantic, rusting, tin fieldhouse moonlighting as a hangar.

Making a visor of his hand, he began a three-sixty of the place. Beyond the landing strip, there was desert in every direction, with just a one-way paved road cutting through it, going from what looked like nowhere to nowhere else. Which, of course, was exactly where Miggsy was headed, metaphorically. But in real life, he needed a cab.

"Need help?"

Miggsy turned to see another huge guy, with *Bruno* stitched to his pocket, towering over him.

"I need a cab. Know where I can catch one?"

"Sure don't," he admitted cheerily.

The remaining Brunos joined their brother Bruno, and together they formed an assembly line to load the remaining crates.

"How do I get out of here?" Miggsy persisted.

"Beats me," the first Bruno mused, heaving heavy packages to the second, who hurled them to the third, who tossed them to the fourth, who threw them to the fifth.

"But what am I gonna do?" Miggsy pleaded.

"You'll figure it out," the first Bruno assured Miggsy, airily.

"Have a little faith!" The fifth Bruno concurred, hoisting the last carton onto the pick-up. The others murmured agreement, though it sounded like sawing logs.

And that was that. The Brunos secured their cargo and revved their engine, stirring up a dust twister.

"Thanks for your help." Miggsy coughed and sputtered at them.

"Sure thing!" the five Brunos chimed, disappearing in a cloud of sand.

When the air cleared and Miggsy stopped coughing, he saw it. A sign on the field house wall which read, "EBAN STEBBANS AUTOS + PARTS, SALES! RENTALS! FOLLOW THE ARROW."

He followed the arrow, which snaked around the building, to a cluster of the most pathetic looking excuses for cars he'd ever seen, bleaching in the sand.

They seemed all "+ PARTS." Assuming there had to be at least one working car in the junk heap, he could lease for the day, Miggsy picked up speed, but his leg gave in again, and he almost fell, would have fallen, except for the eyes he felt were on him.

From inside the field house, Eban Stebbans saw his first outsider in weeks, and it was sweet. He was the sucker's only ticket out of the desert.

Then he noticed the limp. Had the guy been in an accident? Was he born that way? Did he have a wooden leg? A club foot? He had a story, that was for certain. And he was so short. It was more than Eban could really stand. But he couldn't take his eyes off the gimp leg. The little guy was walking toward the cars in an annoying gimp, limp, hop, step. This did not sit well with Eban. He was a simple man. Liked his three-squares a day. And no complications. This hip, hop man looked to Eban like a bundle of complications.

Dismembered car corpses were scattered all over the sand. Miggsy skip hopped from one to another and was about to go with a rusted-out Chevy, when he saw a faded yellow VW van on a sand dune a few feet away.

The sun shifted and shafts of light bounced off the van. Set apart on the parched hill, it looked like a sizzling sunny-side up. Miggsy took a deep breath and headed for it.

Eban Stebbans also took a deep breath. He was a patient man, but this was too much. Watching that guy climb that sand dune was like watching molasses pour in a freezer.

Miggsy finally got to the van and opened the door. There was a key in the engine.

"Looks shot but there's a thousand miles in her," something buzzed in his ear.

Miggsy wheeled around and stared up at the ragged, crusty shell that once housed the dreams of Eban Stebbans.

"You must be Eban Stebbans. I saw your sign."

"That's *Eeban Steebans*, like *Even Stevens*," the man corrected, "and, like my name, I'm as honest as the day is long. Now, as I said—"

"I know what you said, but I just want it for a day or less. Think it will last that long?"

"I *know* it'll last forever, cause what ya got here's your *gen-u-eye-en*—"

Miggsy couldn't believe the geezer pronounced it with four syllables, like it rhymed with lyin', which is what he said next.

"Yessiree Bob, and I ain't lyin' cause you're lookin' at a *classic* VW Panel Van."

"Fine. But I'm not looking for a collector's item. I'm just trying to get out of here," Eban Stebbans pointed his bony finger over Miggsy's head towards the desert.

"Ya wanna get outta here? This van's yer best shot. But it ain't for rent. It's for sale." Eban definitely did not want this guy to come back. His steely eyes dared Miggsy to turn it down.

Miggsy held his ground by starting to move very, very slowly.

It was just too agonizing. Eban Stebbans was getting the heebie-jeebies.

Miggsy could read Eban Stebbans's mind, not because he was psychic, but because he'd seen the same look on faces every day of his post-accident life. So, of course, he knew that all the guy wanted to do was to get him to stop.

"I could let you have it for fifteen hun—"

"Oh, please." Miggsy reached in and turned the key in the ignition. The van coughed a few times, then choked to a start, surprising them both. Blue smoke rose from the exhaust.

"It's not worth half that much," Miggsy coughed, while the van sputtered.

"Hell, it's not. It's a classic. Its even got its original, working radio! But I tell ya what. It's a hot day. I'll make you a deal. Give me an even thousand, and it's yours forever."

"I already have a car," Miggsy coughed again.

"Of course, ya do," Eban Stebbans sneered. "Ya got a great ole car at home. But you're not home, are ya? And here in the desert it ain't bad to travel with your house on your back, if you catch my meaning."

"You don't even know where I'm going."

"I know it ain't close. Tell ya what. Go on and give me eight—"

"I'll give you five, if you tell me how to get out of here."

"Fine." Eban Stebbans agreed too quickly. He had no real proof of ownership, and he didn't want to press his luck, especially while the van was still running.

Miggsy got in, sank into the driver's seat and kept sinking. Someone had made quite an impression. "And throw in a pillow."

Eban Stebbans threw in a dusty pillow and an outdated map in exchange for five one hundred dollar bills that Miggsy surreptitiously extracted from of the false lining he'd had sewn into his jacket. He knew he overpaid, but figured he'd just take it off the price he'd offer on the restaurant if the van ever got him there.

Eban Stebbans couldn't suppress a thin, rickety smile. He only paid one-fifty for the clunker to a guy he knew, who had neglected to mention where and how he got it. And due to his own top notch bargaining skills, he was walking away with five. He would have used it for parts. Never thought he'd unload it at all, let alone all at once. But he had just tripled his investment. Not a bad profit from a gimp freak on a hot day.

Following Eban Stebban's grease-stained map, making use of the tarnished brass compass hanging from the rear-view mirror on a tarnished silver chain, Miggsy traveled at a dispiriting top speed of forty-seven miles per hour to something designated Ten Mile Junction, where two highways had once transected. From there, he turned onto the one called The Mother Road, a name which dislodged *The Grapes of Wrath* from wherever it had been wedged in his memory since Sixth Form, fueling his suspicion that he was now driving on historic Route 66.

He was looking out for signs when a torrential sandstorm whipped up out of nowhere, blacking out daylight, savagely lacerating the van, forcing it to a crawl.

The needles went haywire inside the brass compass, then settled back down and pointed north.

The van crept along in that direction for twenty harrowing minutes, spindly wipers squeaking valiantly against the windshield, but all Miggsy could see in the weak, yellow headlights was the flickering, amber silhouette of what appeared to be an endless line of cast-off people, kneeling on both sides of the road ahead of him, the wind keening through their open mouths and, rising from their misty midst, the specter of Tom Joad wailing, *"We've all come to look for America,"* quoting Paul Simon in Henry Fonda's spidery voice.

The song ended, the storm subsided, and the desert settled back down into itself, as if nothing had happened. The Mother Road turned into National Old Trails Highway and meandered uneventfully for miles after that, past an assortment of deserted gas stations and motels.

Just when he was despairing of ever finding it, Miggsy caught the remnants of an exit sign for New Nebo and swerved towards it. The remains of a small town rose in the near distance, like an abandoned Avalon. The old van labored toward it with a will of its own.

Checking his map, Miggsy turned onto New Main, a street on a small hill dotted with the shells of old, deserted stores. Like everything else about this trip, as he got closer, things got weirder. Though vacated, they weren't empty. Something had been left behind in each. One had wan, whey-faced mannequins, spectral in shreds of what must have once been the latest tie-dye styles, another had a deteriorating display of Beat Poetry, featuring faded, dusty copies of *On the Road* stacked precariously atop faded, dusty copies of *Howl!* Still another, "Mae's Drye Goodes," had conflicting signs that boasted, "Open 24 Hours A Day 7 Days a Week," and confessed, "Sorry, Gotta Eat! Be Back Soon, Friends!" But when? Miggsy couldn't shake the feeling that these stores had been holding on all these years, waiting for their people to return.

But before he could pursue this insanity any further, something else caught his attention, something he couldn't quite make out, on top of the hill, blinking in the slanting afternoon sun. Some sort of Morse Code for "turn back before it's too late," Cowardice suggested.

The van huffed and puffed up the hill, hiccupped and lurched around a curve, and Miggsy was face to face with the back side of *ma's Café*, which he mistook for the front. And the second Miggsy laid eyes on the cinder block wall, he knew from the way his stomach knotted, it was perfect.

"Perfectly awful, but in a *Shavian* way," Noel Cowardice popped up again. Multiple times in one day. This did not bode well, unless it was just a lapse, like a short circuit, not another full-scale attack.

"One *could* hope," he thought, wondering whose thought it was.

"Haunted by ghosts or bats in my belfry?" he queried himself.

"Dear boy," Cowardice answered, in that patronizing way of his, so reminiscent of Mills's oldest and most supercilious tutor, a George Bernard Shaw scholar, "what was that Henry Higgins line, when he first laid eyes on Eliza Doolittle. What *was* it?"

The trouble with Noel Cowardice was that it didn't matter what the condescending prig, who'd gotten more and more condescendingly priggish with age, actually said. No, the real trouble with Cowardice was that whenever he showed up and refused to leave, Miggsy was about to take a fall.

"What *was* it? 'So—so—' so, help me out here, won't you? I beg of you. Such a little favor, really." Cowardice prattled on, easily slipping into grandiose Aunt Aida mode, while Miggsy drove on, trying to will him away by concentrating on the faded silver and black letters that faintly spelled out "*ma's Café*—PARKING" on the blue cinder block wall that may have once been intended to blend in with the sky.

"The place doesn't even have windows!" Cowardice hyperventilated claustrophobically.

Okay, okay, so *ma's Café* looked like a like a jail. But so, what? If he wanted to fail in this particular way, it was his own business. It just sounded so dismal coming from someone else, even if that someone else was only a fabrication of his own sick imagination, he brooded, mumbling in spite of himself, "So deliciously low. So delightfully dirty."

"Yes!" Cowardice pounced. "Fits this place, don't you think, this *ma's*? Not to mention the rest of this godforsaken town, or should I say ant hill?" He spat out the words "*ma's*," "town" and "ant hill," like they were ill-advised sips of sour wine, with pieces of cork in them. "Have you seen anyone *else* for miles?" He demanded, composure regained.

Miggsy checked his rear-view mirror and saw his father's withering glance flash across his face. No doubt about it. Cowardice was back with a vengeance. If he had a brain left, he'd get out now—while he still could.

"And of course," Cowardice quipped, "it has that added benefit of being *so* low, we won't have too far to fall this time."

Miggsy recoiled. From himself.

"I'm assuming, of course," Cowardice trilled, having hit his mark, "that we only intend to stay around long enough to fail miserably."

"Take a hike," Miggsy chided. "You're not dressed for this town."

"This is *not* a *town!*" Noel Cowardice sighed with world-weariness. "It's merely a faint capillary of a forgotten artery of a moribund highway."

"Oh, shut up!" Miggsy ordered his alter ego, furiously jabbing at the allegedly working radio to fill his ears with anything but Cowardice. The radio crackled, sizzled and sputtered. He turned it up full blast.

"Obviously, the subtle approach hasn't achieved the desired effect," Cowardice ripped through on a static signal. "Indulge me, if you will, my dear boy, in a Don Quixote moment. Let's take a peek in the mirror at ourselves, shall we?"

Miggsy reluctantly stole another glance at himself. His complexion was pasty. His eyes were sunken above dark circles. He definitely should have tried to get out more.

"Frankly, you should never have gotten out of grandmother Beryl's chair," Cowardice observed.

The radio shorted crankily and went dead, taking Cowardice with it, leaving Miggsy alone, still staring at the cinder block back side of *ma's Café,* still thinking it was the front.

Even with no expectations, Miggsy had expected more.

Then he saw the faint happy face next to the fainter words, "ENTRANCE—AROUND FRONT!"

"Turn back while you still can!" Cowardice returned for an encore. And for once, Miggsy wanted to listen. But, against his own better judgment, what was left of it, he overrode Cowardice, because the van seemed to be overriding him.

Trudging around to the front of *ma's Café,* it crawled into a parking space under a weather-beaten canopy and gave out.

Ma's was so empty BJ could hear his own thoughts bouncing off the walls. He was behind the counter, polishing the soda fountain like he'd done at least once a day since Mama popped out, so it would be ready for her whenever she popped back in, in the same shape she left it, which was as good as the day she bought it. Because there was one thing about Mama. She kept her equipment clean.

Mama! Even now, she floated through the waters of his desire like a regular Cleopatra on her barge. He could not think of her and keep his mind off her succulence. She was a ten-course meal of a woman and he was a man with a hardy appetite. But as big a banquet as she was, what he loved about her most, the main course of Mama, ya might say, was her great big heart. In all their days and nights together, which is exactly how they always wanted to spend them, he never heard her say a harsh word, or saw her turn a soul away. Couldn't even count all the people she put up in ole SunnySide Up, helping them get back on their feet. The cozy van, herself, semi-retired when Mama bought the roomier Airstream, was therefore available as guest room, safe haven, sanctuary and all-around refuge.

He knew he shouldn't dwell on it, but it would never, ever be right that things at *ma's* had gone so wrong, what with all the good that went into it. He reminded himself again that if he'd learned one thing going up and down Route 66 in his vagabond days, it was that fair had nothing to do with it. Never did. Never would. And if he was looking for fair, well, he'd better get over it.

Let go and move on. That was his motto before he met Mama and she stopped time. But now it was time for him and Mama to let go of *ma's* and move on to a place where Mama could transmit and receive to her heart's content. They could pay off *ma's* debts and start a new life in a new place, maybe even with a little nest egg. The minute they settled in, he'd line up steady work, and they'd keep going. No one would be worrying about making ends meet anymore. Mama could commune with the Doo Wops from now till the last Tuesday of eternity and she'd always be okay because he'd be looking after her, and whatever it took to take care of Mama, that's exactly what he wanted to do. She was his Doo-Wop goddess. Perfect to the marrow. And oh! How she moved him. Now it was time to move her.

As if summoned, the door opened.

And, framed by the afternoon sun, in a shimmering halo of fire, stood an angel, a very tall, very skinny, undernourished angel.

"Excuse me," she said, tentatively, "excuse me, but are you looking for a waitress by any chance?"

The angel on fire stepped inside and closed the door. The fire vanished and standing in front of BJ was the girl etched from it. Her skin was porcelain. Her hair fell around her like cotton candy spun from gold. Her lips were heart shaped. Her eyes were bluer than the Mojave sky on a perfect day. They were the clearest blue he'd ever seen. And the saddest, even though they shimmered along with the rest of her, even after the door closed, blocking out the sun.

Before he could speak, she walked—actually, glided was more like it—towards the counter, looking up at him. Tall as she was, she still had to look all the way up to look him in the eye, which is what she did with those big baby blues, and they were pleading with him, in spite of themselves, telling him that if she didn't get this job, she didn't know what she'd do.

And that did it. He felt that tug on his heart-strings that he got time and time again from the strippers, after some sort of curtain opened and he saw past their substantial assets and hard exteriors into their fragile, breaking hearts. He wanted to help her. But what could he do? Things being what they were, what on earth could he do?

"Well—" he said, trying to think of a nice way to tell her that there could be no job at *ma's Café*, since there would soon be no *ma's Café*, but he'd put in a good word with the new management, if there was a new management, when he saw a single tear run down her delicate cheek.

"Well—" he repeated, "as you can see, we're—uh—slow. In fact, we're closed for lunch."

"Oh, I don't mind working dinner. In fact, I'd prefer it! It would be perfect!" She gushed.

Once, BJ had thrown a line to a guy and saved his life. The guy had the same look on his face that this girl had. From hopelessness to hope in a flash. To disappoint her now. Well, he just couldn't.

"Tell you what," BJ said, "we're making some changes."

Her face began to fall. Her eyes began to fill. This was too much.

"But I'm sure we can find something." BJ heard himself say this, knowing it was more of a wish than a job offer.

"I can start right away! I've even got a waitress uniform. I'll change into it and come back in time for dinner! Thanks for giving me a chance!" She danced over to BJ, leaped up, gave him a peck on his cheek, and was out the door in a blur.

Oh well, he'd just have to make her part of the deal. Buy the place, get the waitress.

Jane Angelina stood on the other side of the door, catching her breath and feeling a lot happier than she had in she didn't know how long, not really knowing why. It wasn't just the promise of the job. Anyone could see the joint wasn't exactly jumping, and if she had to live on tips she'd surely starve.

But there was something about the big man who had just hired her—maybe because of his size. She estimated he was about six-ten, weighed, maybe, three eighty-seven, mainly muscle. And she knew she was close because numbers were her thing. Or maybe it was his shoulders, which were broad enough to hold up the world, or his eyes, which seemed to have infinite patience. He had countenance.

Countenance.

Now there was a word that didn't come up a lot. As a matter of fact, the minute she saw him, she actually felt the word surge through her all the way from Teenage Bible Study Class.

Every Sunday, every single Sunday during her mother's long, prolonged, interminable religious phase, she had insisted on trundling Jane Angelina off to Church and then Bible Study Class, as if her attendance at "BSC with an emphasis on the BS," as it was rudely, but aptly, nicknamed, somehow made up for her mother being too weak to pick herself out of her torpor, and her father being too far away to do much more than phone it in.

She was their sacrificial lamb. But she wasn't the only one. All her friends got stuck in Church and then Bible Study Class, all forced to sit there and listen to whatever B. S. Pastor William was selling that week. Of course, they never listened. Instead, they passed gossipy notes that made fun of whatever they were supposed to be taking seriously. But even when they were all joking around, Jane Angelina could feel the desperation simmering just under the surface, which made it harder to laugh. Because in the small, broken-down community that the Parish Church of All Saints ministered to, Jane Angelina knew everybody's story.

Just like she had a talent for numbers, she had a gift, not just for keeping secrets but for listening in a way that made people feel somehow better, and not only for the moment of the telling. Somehow, everybody seemed to sense this, because everybody told her their deepest, darkest secrets. She knew, for example, that Lenore's mom and Rosalee's dad, who both could quote the Bible from Genesis to Gospels, and often did, in Rosalee's face, had been going at it for so long, Rosalee and Lenore didn't know if they were actually half-sisters, that Lulu's dad had been arrested for holding up a liquor store somewhere in Carson, that Esme's dad liked to sneak into her room at night. And on and on it went, until all the secrets seemed to pour out of them into Jane Angelina, who kept those secrets like a sacred trust.

But then she began hearing the secrets no one said out loud.

It started in Church, right after Esme told her about her father, which rocked Jane Angelina to her core. That Sunday, when the congregation lifted their voices in solemn prayer, Jane Angelina heard something else, something that sounded like voices under those voices, screaming for help.

She stood in the back, her second-hand pillbox hat on her head, her prayer book in her white gloved hands, listening to the whole town shrieking their secrets to God.

"Forgive me, Jesus!" Pastor William encouraged.

"For I have sinned," their voices responded in the bland unison of the blameless.

But what Jane Angelina heard was the wild caterwauling of their despairing souls begging, "Forgive me Jesus. Forgive me, for I have fornicated with my sister, my neighbor, a harlot, my child."

"Forgive me Jesus for I have stolen from my brother, my father, my neighbor, a stranger."

"Forgive me Jesus for trying to inflict my pain on the ones I am supposed to love."

She heard this as clear as day, and without meaning to, she counted up the sins and divided them by people and came up with such a deficit that it always made her weep.

And then came the appeals.

"Shine Thy Countenance upon me and make me whole."

"Shine Thy Countenance upon me and set me free."

Jane Angelina was afraid that even Jesus and His Father, Almighty God in Heaven Above, Himself, couldn't do this for anyone in the congregation, including her, couldn't make them whole, or set them free.

But this big man, this BJ, he had shined his countenance upon her and somehow, for the first time since her father had to leave, she felt uplifted.

And she was thinking she could just stay there in the doorway of *ma's Café* forever, under the canopy of BJ's good graces, when the door squeaked a warning and snapped shut behind her, at the very moment the late afternoon wind picked up.

Was it the door? Was it the wind?

Such a weight had been lifted from Jane Angelina, that she rose off the ground.

It was as simple as that.

She just rose and kept going, picking up speed, feeling like she did when she was ten and rode her bike straight off Devil's Cliff, zooming off the edge of the edge, where the dirt road disappeared and there was nothing but sky and a twenty-foot drop, legs pedaling for all they were worth, heart racing, blood rushing God knows where, yelling, "Jeezus! Sweet Jeezus!" at the top of her lungs, until she caught the updraft, and everything slowed down and began to hum, and she threw her legs onto the handlebars and raised her arms to heaven, and sailed on air.

Below, was the scrubby ravine and the dried-up creek that led to the Dead River.

Below, was the caked dirt that always got into your nails and hair and lungs. So, the whole town suffered from the same dry cough, the percussive signature for a place so dry, that not even crabgrass grew, and wherever you went, you could hear dry coughs echoing down the dry streets.

Below, everyone was speckled with light layers of dust, which on really windy days blew off them like swirling, twirling, whirling dervishes that sick of being stuck in that clay-baked town with everybody's pent-up pain, decided to up and leave.

Below, was another Jane Angelina dreaming of being her own dust dervish, achieving lift-off and flying away.

Careening through the air high above Dead River Ravine, for that narrow, swirling piece of time, she had achieved her dream.

Her mathematical mind, of course, always demanded an accounting, insisted on measuring velocity, distance, lift. But she would not let it. She just soared like a leaf in the arms of the wind, allowing her mathematical mind to join her only exactly when necessary, to drift into a perfect landing along the dry river bed, feet back on pedals, wheels spinning so furiously that even when she reached the ground—kicking up a dust storm in the process—she was still soaring.

Soaring!

The wind picked up again and blew Jane Angelina smack into Mills "Miggsy" Miggston the Third.

Falling backwards, she thought of something cool and wet, like grass.

Miggsy was just exiting the van, had turned around to shut the door, when a girl with a Botticelli face soared out of nowhere and slammed into him.

The next thing he knew, he was falling backwards and she was falling backwards, about to land on her head. Forgetting that due to extenuating circumstances, like his gimp leg, and that having just been launched in the opposite direction, he was in no position to help, he tapped into reflexes that had long ago given up on him and praying for a miracle (not that he deserved one, but he was sure *she* did), he reversed himself in mid-air and leapt to her assistance, grasping her willowy hands in his just in time, lifting her up, gliding back down onto his good leg, uplifted himself. She was light as air. Her eyes, which never left his as she rose above him, in their curious, windswept pas-de-deux, held the answers to all the questions in the universe.

"Thanks," she said, breathlessly, not taking her eyes from his. "Really."

"It's nothing," he heard himself say softly, not taking his eyes from hers. "Really."

They stood there while the wind died down around them. Then she politely withdrew her hand from his and blew down the street on a passing breeze.

"Wait!" he shouted, suddenly understanding what Cole Porter had meant by "I've Got You Under My Skin."

"What's your name?" he called after her. But his voice just got waylaid by the wind on its way to the girl.

And it hit him like the flu. He was feverish and freezing, poetic and dumb, graceful and clumsy, absolutely calm and altogether shaky at the same time. He was filled with her. She took up his every pore. And yet, he was hollow and empty without her. She had affected him absolutely. Just thinking about the way she smiled at him made him feel ten feet tall.

He had to find her.

He took a shaky step in her direction and remembered who he was and that he could never have her. What good would it do to find her? Loving her was a lost cause even he couldn't take on. With that settled, he set out again towards *ma's Café*.

Jane Angelina blew down the street thinking about the strange young man. Well, not thinking about him. Hearing his prayer.

"The closer you are—
The brighter the stars in sky."

Just about the time he heard the first strains of Doo Wop drift into the café, BJ had looked up, and when he did, he saw it all, although he sure wasn't sure he could actually explain any of it.

First, he saw Ole SunnySide Up herself, puttering around the corner, which should have bowled him over, what with her being gone without a trace for almost three months. But here she was, and he wasn't a bit surprised. His hunch was coming true. She was coming home to Mama. Who could blame her?

"You went away, but now you're back to stay. And my love for you grows stronger every day!" the Doo Wops concurred breezily, while BJ watched Ole SunnySide slowly swing into her special parking spot under the canopy

that once had *ma's Café* spelled out on it in letters so bright, they outshone the moon. But now, there was nothing left of them except flecks and specks scattered around the faded fade-resistant, industrial strength thermoplastic polymer, like dull stars in a murky sky. He had to face it. Although he had promised and *believed* it would, in the end, even top-of-the-line Fliridescence could not withstand the test of time.

What had withstood the test of time on nothing more than guts and gumption, of course, was ole SunnySide Up, back at last, with some kind of a tale to tell. But she wasn't alone. Because her driver's door had jerked open and a very small, very rumpled young man bounced out.

The thief? Nothing in BJ had registered yes. But before he could ask himself why, the next strange thing happened. The wind howled up a storm right outside *ma's* door, and suddenly, the angel who wanted to be a waitress blew into view and slammed violently into the rumpled little guy while he was closing SunnySide's door, sending them both flying backwards in opposite directions, headed for a really bad fall. But somehow, in the split-second before they hit the ground, the little guy hovered in mid-air, righted himself back up like a gymnast in the Olympics, then reached out and broke the angel's fall. As the Doo Wops were his witnesses, BJ sure did not know how.

"*Do be dum do be do,*" the Doo Wops agreed.

"It's been that kind of day," BJ mused, deciding at that juncture, it would be safer all around if he closed the blinds and minded his own business. But it was not to be.

Seconds later, the door flew open again, and the little guy limped (limped!) through it.

BJ had been hoping the little guy had seen one of the hundreds of posters he'd put up everywhere he could think of, and was just bringing Ole Sunny-Side back, but something in the pit of BJ knew from first laying eyes on him, that he was the one. Only, he was turning out to be the wrong one.

BJ had made a pact with himself the day he placed the ad, that even if he and Mama could actually bring themselves to sell *ma's,* he still couldn't bring himself to pawn *ma's* off on some poor, unsuspecting soul, who was pouring his last cent into the place with false hopes. It would be like stealing. That meant *if* they ever sold *ma's,* it couldn't be to just anyone. They could only sell it to the right one: someone rich enough to buy it, and strange enough to want it, even though it was a losing proposition, on land that was worth less and less with every tick of the clock. Figuring it would be cold in hell before that happened, BJ went on tending to Mama and *ma's,* doing what he could to keep money coming in, praying for a miracle that would grant them absolution and allow them to stay.

Then the call came from Mr. Mills Miggston the Third, and BJ knew someone with a name like that wouldn't be pouring his last penny into *ma's.* Someone with a name like that probably needed a tax write-off. In the end, they would be helping each other. So, he gave Mr. Mills Miggston the Third directions and waited for this day with hope and dread.

The little guy stopped in his tracks, something BJ was used to, when people got a gander at how far up they had to look to get to the top of him. But in this case, it took twice as long, giving BJ even more time to regret his decision. The little guy certainly didn't look like he had a bank account as big as his name. Hopelessness was pouring out of him like he was a shot up water barrel in an old western. But there was something else, something that reminded BJ of his darlin' strippers—a tiny filament of hope that was still flickering inside of him.

"Mr. Mills Miggston the Third?" BJ asked, trying to sound cheerful, hoping the little guy would say no.

"Ma?" Miggsy responded, trying to sound casual, hoping the big guy would say no.

"Nah, I'm just BJ," BJ laughed, creating a small tsunami, which fortunately, blew over Miggsy's head, rattling some utensils and glasses on the tables behind him.

BJ extended his hand which, from his prospective looking down, unfortunately blotted the little guy out completely.

"And I'm Mills Miggs—just Miggsy. Call me Miggsy," Miggsy corrected himself, peering around the gigantic hand, extending *his* hand, giving BJ an unusually hearty shake. They locked eyes, each taking measure of the other. Then BJ watched Miggsy eye the empty room.

"Brisk business," Miggsy observed, with Cowardice's edge in his voice.

"Used to be busier," BJ admitted, "But ever since Mama's accident, things kind of petered out."

"*Accident*?" Miggsy and Cowardice shuddered in unison, both scrambling to look around for signs of foul play. It was spotless. "Too spotless." Cowardice pointed out, which, he mirthlessly explained, "did not bode well, did not bode well at all." Rather, it led to the assumption that someone, probably this colossus, had recently dismembered his victim—probably the suspiciously absent "Mama"—and then cleaned up the blood right where they were standing. "It's the very absence of evidence that is the evidence." Cowardice waxed Sherlock Holmesian. But he was interrupted by a rumbling. The big guy was still talking.

"Ya see," BJ went on, "Mama's accident was that she got hit in the head by lightning and that kind of spooked people around here."

"That she got hit by lightning?" Miggsy asked, relieved there was no foul-play involved,

"Yeah. And then she started hearing voices, though no one else knows about the voices but me and Mama—and now you." BJ rumbled on, going for full disclosure.

"Let's get out of here! Now!" Cowardice demanded, trying to get Miggsy's feet to move. "Did you hear him? Were you not listening? She hears voices!"

"Well," Miggsy huffed, "who doesn't?"

"Don't for a second, dear boy—don't for an iota of a whit of a shred of a nano of a second—delude yourself into believing that the absurd synchronicity of crazies—" Cowardice gave BJ a quick up and down, "bumping into each other in the middle of the God forsaken Mojave Desert, will lead to anything other than unmitigated disaster."

"Don't be so negative," Miggsy silently ordered, demanding the impossible.

"Do you not get the point? These people are demented, disturbed and deranged—at *best*!" Cowardice frantically pontificated inside the lecture hall of Miggsy's mind, forcing Miggsy to remind him to put a lid on it, since he, the great and terrible Cowardice, was in the harsh light of day, no more than a mere figment of his own imagination.

"So, you think," Cowardice sniffed, about to do a riff on all the possible disasters lurking in any future concerning *ma's Café,* when strains of "This Magic Moment" drifted in from out of nowhere, drowning Cowardice out, and taking Miggsy for a ride on the gossamer wings of its irrepressible harmonies—to nowhere else in particular—but it felt like cloud nine.

When the song ended and Miggsy returned to earth, there was BJ staring at him oddly. How long had he been swaying back and forth with his eyes closed, forgetting himself totally? That was easy. Three minutes. The length of a song. No wonder the guy was staring.

"Nice jukebox," Miggsy tried to sound nonchalant.

"Oh, that's not the jukebox you're hearing," BJ explained. "It's Mama's voices."

"Come on, I'll give you a look-see." BJ offered, in his most business-like growl, leading Miggsy towards the kitchen and reluctantly away from the lingering harmonies of "This Magic Moment," which vanished behind him like the last wisps of a vapor trail.

BJ held the swinging doors open, urging him into the dark room.

"As you can plainly see—" BJ beamed into the pitch blackness, turning on two rows of overhead fluorescent lights.

And Miggsy was suddenly faced with blurry visions of himself everywhere, all sizes and shapes of him, reflected on the walls, cabinets, counter tops, refrigerator doors. And even, when he looked up expecting relief, the ceiling. He gasped.

"It's a one hundred percent riveted, stainless steel kitchen! And it sure takes *my* breath away every time!" BJ said proudly, before honing in on one particularly precious piece that had caught Miggsy's eye, but was definitely not for sale, a sterling silver kitchen timer, shaped like *ma's Café,* with the Marine Corps insignia engraved on it.

"Sorry, but Mama could never, ever part with it," BJ explained, picking it up and showing it to Miggsy. "It's a one of a kind, personally presented to Mama by Base Commander, Major General Vince Alan Murdoch, in honor of how all the wonderful flavors of *ma's Café* always snuck up on them like a taste of home when they needed it most, and for making her traditional herb-crusted, Coca-Cola basted ham for all the boys every Christmas for over twenty-five years." BJ enfolded it in his huge hand, remembering all the meals it had helped make great.

"It's calibrated to Marine Corps standards, accurate to the nanosecond, which, like Mama likes to say, is all it takes to make or break anything, from an egg to a heart."

BJ paused, lost in thought again, then leaned down and whispered. "Timing is everything, if you know what I mean."

Miggsy nodded the rueful nod of someone who has lost his timing and misses it every nanosecond of every day, and a dozen fun house Miggsies nodded back, unnerving him.

But BJ went on, unfazed.

"Right here is our fully functional, top-of-the-line, Stevenson grill, a real beauty of a grill by any man's standards. And what you're standing in front of is our special double-wide food prep area."

BJ was unable to stop himself from remembering how Mama had asked him to build it exactly to his own double-wide specifications, so he could take his quote—"considerable knife wielding know-how"—at least that's how Mama phrased it at the time—and put it to good use, chopping, slicing, dicing, and filleting away, while Mama did her magic right by his side, which suited him just fine. The best part being that whenever he looked up, wherever he looked, he saw Mama's robust and genuinely fine form formulating her "flights of culinary fancy," which was how Mama always put it, when she was just about ready to take off and start cooking.

"Nothing but the best for Mama," he purred, lifting his prodigious arms to take it all in, in what seemed to Miggsy to be an enormous embrace, which ricocheted off every riveted stainless-steel panel around them.

There was so much to take in: intimidating cast-iron skillets and copper pots and pans blackened from use, dangling on hooks, over a six burner, *Super Chef* stainless steel range that looked like it could feed an army, and evidently did, cabinets stocked with an assortment of canned goods, condiments and cleaning supplies, drawers filled with a variety of utensils, bottle and can openers and a serious arsenal of knives, sharpened to a razor's edge, shelves lined with glasses, plates, cups, saucers, and platoon of riveted stainless steel napkin and menu holders with matching straw and toothpick dispensers, all exact replicas of the front of *ma's Café*.

BJ was pointing to each and every gadget and gizmo *so* lovingly that Miggsy could not help but think there were people in the world who had never been loved as much as BJ loved his appliances. He had once felt like one of those people, unloved, undeserving of love. Then, thanks to Wilde and Will, everything had changed, until he ruined it all.

No. It wasn't the hardware that was moving this mountain of a man. It was the memories.

Memories.

Hah!

Other people had memories. What Miggsy had, thanks to no one but himself, were self-inflicted wounds.

That was it. The start-up to the count-down to the tailspin that would plunge him back in the saddle, back in the race, back atop Wilde, feverishly trying to outrun fate, crashing head first into the impenetrable, unalterable past. Even though it was all his fault and his burden alone, it was too much to bear. In the dark of his darkest nights, he had secretly wished, above all, not just for a time-out, or even a black-out, compliments of the right brew of drugs and recklessness, but for a moment of grace. And miraculously, he'd been granted his wish, just a magic moment ago, but somewhere between the café and the kitchen, the Doo Wops had given up on him. And now he was as bereft of their harmonies as he was of Wilde and Will and, oh yes, that flickering flame of a girl. Wanting them all back, aching for them, but reminding himself that he didn't deserve any of them, he fretted himself into a boil.

The very second Miggsy was about to blow, BJ leaned down to put in a good word for a very special feature on the dishwasher, and the fabulous falsetto of "Could This Be Magic?" mercifully swooped down from somewhere around the top of BJ's head, immediately lifting Miggsy out of his self-induced morass, and carrying him away on a magic Doo Wop ride, in such perfect harmony with the universe, that strange and wonderful visions of sprucing *ma's Café* up to its former splendor, whatever that was, danced him right out of the kitchen and up to a shiny, vintage soda fountain, sparkling behind the counter, that he hadn't noticed before.

He couldn't believe he also hadn't noticed before how charming this place was. How it gleamed. It was true the booths needed recovering, the counters and table tops were faded, and the front could use a little landscaping, but—"

"A *little* landscaping?" Cowardice, aghast at having been asleep at the wheel for too long, shrieked so sharply, he severed Miggsy's Doo Wop connection.

"All the grounds-keepers at Miggston Farms couldn't revive this dump! Get a grip!" Cowardice admonished sternly.

"It's not a dump. It has possibilities." Miggsy insisted.

"Pardonez-moi for interrupting your delusion, dear boy," Cowardice cut in, hissing in his head, obliterating any last vestiges of Doo Wop still lounging in the air, hurling Miggsy down to earth so fast, he got whiplash. "But, in case you haven't noticed, we're on the outskirts of oblivion here, which means *NO CUSTOMERS! EVER!* So, let's cut to the chase and beat a hasty retreat from this dust bowl debacle before you go stark raving mad and take me with you."

This thought painted Miggsy into a corner of confusion, since he already was stark raving mad, as the songs he'd been hearing that weren't there, and his continued contretemps with Cowardice certainly evidenced, especially since at this very moment, Cowardice was attempting to take over his body, and move him towards the door.

"Let's see, now, what's left? We've got oversized goods, and the like, stored in the back, and there's a cooling pantry behind that door over there. We've got all the staples. Ya know, salt, pepper, sugar, flour, mustard, ketchup, and the like. We've got a big storage area out back, which comes in very handy. And speaking of handy, we've got our own generator in case of emergency," BJ beamed, totally involved with every single item he itemized. "And oh yes, one waitress. We've got one waitress."

Miggsy looked up at him, trying to hold his ground against Cowardice.

"I gotta be honest. *Ma's* hasn't been doing so well, lately. Truth is, we haven't exactly been holding our own. There's past due bills. Lots of them. And back taxes. I can show you the books," BJ offered, watching Miggsy losing the struggle with himself. "That is, if you're still interested—"

"Just say no!" Cowardice urged.

"No!" Miggsy retorted.

No?" BJ repeated, instantly, albeit temporarily relieved, because as much as he wanted to take Mama to a safer place, now that it was really happening, he realized that even if it wouldn't kill Mama to leave, which it would, it would kill him. Showing Miggsy around had clinched it. BJ couldn't, even in his wildest dreams, imagine how he could bear to part with any part of it. He loved every square inch. Because, no matter what shape it was in, *ma's* was a part of him and Mama, like family. And you don't abandon family. He said a silent prayer of thanks that Miggsy had stopped him from making the biggest mistake of his life. But, just to make sure, and put it all to rest, he asked again. "You said no, right?"

"That's right. I've changed my mind," Miggsy assured him so firmly, Cowardice breathed a sigh of relief and relaxed his grip.

"I don't want to buy you out anymore," Miggsy confirmed, as a self-satisfied Cowardice slipped into a drawing room, somewhere more civilized, in the back of Miggsy's mind, where a Courvoisier was waiting.

"What I want to do is stay here and be your partner," Miggsy continued, when Cowardice was completely out of range, hearing words he certainly had not planned to say, roll out of his mouth.

"Partner?" BJ questioned, his eyes actually blinking in surprise.

"Here's what I'm prepared to put on the table," Miggsy said, as if he was prepared to put anything on the faded Formica. Which he wasn't.

"I'm prepared to give you a fair price for the value of your establishment and property, and pay all your bills from the past into the indeterminate future."

Give them actual money and pay their bills forever? What was he saying? Worse, what was he doing? Where was Cowardice when he needed him? Temporarily done in by the sheer force of Miggsy's will? Highly doubtful. More likely fainted dead away from the prospect of being stuck here and dying a slow, painful, tacky death. Or maybe this was a hideous joke. Finally give the kid something he wants. Hoist him by his own petard.

"I'll bankroll *ma's Café,*" he heard himself say, as if he hadn't said enough.

BJ was taking it all in, understanding the words all right, but not the trick behind them. Because he was being offered exactly what he wanted.

"You serious?" He asked.

"Yes—" Miggsy's mouth opened and this strange new voice came out, not exactly in sync with his lips, but somehow, amazingly, in sync with his heart. "Yes, I am." Miggsy assured him, pulling himself together, rising to his former stature, looking BJ straight in the eye as only a Miggston could, convincing him, without a shadow of a doubt, that he was serious.

He held out his hand to BJ, who was just slightly more shocked than Miggsy himself.

"So—" BJ asked, withholding his handshake before sealing the deal, bringing everything to a screeching halt, "why are you doing this? What's in it for you?"

"What's in it for me?" Miggsy reiterated dumbly, hoping that saying it out loud would be an invitation for an answer to land in his vicinity.

"Yeah. What's in it for you?" BJ threw the whole thing back into Miggsy's court. "What are you here for? What's here for you?"

And then it came to him. The answer he sought was as simple as the chords to "Heart and Soul."

"Harmony," Miggsy said.

"Well then!" BJ smiled his coast-to-coast smile. "If Mama says the word, we got ourselves a new partner."

Thrilled beyond his own comprehension, Miggsy thrust out his hand again. This time, instead of shaking it, BJ scooped him up in the air and hugged him

"This magic moment—will last forever, forever, till the end of time," the Doo Wops observed, sealing the deal.

Mama was mamboing with the cha-cha of the cosmos when the two pulled up in Lucille. The Doo Wops had been gone awhile now, as far as she could tell, though time sure wasn't what it used to be. So, thinking maybe they'd taken off with BJ to clear her personal wave length, she'd tried to blow the whistle on the drunken party being thrown by all her new wild ideas, so she could tune in to that apple pie recipe transmission. But all she got was static, which pinged off the ping and pong trampolining inside the receiver that once was her brain, until she got the picture. There were perturbations in the universe. The apple pie recipe was temporarily on hold.

To double-check, Mama rotated her head, which had now taken to blowing off steam at regular intervals like Old Faithful, and immediately honed in on a hum. But it wasn't an apple pie hum. It didn't seem to have apple pie anywhere near its wavelength.

It was coming in from the charred garden path, where BJ was quickly gaining on her with his odd sidekick, who reminded Mama of some sort of an amusement park ride, tilting and whirling frantically to keep up, an impossible task for a normal sized guy, yet, somehow, actually doing it. And she was getting lost in the uncanny speed and spellbinding rhythm of the little guy's limp. But the minute that big guy of hers put his Paul Bunyans across her threshold, riveting her attention, full transmission recommenced. Spaceship Mama was once more operational. She was back in business.

"Daddy's home!" the Doo Wops crooned the obvious.

Meanwhile, BJ and the Tiltawhirl Man kept coming at Mama like she was a bank that was about to close and they needed to cash their pay checks in a hurry.

And the closer they got, the more something about the Tiltawhirl Man steamed up and down her insides, and the more she could swear she heard calliopes.

Calliopes! The sounds popped up in her head. And ping! She knew why. It was because she happened to be passing through Carson, the day the Carson City All Girl Calliope Band, in a startling upset, beat their bitter rivals The Kylee County Calliope All Stars and walked away with the Western Regional Calliope Band Play-Offs.

Another gander at the Tiltawhirl Man and ping! Mama was back at the play-offs savoring every lick of a double-dip, rocky-road, when she was suddenly sidetracked by a commotion coming from the general direction of Town Hall Auditorium, and never being one to shy away from a party, she immediately joined in.

It was bandemonium! The Carson City All Girl Calliope Band, formerly the Carson City Chapter of Weight Watchers—who, as legend had it, at one historic meeting, decided that, since none of them had lost so much as five pounds in three years, they had to do something else at their weekly meetings besides weighing themselves, lying about their diets, and exchanging fat free recipes they'd never try—were being paraded down State Street playing their calliopes for all they were worth!

The amazing sight and absolutely awesome sound of a chorus line of the fiery red contraptions arranged back-to-back on three recently repainted bright blue flatbeds, with all those Weight Watcher drop-outs bursting out of their tidy, red, white, and blue uniforms, whomping away on their keyboards, thumping the Bejeezus out of their show-stopping rendition of "Forget Your Troubles Come on Get Happy," which whooped out of shiny brass whistles in dozens of whooshes of steam. Well, that's something you don't forget. It was like being in a hundred circuses all at once.

But the thing that caught Mama's eye wasn't all the glitter, glitz, and happy-go-luckiness of the tunes. It was the turbulence and the agitation of the steam roiling itself into music.

No doubt about it. Tiltawhirl Man was a calliope of unrequited oom-pahs. She could feel it parboiling inside of him, hear its familiar whoosh and hiss. Like Mama's mind, the boy was ready to pop. But would he make music or blow his head off?

"So, the thing is, Mama—" BJ broke through from the great distance of his fabulous expanse, suddenly right there, whispering in her ear, "—the thing is—"

The thing was, everything had changed around and back again, and it was all luge-ing around in BJ's current state of mind. The thing was, Mama could feel his gears shifting, like he had a plan and then the plan had changed while he was in the middle of having it.

Now, if you asked Mama, BJ was not a man who stripped his gears. He was, in fact, so well-oiled from the inside out, that everything he put his hands on just purred and hummed away, and Mama was bobbing up and down on the purring and humming, and she just kept on gyrating inside of BJ's insides, right up into the secret dream portion of his copious inner self, where she and BJ were traveling in the Airstream, pulled by good ole SunnySide Up, who surely had one more trip left in her. But there was something bumpy about this ride, and suddenly, Mama was hurled right off it into the over-seasoned stew of the smile of the Tiltawhirl Man, and she didn't have to be struck by lightning again to get it. The little guy would be appearing on the menu right alongside her and BJ.

BJ's mouth was opening and closing, still trying to tell her something. But the Doo Wops, returning with a flourish, drowned him out with a chorus of "Save the Last Dance for Me," which sounded like a good plan to Mama, except Tiltawhirl wanted to cut in. He was holding out his hand and Mama, politeness built in, thanks to her momma, held out hers.

Tiltawhirl's small, fine-boned hand grasped Mama's, and he had a grip so astoundingly powerful, it momentarily terminated all other transmissions, giving Mama a window to peer through, between the cracks in the universe, to take a gander at the guy.

And everything shifted just slightly.

He was still small, but he was no longer lopsided. He was straight and lithe and strong, with a heart so pure—in spite of an ache so sharp it almost cut right through him—that there was nothing else she seemed to need to know. Although for what, exactly, escaped her at the moment. He, among other things, not being a she, was surely not the angel Mama was on the lookout for, although out of everybody she remembered she knew, he surely had the most need for wings. She listened for anything to the contrary from the Doo Wops, picking up on her ground radar that something big was happening right in front of her and she was a big part of it, and it had to do with the Tiltawhirl Man and his vibrant blue eyes, and his tortured soul, and that mighty grip of his which could reach down and pull you out of a hole one-handed. Though he sure couldn't do the same for himself. But then again, who could?

"So, Mama—" BJ was saying, maybe had been saying non-stop. There was no way to really tell, "– just say the word."

"What word is that?" Mama heard her voice piping in.

"*Sh-Boom—Sh-Boom,*" the Doo Wops offered.

"Oh. In that case, it's fine with me," Mama purred, relaxing back into her apple pie vigil, feeling overdue to start *Sh-Booming* with the Doo Wops, knowing whatever it was, BJ would take care of it.

> *"Life could be a dream, Sh-Boom*
> *If I could take you up to Paradise above..."*

The Doo Wops drifted away from BJ and began wafting to and from the kitchen like the aroma of freshly baked pie, which under ordinary circumstances, would have made Mama's mouth water just thinking about it, but she was too busy being distracted by her momma, waving at her from her mind's front porch.

"Hello, hello again.
Sh-Boom, here's hoping that we meet again."

"Don't forget!" Her momma was saying, waving good-bye like she did the day her baby, her Norma Lee, went away for good. "Never forget."

"Forget what, momma?" Norma Lee had asked, her head filled with the future, her heart wanting these last words of wisdom to carry her all the way to wherever she was going.

"How to make apple pie, of course," her momma had said.

"Sh-Boom!"

Norma Lee Walters was setting out like her poppa had done so many times, she couldn't remember all of the goings and comings. So many, that they were routine. And it got so she and her momma barely even got that pang of good-bye so much anymore. Because they knew his leaving wasn't personal. It just was.

So, of course, when the time came for their Norma Lee, her momma and poppa knew they would have to let her go, and that it would be all right, because of that guardian angel they swore they saw on her shoulder.

But Norma Lee didn't think she really needed an angel to protect her, because in her secret dreams she saw herself as a big ole float in her family's personal parade, floating high and away from the people on the ground, who were, well there was no other word for it—*grounded*—and couldn't get lift-off because they didn't have that special way of seeing, like Norma Lee and her poppa did.

But, as time closed in on her, and going was just heartbeats away, she realized that she wasn't a float at all, bobbing at the end of her momma's string, so wherever she went to, she would always be just a tug away and that close to home. She wasn't even a moon, orbiting safely within her momma's gravitational pull.

No, the day Norma Lee was set to leave home was the first day of her life she didn't feel floaty in the least bit.

All morning, as she double-checked her duffel bag, and triple checked the inner pocket her momma had sewn into her brassiere to hide her money, to make sure it was all there, down to the dollar, and quadruple-checked her map, all she could think about was that she was already feeling cut loose from home, but not in the way she had imagined.

Sitting in her beloved room that, though small from the outside, always seemed to expand around her to accommodate all the parts of her, she had the saddest feeling that when she left it this time, she would never fit into it again.

When the time came, she got up from her canopy bed, which her momma had put together from cast-off prom dresses, petticoats and crinolines, and paused in the door frame to honor times gone by together. Then, her dear room, she was sadly departing, which had shared all her big dreams with her, shuddered its bon voyage, and shrunk back into itself.

Norma Lee sighed deeply, stepped away, and called ever so casually into the kitchen, where her momma had just finished cooking up a storm for her to take on the road.

"Momma! Poppa! G'bye!"

Her poppa was in his favorite chair, the one her momma had fashioned entirely out of tossed away quilts during the coldest winter he was gone, because he would need a warm place to settle down into when he got home, which is exactly what he had done. Norma Lee told him not to get up because she wanted to remember him staying put for once, and they both laughed the private laughter of wanderers.

"Norma Lee," he said, tears of pride in his voice, "it's not every father's daughter who can follow in his foot-steps." And that's when he gave her his brass compass, his mantle he was passing on to her, "So you can always find your way. Whatever way it is."

Norma Lee worried for a moment that if she had his compass, then what would he do? She was kind of hoping that maybe he would retire from the road and stay home with momma. But, of course, she knew that was a story she was telling herself to make leaving easier. The road was so ingrained in her poppa by now, that he was his own compass.

She was pondering all this when her momma came out of the kitchen with her handiwork all wrapped up in waxed paper packages and enfolded in her favorite table cloth, her masterpiece that she'd sewn from the finest remnants of red damask she'd collected over the years—unbeknownst to Norma Lee—just for this day.

"There's a special gift in here for you," her momma whispered, the enticing aroma already encompassing Norma Lee in its special kind of protective coating.

She kissed Norma Lee and hugged her when she handed her the beautifully rendered meals that she hoped would fill up her daughter's insides and keep her well. And Norma Lee was sure that was when her momma would fill up her heart and soul with wisdom and good advice. But her momma said nothing, just looked at her, memorizing that exact moment of Norma Lee, who was feeling herself filling up with the journey ahead, ready to drift away from her momma and her poppa and her home, but still waiting for her momma's words that she could take and carry with her everywhere.

But her momma just stood there, rooted to the spot, while Norma Lee waited and waited for the final benediction of her good-bye. When nothing came except the apple pie advice, she just turned and headed out the door and down the road, feeling cut off and cut out, deflated and rejected, even though leaving was her own idea.

And those feelings confused Norma Lee, who had never felt anything like them before. They tilted her balance, which is not a good way to set out on the journey of your life. So, she purposely wrapped those confounding feelings in that apple pie recipe, as carefully as her momma had wrapped those meals, that magically had lasted her the better part of a month, tiding her over until she found her road rhythm. And she kicked that recipe and everything wrapped in it right out of her memory bank and buried it deep down in the basement of her mind, from which she was now trying to unearth it.

But the recipe kept getting all tangled up in the way the glittering grains of sugar her momma had poured into the oversized silver spoon she once found inside a thrown-out swath of blue felt, reminded her of how the riot of stars that speckled the desert sky at night spilled down on the sand, like some painter had aimed his paintbrush up instead of down, so stars were dripping all around her and she couldn't stop herself from closing her eyes, scooping them up in her arms in a luminous bouquet and making a wish. And, in one blinding flash, there she was again, on the doorstep of her future, looking into her momma's eyes, seeing only herself, caught in a Mexican stand-off, listening hard for the words that would send her on her way.

But how could she hear straight with all her own, excited, unsettled thoughts zooming around, like she had already been hit by lightning? All this time, convinced it would be easy to leave, because she was just like her poppa. Shocked to find out—at this very late date—that she was also just like her momma, as rooted to home as she was lured by the road, that she would not be floating away at all, but uprooting herself, and that the only way to get off of that doorstep was to wrench herself away, tear herself out, like a page from a book that would never be part of that story again.

And, with all this going on, how could she have heard the prayer her momma was offering instead of advice, because everything her momma knew about life, she had already passed on to her daughter. And it was not that she had run out of advice, but that everything else Norma Lee had to learn from there on out, she could only learn by experience. All she had left to offer was the prayer that the world her Norma Lee was so intent on heading headlong into, would be a better place than she knew it was.

Hearing her momma's prayer for the first time, Mama's eyes welled with tears. From where she sat, the world had not turned into a better place since she left home. But by all accounts, had become a more and more miserable place to be. Sadly, her momma's prayer had not been answered.

And sadly, when she listened closely, with her new way of hearing, through the vent in her mind, the desert sky was as filled with unanswered prayers, as it was with invisible stars. And the ones coming in the loudest and the clearest were from all the mothers praying that the cruel world would be kinder to their sons and daughters than they knew it would be.

It was too much to bear.

"Where do I go from here, momma?" Mama finally asked the one question she could not ask then.

And the recipe came to her like it had never left.

"So, Mama, darlin'—" BJ whispered in her ear, his warm breath tickling her fancy, "ya didn't happen to get that apple pie recipe yet, did ya?"

"That man," Mama thought, her insides all a flutter again, "always did have prodigious timing."

"Matter a fact, I did," she said, matter of factly, as if they had never stopped conversing, which in a way they hadn't. "Why'd ya ask?"

"Remember that angel ya told me to be on the look-out for? Well, I hired her to be our waitress a little while ago, and me and our new partner, Miggsy, here, we gotta go meet her just about now, cause she thinks she's starting tonight. And Mama, it sure would be nice if she had some customers to wait on, if you catch my drift."

Mama, of course, always caught BJ's drift and frankly could have coasted on it till Kingdom come came and went. But in this instance, firing up the engines on the apple pie enterprise "AYSAP" as the Marines liked to say, made perfectly good sense to Mama, a part of her conjuring up some sort of a strange reunion at the café, the rest of her listening to her momma's apple pie recipe hum through her like a lullaby.

Well, well, well. There was an angel coming.

No doubt about it.

It was time to bake.

Everybody has a prayer, Jane Angelina was thinking, running up to *ma's Café*, praying that she wasn't late. She had on her uniform from her last actual waitress job at Calico's Cozy Corner, which, in her enthusiasm to get whiter than white and just like new, she may have over-starched, as it was standing away from her lodgepole pine body like a sandwich board.

She had gotten it as a hand-me-down from Sharl, on the occasion of Sharl's leaving Calico's after winning enough in the local lottery to retire on. Sharl gave Jane Angelina her entire wardrobe of uniforms, having worked in the "tray trade," as she called it, "for forty *odd* years—with an emphasis on the *odd*." Most of the uniforms were almost threadbare, held up only by starch and vanity. But a few, like this one, Sharl's Saturday-Night-Special, in particular, were in almost perfect shape. "Ship-Shape," as Sharl said every morning when people asked how she was, even though she was pushing the short end of seventy by the time she got lucky and her ship came in.

Jane Angelina was hoping to feel ship-shape on her first night on the job, but she was feeling more ship*wrecked*. "If you could be a shipwrecked sandwich board," she reflected, struggling uphill against her clothing, until, caught on a gust of wind, the uniform became a sail skimming her along the street and up the steps to *ma's Café*.

"Here she comes—" BJ said, with a double-dose of his infectious exuberance, hearing her at the door, pushing Miggsy in from the back, where they'd just parked Lucille, "—our new waitress!"

To be totally honest, Miggsy was in no mood to meet anyone. He didn't even necessarily want *ma's* to have customers. He just wanted to be near the music.

"Ah the joys of being a restaurateur!" Cowardice, back with a vengeance and invigorated purpose, sniffed. "How do you like it so far, dear boy?"

The jolt of perverse pleasure in the newly perked Cowardice shot through Miggsy like a spasm. He grunted.

BJ looked down.

Cowardice laughed.

"No way around it. It's time to meet the help." Cowardice taunted, loving every rancid minute of Miggsy's discomfort.

And then the door opened and *she* blew in and Miggsy's heart stopped dead in its tracks. Again.

"This lovely lass," BJ lilted in a newly acquired Irish brogue, a glow in his voice that spread to his state-wide smile, pleased as punch that fate and Mama had brought these two souls together under this particular riveted steel roof, "is our new waitress—uh—"

Jane Angelina was busy settling herself back on solid ground and getting her waitress legs again, when BJ abruptly stopped talking, looked at her strangely, and spread the King Kong palms of his take-care-of-everything hands out like he'd forgotten something big. And it dawned on her that he was waiting for her to tell him her name because, among other things she hadn't taken care of in a professional, business-like manner, like she normally made a point of doing, she hadn't told him her name. But instead of figuring out why, some other Jane Angelina was whispering in her ear, that as of that very moment, she could be whoever she wanted to be.

"*Deirdre*," Jane Angelina said impulsively. "My name is—*Deirdre*."

"Well then—*Deirdre*—I'd like you to meet Mr. Miggs—"

"Miggsy!" Miggsy cut in, petrified of being introduced to her with his full name and everything it implied. "Just call me Miggsy. The name's Miggsy."

Deirdre looked down at him through Jane Angelina's eyes and smiled with a radiance that warmed him from the inside out. "We met," she said, softly.

All he wanted to do from that moment on was live up to his feelings for her.

"Now I can thank you properly," she said. "Thank you, Miggsy."

He was stumped for a reply. Even the mere, "you're welcome," escaped him. But it didn't matter. Her voice lingered in the air and serenaded him after she stopped talking, rivaling the Doo Wops in sheer sweetness.

He wanted to, needed to be perfect for her, to take her hand in his and say, "it was nothing," in a way that would make her think it was everything, *he* was everything. Unfortunately, he was rendered mute and just stood there, staring up at her like an orphaned puppy.

BJ watched his new partner again fall for his new waitress and decided to step in before he hit the ground.

"Ya see, Deirdre," BJ helped out, "he doesn't like to brag but—he's actually—well, I'll let him tell you himself."

Miggsy was sinking fast.

"Miggsy here's just a bit modest, ya know, but he's really—" BJ continued, indicating that Miggsy should speak for himself; let the girl know that he'd just become BJ and Mama's partner in the café, and therefore, her new boss.

He was trying to throw Miggsy a lifeline. But Miggsy was incapable of grabbing onto it because his life had already started flashing before him and it was not a very pretty picture. How could he allow himself to have feelings for her? He wasn't worthy of anyone's love. He'd already proven that. Because, as a friend, as a human being, no matter how he looked at it, no matter where he looked—

"Miggsy here's—" BJ tried again.

—At every turn—he came up—

"Short!" Miggsy blurted.

"Short?" Deirdre repeated.

"Short?" BJ echoed.

Short! The word reverberated in the air in front of them, bouncing off the riveted steel walls in a scene directly out of his worst nightmare.

Could it possibly get worse? Of course, it could.

While Miggsy's mind cast about wildly for a way to salvage itself, Cowardice reappeared to complete the humiliation.

"See that look of *concern* in her eyes, dear boy. It's verging on *pity.*" Cowardice taunted, bubbling over with tart revenge. "Your life here is about to become a living hell, unless of course, you can—which of course you can't possibly—come up with something in *short* order."

Miggsy's eyes lighted on Mama's shiny grill.

"Yes! That's it!" Miggsy said, triumphantly. "I'm the new *short order cook*!"

"Oh!" Jane Angelina and BJ said in unison, both relieved that Miggsy's sentence had ended well.

"So, we'll be working together, Miggsy," Jane Angelina said, unable to stop smiling. "I bet we're gonna make a great team!"

BJ watched his and Mama's new waitress, who, he was sure, had just given herself a much fancier name than she was born with to stretch into, not that she needed any stretching or changing in any direction, since she was just about perfect as is. But anyway, there she was, lovely as the month of May, smiling at their new partner and short order cook, who had picked the smallest part of his name to shrink into, in order, BJ reckoned, to grow out of it. And he knew there was balance in the universe.

But not for long, because just a half-mile downhill, with a ping of enormous proportions, Mama was abruptly ponged into another dimension, throwing everything off-kilter again.

"Well, well, well, if that's not a case of the cosmic jitters, I don't know what is," she observed, shaking that into the galactic martini that was being mixed in her mind.

There was a disturbance in the universe. Deirdre, who so recently was Jane Angelina, felt it.

"Did you feel that?" she asked Miggsy and BJ.

"What?" each echoed the other.

"Men," Jane Angelina thought, "lovable but obtuse."

"Unless you mean that little disturbance in the universe." Miggsy said off-handedly, having met Mama.

"Oh that," BJ confirmed nonchalantly, "must be Mama goin' off again."

Indeed, Mama was now picking up minuscule perturbations, hiccups in the heavens, fossils from the birth of the universe, fifteen or so billion years ago, when that fiery cataclysm, better known as the Big Bang—in a moment of divine over-achievement—jump-started space and time.

"'In the beginning,'" Mama intoned to a Jack Rabbit and a few passing lizards, her voice rising from her supine body, "'the earth was without form, and darkness was upon the face of the deep.' In the beginning, there was a void, a vacuum, containing no space, no time, no matter, no light, no sound. Nothing. But the promise of everything. Then there was something, a singular spark, a tremendous flash of light."

"And then there was a burst of heat!"

"And the planets and the stars baked in the molten oven of burgeoning solar systems, like apple slices bubbling into something thick and syrupy."

"Amen."

The three new friends held their breath waiting for the universe to settle back down again. When it didn't, Miggsy and Jane Angelina, who was still getting used to being Deirdre, turned to BJ, the resident expert, who had sounded so nonchalant, for assurance.

It was true, BJ had sounded very casual about it all out of habit. But, on further consideration, he wasn't feeling so casual.

Sure, if there was anyone who was an old hand at these things, it had to be him. Sure, he always knew when Mama was going on and off, and that's when he dropped everything to check in on her—even though she really never needed checking in on, being cosmically connected, and all. But this time, it came to him like a jalapeno attack—in such a hot gust of aha!—that he had a feeling something had changed.

Well, of course, it had, he reminded himself. Everything was finally in place, like at the end of a scavenger hunt that he had won just by not giving up.

BJ considered himself a simple man. He was not the type to commune with the universe over questions of a philosophical nature, like maybe Mama was doing right now. He was just a hard worker, happy to do anything he could for Mama, because to make Mama happy, well, that was more than fine with him. So, he had gone about collecting all the items on his list of things necessary to save Mama. And Lo! And Behold! He had saved *ma's Café*, somehow. Although the odds had been against it, he now had everything: the money—or at least the promise of it from their new partner, who was also their short order cook. And of course, the angel, who coincidentally, was also their waitress.

All they needed now was Mama and her apple pie to complete the picture.

That was it! Mama was the missing ingredient, the reason the universe was out of sorts this time. He was as sure of this as he was sure of his undying devotion to her. *Ma's* needed Mama and Mama needed *ma's.* And he could handle this. It was just a matter of transportation.

But first things first.

It was time to let his new friends in on what they'd just got themselves into.

BJ looked down at his friends' expectant faces, at the short order cook, who had no one to cook for, and the waitress, who had no one to wait on, and he began to talk.

"Ya see—" he started slowly, building up steam, "we're waiting on a special recipe for apple pie that Mama's kinda been gone getting. But now she's back, in a sort of way, although she never really left, and she's as good as got it. So, we gotta get ready to help her bake it, since she's not exactly mobile."

BJ reached up to a cabinet so high, Miggsy, sure it must have been made only for him, removed industrial strength cleaning supplies. "I'll just give everything a once over."

"I can do that!" The brand-new Deirdre jumped in, thrilled to help, thanks to Jane Angelina's know-how.

"I couldn't—" BJ protested.

"I insist!" She smiled, so genuinely overjoyed to pitch in, he didn't want to ruin it. He relinquished his paraphernalia to her and she immediately began filling the pail with soapy water.

"But first, allow me." BJ said, whipping a mammoth sponge out of nowhere, dipping it into the sudsy water, and handily wiping down the shiny ceiling and walls in four swipes, making everything even shinier.

Miggsy watched Deirdre take the cleaning supplies in hand, sweetly declining his offer to help. And although he yearned to help, he didn't push it, because he could tell that he would only be in the way. The sheer economy of her every movement took his breath away. From left to right, top to bottom, she did not miss a spot. She was the Einstein and Astaire of cleaning, a mad genius of Clorox and Comet, whipping everything into a frenzy of efficiency.

Whoosh. Whoosh. Her sponges danced over the riveted steel panels covering the cabinets and counter-tops, and he could not take his eyes off her once again. She was everywhere, glimmering in every panel she polished, her body singing and dancing a glistening rendition of something he couldn't quite catch the tune of, but he was right there with it, swooped up along with the sponges and the soap bubbles.

When she got down on her hands and knees to start on the floor, her sponges splashing in the sloshy water, he saw it, or more accurately, caught the image in the same way someone stranded on a street corner in rush hour catches a glimpse of a taxi cab. Out of the corner of his eye at first, disappearing at a blink. But then, a doubletake to get it back, to retrieve and make sense out of what was only barely there, if there at all. And then, an exerted effort to track it down, whistle it down, hail it, and wait impatiently

for it to reappear—the split-second vision that popped up out of the concoction of soap powder and bleach that glittered in her curls—of a porch
swing under a sky freckled with stars.

"Consider this a run-through—" BJ said, when the kitchen gleamed, handing out crisp white aprons, a real bounce in his voice that went all the way
up through the roof like a Spalding ball, "a run-through for apple pie. So,
we're all ready for Mama."

"The fact that Mama is a mile downhill, melted into her lounger, blowing steam out of her head, doesn't seem to faze any of you in the slightest,
does it?" Cowardice lamented loudly in Miggsy's head, trying to be heard
above the pounding in his own head, which got louder when BJ went over
to the oven and turned it on. And nobody stopped him!

"Apple pie. How unutterably pedestrian," he sneered, apoplectic that
anyone from *his* station of life should be in the same room as—let alone
trapped into helping concoct—a dessert that didn't have the words brûlée
or glacé attached.

One by one, the motley crew of would-be Julia Childs put on their
aprons, and then, to Cowardice's utter horror, it was Miggsy's turn.

The humiliating image of relinquishing his impeccable, Brooks Brothers
smoking jacket for a soon to be apple pie-stained apron came over Cowardice like a hangover. There was a strange ache around his temples. He was
getting a migraine. He'd never gotten a migraine before. He only gave them.
"You're not *seriously* considering putting that *thing* on!" He demanded in that
perfect blend of mordancy and disdain that always brought Miggsy to his
knees—and then, to his senses.

No answer.

"Are you paying attention, dear boy?"

Still no response.

Had he lost his grip on the kid?

In the sparkling clean kitchen of *ma's Café*, a trinity of sous-chefs awaited instructions.

In the kitchen of Mama's mind's eye, what looked to be three strange angels floating into focus, turned out to be BJ, the Tiltawhirl Man, and towering above him, a shining girl, whose spun gold hair floated around her like a halo. Falling into frame, all three were crisp as apples, in blindingly white aprons that flared out in back like wings, swaying slightly to their own inner sound tracks, her own falling angel choir, just waiting for Mama to orchestrate them into more than the sum of their parts.

Of course, there was the slight hitch that she was down here with the recipe and they were up there with the ingredients. And she wasn't exactly sure where the actual apples were. But she'd had patience for so long, it had long ago turned into faith. And if there was one thing she'd learned from the Doo Wops, it was that whatever it is you're looking for, it's probably already here, somewhere in the great everywhere and so, the universe would most certainly provide—one way or another.

Honing in on her choir of angels, she lifted her arms like a maestro starting a symphony, and their voices rose in her mind's ear, in a chorus of apples, of Gravensteins and Granny Smiths, of Cortlands, Empires, and Coy Orange Golds—

"*Ah, ah ah!*" She heard her momma rhapsodizing from somewhere on her mind's front porch, in perfect harmony with the falling angel choir, "the wonderful thing about recipes—the *most* wonderful thing, Norma Lee—is that they never disappoint. No matter how bad your day may be turning out, no matter how gloomy, dark, or dreary everything may seem, or even be, your recipes will never, ever let you down."

The falling angel choir began singing of Roxbury Russets, and Rhode Island Greens.

"The secret to apple pie, Norma Lee—" Mama's momma was humming, the rainy morning, when Norma Lee had just turned nine-and-a-half, and her momma had one of her never wrong "sneaking suspicions" that poppa would be returning from an especially long one very soon and that apple pie would just hit the spot.

"The secret to apple pie, Norma Lee, my darling, has nothing to do with the tired old argument over whether or not to add lemon juice or nutmeg or cloves or leave out the flour or dab on some butter, or brown sugar versus white. That's for silly biddies with no taste buds, sitting around with nothing better to do. No. The secret of apple pie is the apples."

That was when Mama's momma went to her shelf of well-worn, thumbed-through, splattered-on, cookbooks and pulled from behind them, a book Norma Lee had never seen before. It had a shiny cover and looked brand new, although she just knew from the way her momma was holding it close, while flicking the pages to the exact one she wanted without looking, that it was as old as the others, if not older. Norma Lee caught the title, "Apple Edens," on the fly.

"It's all in here," her momma said, her eyes dreamy, "the perfect apple pie."

She opened the book.

The falling angel choir burst into a refrain of Northern Spies and Spitzenbergs.

"The spicy Spitzenberg. Thomas Jefferson's favorite," her momma confided, turning to a marked off page with a picture of an apple that surely would have been the downfall of the Garden of Eden. It was so shiny and red, it made Norma Lee's mouth water just from looking at it.

"It positively cries out for someone to take a bite out of it, doesn't it?" Her momma clucked, putting her arm around her daughter.

"Anyone tasting those apples in a pie will spend the rest of their lives throwing cloves into their pie mix to get that taste back, but they never will without the Spitzenberg," she explained in a hushed tone that included Norma Lee only in all the world, letting Norma Lee know that she was being let in on one of her momma's very special secrets.

"And would you just look at this?" she sighed, "the Northern Spy."

Norma Lee looked down on an even bigger apple, bright green with lustrous red stripes, and was practically drooling for it.

"That's the one that gives the *classic* apple pie flavor. Thin skin, firm, tender. Can't you just taste it?"

And, of course, Norma Lee could.

And so, it went. Mama's momma and her Norma Lee sitting together under the soft, multicolored quilt that Mama's momma had fashioned from pieces of velvet cuffs and collars and satin linings she'd saved up from yard sales and throw-outs since she was Norma Lee's age, *Apple Edens* open between them, rain dancing on the window, sun struggling to break through the clouds.

"But even the Northern Spy," Mama's momma said, stroking Norma Lee's quirky curls tenderly, "even that noble apple cannot stand alone without the pear undertones of the White Permains, or the lip puckering pineapple overtones of Calville Blanc d'Hivers." She lingered over every picture and at the same time could not get from one to the other fast enough, so all the flavors she described could linger in their mouths together.

"Ah! Pink Pearls! Just heavenly and tasty too," Mama's momma crooned, pointing to a breathtaking, two-page picture of a tree laden with what looked to Norma Lee like giant pink pearls.

"And finally," Mama's momma said, when they just could not wait any longer, "my favorites, the Belles de Boskoops, so crisp, tangy, and aromatic, the flavor dances in your mouth. Now! Let's get into that kitchen!"

As if on cue, the sun broke through.

Mama's momma threw off the quilt, grabbed Norma Lee by the hand and, holding the tastes in the hearts of their mouths, they hurried into the kitchen, where the regular, ordinary apples, the Pippins and Granny Smiths, were waiting for Mama's momma to transform them into an extraordinary welcome home apple pie.

"Let's bake!" Mama's momma said, gathering the rest of the ingredients, while the sun continued to make its comeback.

The falling angel choir was rising up in the kitchen of Mama's mind's eye, and the Doo Wops were swooping down to join them in praise of apples, and everything was reaching a crescendo when Mama finally got it. Ever since lightning blew a hole in her noodle, she'd been receiving. Now it was time to transmit.

She tilted her soup can coiffure uphill.

A mile away, the haunting blend of Jane Angelina's angelic soprano, BJ's earthy bass, and Miggsy's school-choir tenor, joined their doppelgängers in Mama's mind-blown mind, in a tantalizing chorus of Spitzenbergs and Northern Spies, Pink Pearls, Rhode Island Greenings, and Ida Reds; Baldwins, Braeburns, and Belles de Boskoops, calling them forth from Mama's memories, while there simultaneously appeared on the counter behind the three unwitting friends, by magic, or miracle, or maybe merely mind over matter, mouth watering piles of apples, all of them crisp, plump, firm, sweet, tart and bursting with so much flavor, their tanginess blasted right through the thin membrane between here and now, there and then, and time and space—and filled the room with their spicy perfume, causing everyone in it to swoon.

And then it began.

Mama hummed a tune she had known forever but had never really heard.

And even though Jane Angelina was now Deirdre, she heard the humming anyway, and then she saw it all unfolding in a sun-dappled kitchen: a pudgy little Campbell's Soup Kid of a girl, with copper curls, looking up with the most trusting, wondrous, and startling split pea green eyes, at her momma, who was humming something half-way between a lullaby and a prayer. And Jane Angelina's heart broke and melted back together again, while sunlight spilled through bright kitchen curtains illuminating Mama's momma's silver measuring spoon, as she reached for it.

Then it was a pinch of this, a sprinkle of that—maybe to anyone else. But Jane Angelina counted the grains of sugar and cubic centimeters of pastry dough and numbers of slices of *which* apples at exactly *what* thickness. She saw it all from a myriad of different angles. She couldn't help it even if she wanted to. She didn't know why she saw Mama's vision clear as day, but she did. She was in Mama's momma's kitchen and it was so warm and cozy, she did not want to leave. But of course, she had to. So, she took it with her—Mama's own dear memory that she had stumbled upon uninvited, unannounced, and on unawares.

A sweet tickle was shivering its way up and down Mama's boom-box-to-the-stars body. Someone was making a tender rumpus. One of Mama's planets had loosed itself from its moorings in the laws of gravity and was coming in for a landing right through the window of her momma's kitchen.

And there she was. Basking in the radiance of Mama's momma's loving light. The angel on Mama's shoulder.

Jane Angelina tiptoed back through the chintz curtain of Mama's memory, shook her head to regain her bearings, and turned to Miggsy and BJ, who were all ears, not to mention eyes, watching her golden curls bounce with every shake of her head. But she was looking right through them into a far away kitchen.

"Flour," she said to herself, really, then ran to the cooling pantry she didn't really even know was there, to retrieve a sack of flour, which Miggsy sped to carry for her, while she raced back to the counter.

"Sugar," she said, and without her say so, her arms reached up for ingredients that were exactly where she knew they'd be.

The boys watched her in communal silence, then hopped into service, Miggsy going for mixing bowls he'd seen during his earlier tour, BJ reaching for the sharpest knife Miggsy had ever seen, then taking his place behind the cutting board Mama had him tailor-make for himself in a whole other Nebo.

Jane Angelina reached for a wooden spoon, which Miggsy, grinning like he'd just won the Diamond, slapped into her hand with the precision of a relay runner handing off a baton.

"Thanks," she said, looking into his eyes over the spoon.

And then she saw them shimmering on the counter behind him. The apples of Mama's momma's eye, in all their glory.

She ran to them, smiled broadly and began tossing apples to BJ in exactly the order that Mama's momma had flipped through the pages of her book.

From her recumbent perch somewhere between heaven and earth, Mama saw it all, and knew it was good. Verging on delicious.

With the polish of a pastry chef and the legerdemain of a three-card monte dealer, Deirdre, who was still Jane Angelina underneath, added a few finishing touches to the filling mix, gave the spoon a twirl, and slid the bowl beside a larger bowl, which held the snow-white mountain of flour she'd just sifted, and into which she tossed some shortening, butter and a little ice water, moistening, mixing, folding, and kneading the sticky, gooey mess into two smooth spheres.

"Ready?" She chirped, retrieving the smaller bowl, wiping her hands on her apron.

"Ready!" BJ boomed, tossing the last of his perfectly cored, quartered and peeled slices into another bowl, which he reverentially placed in front of her.

"Perfect." She smiled up at him, pouring Mama's momma's glistening mixture onto the crisp cascade of apples, coaxing the last of it with the spoon, making sure not to waste a drop.

"Here!" She passed the spoon, which was now covered with filling and charged with her lustrous energy, back over to Miggsy and slid the bowl under it, causing inadvertent sparks to fly between them. "When I give the signal—scoop. But first, make sure all the slices are coated."

Happy to comply, feeling her warmth still in the spoon's handle, he began to mix, releasing a spicy sweet aroma that made him pleasantly lightheaded—and strangely optimistic.

Stirring the already stirring apples, he couldn't take his eyes off her hands, as she sprinkled flour through her long fingers onto the squeaky-clean counter, reached for the rolling pin she knew would be in the second drawer on the right, and quickly rolled out one of the two balls of dough into a perfect twelve inch circle, exactly one-eighth inch thick all around, just as Mama's momma had, carefully lining one of Mama's Pyrex pie pans, signaling Miggsy to transfer the shimmering filling into it.

Spooning the thick, slick, and slippery slices from the deep bowl into the shallow pan was not at all as easy as it seemed. Miggsy paid scrupulous attention not to drop one precious morsel.

When the bowl was empty and the pie pan full, he watched her roll the second ball of dough into another perfect twelve-inch circle, exactly one-eighth inch thick all over, carefully drape it over the rolling pin, and lovingly unroll it over the syrupy mountain of apples he'd tenderly constructed.

He watched the long, delicate, tapered fingers of one of her slender hands clasp a lucky knife to trim the overhang, while the equally exquisite fingers of her other hand followed, gently but rapidly pressing the two crusts together, until they were one. He watched as her floury fingers flew around the pie-to-be's edges, crimping, fluting, and scalloping it into something so perfect, it was more of a sculpture than a pie.

She stood back for a second, like an artist assessing her work, then slashed three equidistant, parallel slits in the dough, and it was done.

Jane Angelina, in the guise of Deirdre, nodded and BJ carried it, like a sacrament, toward the warm oven, which Miggsy joyously rushed to open. He'd had no idea what an exact and artistic achievement making a pie could be. In spite of himself, he was absolutely filled with wonder.

There are many things you can do waiting for a pie to bake. Many things can be cramped or stretched into those forty-five minutes.

Mama was stretched out on her lounger, gazing past the mountains, deep into space, and far into the past, which, thanks to the speed of light, was bolting in at a crisp one hundred eighty-six thousand, two hundred eighty-four miles per *second*, announcing, with a rowdy salvo of rapid-firepings&pongs that would blow smoke through anybody's head, that everything around her was already history. The sun she depended on, worshiped, and adored, was always eight minutes ahead of her, which meant that by the time it got down to shining on her, it was no more than a memory. The moon, when it rose, though close enough to touch, would still be one-and-a-half seconds ago, having moved on by then, too. But, of course, if Mama knew anything from her sojourn through the stars, it was exactly what she learned from *ma's Café*, something, she now knew, that her poppa always knew: like it or not, everything was moving on, as it had been since fate snapped its fiery fingers, ignited a fireball of infinite possibilities, and then sent them spinning away from each other, forever outward in the ever-expanding universe, literally until the end of time.

"Those Doo Wops sure are onto something." Mama told anyone out there who cared to listen, her sound waves floating off towards infinity, crossing paths on their way, with the faint echo of the Big Bang's big Sh-Boom, which tipped its hat to Mama from fourteen or so billion years ago, inviting her to forget her troubles, rotate her soup cans, and tune in to those zany airwaves that were once reruns of *I Love Lucy*, now playing with cosmic gusto in galaxies all over the universe, because as fast as they may have been rushing away from each other, as the very fabric of space itself stretched out like transparent taffy, they couldn't outrun comedy.

Meanwhile, back in the turbulent outskirts of the Milky Way, Mama's home galaxy, the three new friends spent the first part of their forty-five pie-waiting minutes cleaning Mama's kitchen, which didn't take long un-der Deirdre's aegis, since Jane Angelina had taught herself at an early age, to tidy up after every stage of cooking. When it was back up to its spotless pre-pie-prep sheen, BJ rumbled something about taking care of some sort of transportation problem and made himself scarce.

Miggsy was sitting on the counter, drying his spoon.

Jane Angelina, whom he knew as Deirdre, was leaning back against the counter, her flour flecked curls falling in disarray around her alabaster skin.

"Here," she said, "I'll take it."

The love-charged spoon changed hands again and their fingers touched.

Jane Angelina shuddered and blinked, and suddenly they were face to face and he was staring directly into her startled azure eyes.

"Sorry," he whispered shyly.

Her hand rested on his. "It's not your fault," she said firmly, her eyes, now as calm and translucent as glacier lakes.

Something gentle and cool blew through him, then. But before he could argue with it, she slipped the spoon in the drawer with an efficient snap, and when she looked up, he caught, in the unforgiving clarity of the vibrating fluorescent light, flickering beneath her stoic grace, everything she never let anyone see—darkening circles of exhaustion, frayed edges of uncertainty, fine lines of despair, the toll of trying to make ends meet—and failing.

Life had been harsh for her in ways someone born Mills Miggston the Third, even if he called himself Miggsy, could never understand. And yet, here she was, still somehow, radiant, as if hope, itself, gave her a special light, which was probably why he'd thought of her as an angel, when really, she was the salt of the earth, so far at the end of her rope, that she'd willed herself a job at a has-been café, and felt like she'd won the lottery.

And all the time that this selfless girl—who infused her lustrous joy into everything, even scrubbing floors—all the time she was struggling to survive, he had been throwing his life away, or at least trying to. He had to turn away from her because he couldn't stand it, that he'd wasted so much, when she had so little, that with all he'd been given, he'd given up at every turn, while with the very little she'd been given, she had never given up.

"Deirdre," he said, his heart going out to her, "that's such a sad name."

"Really?" she sighed, "I thought it was beautiful."

"It *is* beautiful," Miggsy assured her, his voice husky with feeling, "very beautiful."

He turned to face her again and was faced with the very meaning, the very essence of beauty.

"What I meant was—" he went on, lost in azure, "—it comes from an old Celtic legend about a girl named Deirdre, who was both very kind and very beautiful. Actually, in that way, she was very much like you." He felt his face flush; still, he went on. "But then, through no fault of her own, *un*like you, she became a vessel of sorrow, the other Deirdre, not you, of course. It was my mistake, really, to even suggest such a thing," he apologized.

But he needn't have, because Jane Angelina was thinking just then, about all the prayers she'd heard, the secrets she'd kept over the years, and she knew her new name was no mistake. She was thinking, too, of the weary travelers who would stop at *ma's Café* in need of a kind word, a smile of encouragement, a sympathetic ear, how she would take their orders, listen to their stories, and how, if it came to pass, as it had before, she would hear their prayers, and hold them in her heart like a sacred trust. And, at the end of the day, when the stars were out, and she was soaring over the edge of her porch on her beloved swing, she would release them all to the changing desert sky, giving them a head start to heaven.

"Deirdre's not my real name," she admitted, smiling bashfully, realizing that he had called her beautiful—he had called her beautiful—which was something she could have said of him, now that he was so close, of his chiseled face, his turquoise eyes. A slight blush spread across her pale cheeks.

"My real name is Jane Angelina,." she said, holding out her graceful hand.

Miggsy took her hand. Though it looked soft, it was rough and dry.

"I'm Mills," he said. "I was a jockey once."

"I know," she said. "I've heard your prayers."

"What prayers?"

Miggsy was about to say this, or maybe had said it—since, as far as he knew, he didn't believe in God, or at least not any kind of a God he'd want to pray to (that was until now), and therefore, he never prayed, at least on purpose—when the unmistakable aroma of newly baking pie wafted from the oven, distracting him, but not as much as the incandescent smile that started taking over Jane Angelina's face when those delicious flavors started taking over the room.

"Okay. Okay. I'll need oven mitts and a clean apron to welcome the pie properly," she said, opening a drawer that contained both, closing her eyes.

Mama's momma donned her white organza hostess apron with the violet lace trim and took out all three of her best pie plates, which were real porcelain china.

Norma Lee, taking her momma's cue, got the fancy white linen napkins out from behind the paper ones, and fanned them across the small, delicate, beautifully miss-matched plates, like her momma had taught her.

Mama's momma put on her favorite flowery mitt and waited, hand poised above the oven, as the tantalizing bouquet of baking apples filled the room.

"I don't have plans and schemes.
And I don't have hopes and dreams.
I don't have anything.
Since I don't have you."

Noel Cowardice laid back on the uneasy chair he had constructed out of old wounds, took a deep sip from his cup of bitters, and sulked.

Well, if the boy wouldn't even listen to reason, he told himself, why on earth bother? Still, he could not shrug it off. It was too, too disrespectful, this total lack of even a shred of consideration from the boy.

Cowardice felt faint. His study—with its walls of wisdom and self-justification, its leather-bound volumes containing, somewhere among them, the answers to every question that would ever arise, the rationale for every decision, where he could retire in the luxury of his vintage Brooks Brother navy silk robe with the white velvet piping—his *precious* study was closing in on him. He couldn't get out.

It was too, too much, this affront, when what was he, but a rather harmless, though indisputably charming old *butler,* a valet, really, from the old school, when they pronounced it properly with a hard *"t"*—so succinct and to the point—so like the English, crisp and purposeful—keeping the boy on track day after day, morning, noon, and night; never sleeping; always at the ready. He was miffed, frankly, although he was not one to easily or *ever* have his feathers ruffled. *That boy,* when all he ever wanted to do was serve and protect, to be the boy's thin *royal* blue line, as it were. And as the first *and* last lines of defense, was he not there armed with a snappy retort whenever needed. Was it not he, who had risen against the tyrant father? And was it not he, whose primal scream had single-handedly stopped the boy and his horse from crashing into that rail? But, no. Let's not go there. His job was to keep the boy alive, not engender gratitude.

Cowardice smoothed down his slightly ruffled lapel and sighed deeply, a bit too deeply in fact, because all the moments of their lives together suddenly started dancing a maddening gavotte in his head, beginning with the moment of his own birth, kneeling at the keyhole, then rising from the ashes of the boy's despair, taking the dear, shattered child in hand, guiding him down to the utility kitchen to smash his toxic cocktail, his pituitary remedy to shards, and arise from his tainted future like a phoenix.

Could the boy not perceive with all that intelligence of his, all that brainpower that some demented God had poured into him instead of height, that the person he was now shutting out was the very one who had always done everything in his power to keep that fragile heart from breaking—no matter what it took.

"Dear, dear, boy," he said through gritted teeth, taking a gentleman's taste of the bracing bitters, trying to make contact, "it's not too late!"

Nothing.

He couldn't compete with the undivided attention the boy was giving to a pie. A pie! For God's sakes! And it was all that waitress's fault! That waitress!!

After all the times he'd helped the boy rise if only to fall again, a fall from the height and the very efflorescence of that waitress's smile would be too, too precipitous to survive.

He had to think of something before it was too late.

He took another snort of his bitters, then another and another and an-other. But he couldn't shake the shaky feeling that something had changed ineffably, unutterably. Oh, but look who was getting all sentimental and shrinking from the occasion, Cowardice chided himself, smoothing down the velvet piping.

Cowardice in retreat? But never!

There was still time to save the boy.

He breathed deeply about to take one more snort—for luck—and then it hit him—sweet, tart, warm, irresistible—apple pie!

"Apple pie!" Mama's momma sang, her hand in her flowery mitt poised above the oven. And just as she reached for the door, the timer went off.

"Apple pie!" Jane Angelina echoed, exalted, confirming what their noses already knew.

"Do I smell apple pie?" BJ loped in exactly on time.

Mama's momma lifted up the bubbling pie, releasing a gush of everything warm and wonderful that had ever been cooked up in her kitchen. And arm-in-arm, Norma Lee and her momma watched the spicy steam slip through the open window and head down the road to a rendezvous with her poppa, who was already there—when the last dessert fork was placed on the last doily—on the other side of the door, ready to be a family again.

Jane Angelina opened the oven and out gushed everything warm and won-derful, that had ever been whipped up in the hey-day of *ma's Café*.

Delighted, she swirled around, holding the pie in two flowery oven mitts.

She was wearing an organza apron with violet piping she'd found in the drawer, over her over-starched uniform, and she looked to Cowardice, who just couldn't resist taking a peek, like an angel Betty Crocker on a Norman Rockwell cover for the Saturday Evening Post.

And the pie, itself, he had to admit, if only to himself, was the work of art its preparation promised it would be. Its rich, golden crust could barely contain the glistening, bubbling, thick amber filling, overflowing with per-fectly tuned apples. Cowardice was beside himself with dazed confusion.

"We have to let it cool." Jane Angelina said, in a hush of religious propor-tions, placing the precious pie down on the counter near the open window, like Mama's momma had.

Unleashed at last—from the incarceration inside Mama of the mis-placed, lost, forsaken, and all but given-up-for-dead recipe—the heady scent of simmering apples, doing what Mama's momma originally in-tended, percolated up from the pie, glided past an absolutely enchanted Miggsy, drifted across a positively buoyant Jane Angelina, caught a more than willing BJ on the fly, filled the café with the essence of home, soaked up a chorus of *Sh-Boom,* compliments of the heavenly Doo Wops, then caught up with a breeze blowing outside the open window.

BJ pulled on his very own flowery—and appropriately enormous—oven mitt, made by Mama to match hers, gingerly lifted the pie, still in its very hot plate, from the windowsill, and cradled it in his now double-padded palm, like a baseball in a catcher's glove.

"Quick!" he urged his waitress and his partner, rushing them out back towards the short cut to Mama's, which to Miggsy's chagrin, turned out to be at least a mile straight down a very steep hill, with absolutely no discernible path.

"Couldn't we take the truck? I don't mind going the long way," Miggsy begged, as BJ pushed him along to the edge of the hill.

"What?!" Was all Jane Angelina could say before the door snapped shut behind her, and BJ and the pie dashed on ahead of her, sweeping her along in their wake.

"Of course, no one could keep up with Mr. Seven League Boots," Cowardice, miraculously revived by a few whiffs of pie, tried to gripe. But before he could work himself up to a serious harrumph, or even begin to grouse things up, Jane Angelina's waitress uniform caught a downdraft and, grabbing Miggsy's hand in hers, she took off.

The next thing he knew, they were soaring downhill to Mama's in BJ's wake.

"Hold on!" Jane Angelina shouted, a little after the fact.

Soaring out from the edge of the hill, locked onto Miggsy's powerful grip with a powerful grip of her own, Jane Angelina was pleased as punch that Sharl's over-sized, over-starched, baby doll sleeves had come in so handy, as she knew they would, catching the wind like sails, allowing her to control both velocity and direction by moving her arms.

Unable to resist, she lowered her arms a few degrees, stepping up their descent just enough for a slight thrill.

Exhilarated, she looked over at Miggsy, who was grinning from ear to ear, having so little trouble staying aloft, it crossed her mind that like her, he was born to be airborne.

BJ, of course, was way ahead of them by now, on his way home to Mama, and gaining ground fast.

"Wanna catch up?" She asked, pointing to their mammoth, yet quickly disappearing friend.

"Absolutely!" Every part of Miggsy shouted with unmitigated joy. "Follow that pie!"

Hand-in-hand, Jane Angelina and Miggsy lowered their arms and zoomed downhill, dizzily trailing BJ, roaring with laughter.

BJ powered down to Mama's in seven league strides, pie held high, co-cooned in the luxurious safety of his double-padded oven mitt, its spicy steam escaping in a twirling, swirling, whirlwind.

Whooping it up and down the hill like a jail break, enticing Jane Angelina and Miggsy to further flights of fancy, those heavenly, divine, and altogether irrepressible flavors hitched a ride on the already pie-driven wind, and high-tailed it out of Nebo, like they were on a mission from God. Which, of course, they were.

Mama was convening with the great and awesome silence of the universe when it hit her. Pie was in the vicinity and closing in. But there was a definite absence of Doo Wops.

Come to think of it, Mama thought, rotating her soup cans to regain transmission, the Doo Wops were last seen crooning above BJ's head, heading across her blistered backyard with him, and hadn't been heard from since.

> *"It's just like heaven being here with you.*
> *You're like an angel, too good to be true—"*

They had harmonized their hearts out for her, letting her in on it—in case she missed it from BJ actually saying it three or four times—that they were going to meet her angel. So, she wished them well as they went on their way, and they vanished between the charbroiled cactuses like rumors from God.

And it was all right with Mama at the time, busy as she was making friends with her memories. But now that she had her apple pies lined up like ducks in a row, cooling off on the windowsills of her mind, it was time to make a move, time for another crack in the universe to let her through.

It came as no surprise to Mama to see her angel coming in for a two-point landing at the bottom of the hill, right behind a newly materialized BJ. But it did surprise her to see, flying behind BJ and beside the angel, hand-in-hand, in perfect formation, none other than the oddly aerodynamic Tiltawhirl Man, who touched ground with a lightness he sure didn't have before. Mama sighed, contended. Her falling angels had landed safely.

And her man was coming home to his Mama.

"That BJ always did know how to make an entrance," she mused, watching his feet eat up the desert on his way back to her, while more of the sublime harmonies she'd been longing for echoed in the wind whipped up by his mighty strides.

> *"This I swear is true—*
> *My love for you will last*
> *Till time itself is through.*
> *Oh, my darling, oh my darling—*
> *This I swear is true!"*

The Doo Wops piped up from around BJ's immense shoulders, echoing what was in his heart, announcing their return with a flourish.

No other words changed hands at that point. Instead, Mama took it all in—the girl, the boy, the Doo Wops, BJ. And the pie.

Often the bouncer, but always the host, BJ stepped in. "Mama, darlin', you remember Miggsy, of course."

Mama nodded. Indeed, she did. It was Tiltawhirl all right. But no doubt about it, someone had taken the pressure right outta his cooker, the tilt out of his whirl, put a twinkle in his eye. And Mama had a pretty good idea who that someone was.

"—Our new waitress—" BJ was beaming, gently nudging Jane Angelina forward.

"Oh, we go way back." Mama winked at Jane Angelina. "Make yourself at home, angel,"

She said, confirming what BJ already knew, before he could properly finish the introductions.

The smile that radiated across Mama's face when Jane Angelina caught sight of familiar split pea green eyes, was so warm and welcoming, and in spite of singed hair, burnt-out soup cans, and the wear and tear of age and time, she was so unmistakably still the plucky little girl in the sun dappled kitchen, that Jane Angelina couldn't help smiling right back.

Of course, watching a smile break out on Jane Angelina's face, Miggsy couldn't suppress a grin of his own, which of course just made BJ beam even wider.

"And Mama—"

BJ kneeled in front of Mama, mainly to be on the same level when he presented the pie to her, but to Jane Angelina, it looked like the height of gallantry.

Mama was, of course, as Mama had been for the last three months, happily ensconced in her lounger. She'd lost a lot of days and nights popping in and out, she was sure. But that didn't mean she'd lost her manners.

"Well, what're we waiting for, BJ? How about getting some plates and forks and offering our guests some pie!" She enthused, as if she'd just been sitting around expecting them, which, in a way, she had been.

And so, the three new friends sat around Mama's lounger, cross-legged, like kids around a campfire, basking in her warmth, the still bubbling pie on the melted, Gaudiesque glass table, that was as permanently melded to Mama's equally melted, Gaudiesque bottle of Wild Turkey, as Mama was to her trusty chaise.

Mama nodded and BJ cut the pie, emancipating a giant whoosh of flavor that made them swoon in unison again. He slid the first slice onto one of Mama's special occasion plates and offered Mama the first bite like he'd been doing ever since she got fried. But this time, instead of drifting off, or popping out, Mama took a bite.

Mama took a bite and she was back in the sun-drenched kitchen again, basking in her momma's love.

Mama looked at Jane Angelina, her angel, her eyes welling with tears. "It's my momma's pie, all right."

BJ slid the other slices onto the other special occasion plates and one at a time, the new friends tasted the pie.

Jane Angelina found herself on a swing under a star freckled sky, being pushed high into the air by her father, who was saying what she felt, which was that this must be what heaven was all about.

Miggsy was in the barn with Wilde and Will, sharing pulpy apples.

BJ took his bite and he was right there, where he was, his great heart filled with Mama, his new friends, and apple pie.

"Well," he said, reaching for another piece, "if this can't save the world, nothing can! Seconds?"

As dusk skipped into night, and night crept into dawn, the heavenly scent of apple pie, fresh from the oven, drifted over the Airstream and Mama's barbecued backyard like a vapor embrace, like one of Mama's momma's special hugs, tucking them all in, while the Doo Wops lullabyed them to sleep.

Jane Angelina, the self-proclaimed Deirdre, dreamed of horses. Miggsy dreamed of porch swings. BJ dreamed of Mama. Mama, having already dreamt them all, took a brief time off to croon with the Doo Wops.

> *"Life is but a dream*
> *It's what you make it—"*

Miggsy couldn't sleep, hadn't slept a full night in years. So, he opened his eyes to check on Jane Angelina, who had fallen asleep leaning against his shoulder, to see if she was still there, since she was so light, she could easily have floated away. Struck by the way her tousled hair fell around her delicate face like a princess in a fairy tale, he ached to kiss her awake from whatever nightmare her life had been up till then, and keep her safe forever. Then she stirred.

She opened her drowsy eyes, looked up at him in a blur of blue, sighed, "Ya know, Miggsy, I grill a mean burger and I can help you out, if you ever need me to." She smiled a dreamy smile and closed her eyes again.

And then she opened them again. "Or, if there's anything else I can do—"

"Well," Miggsy whispered quickly, before she closed her eyes again, "– it's about hearing my prayers—"

"I call them prayers. Sometimes wishes and hopes get mixed in. Sometimes I hear them, especially on Sundays," she yawned, half-asleep.

Had she been more awake, she could have told him how they came in on different wave lengths, in infinite harmonies, like the contrapuntal music she'd loved to sing in Church Concert Choir, and that thanks to her mathematical mind, she knew the exact number of hopes versus wishes versus prayers, as well as the approximate radii within which she usually heard them; but she didn't know why she heard some and not others.

"You heard—mine?" He pressed, feeling a little like he was stepping off a cliff he hadn't known was there, apparently the theme of the day.

"When we first—when *I* first—" she struggled to find the right word, then settled on "crashed—when I crashed into you, you prayed that *I* wouldn't fall, that you would catch me. And you did." She sat up, faced him. "That was very unselfish of you, praying for a stranger, who knocked you down."

"*That* was a prayer?" he said, amazed.

"That's the thing about you. You never really pray for yourself." She blushed and rushed on. "Mainly you pray for your horse and your friend."

"You hear me pray for them, for Wilde and Will?" Miggsy was beginning to wonder what was in that pie.

"It's your constant prayer, really, for their well-being." Jane Angelina whispered, hearing it now, his leitmotif. "Especially your horse, because of the accident."

"You, you know about the *accident*?"

Wasn't it a minute ago that she was asleep in his arms and he was in heaven? Now he was plummeting down that cliff he hadn't known was there, on a rearing horse—on Wilde—skidding wildly into the rail.

Jane Angelina, feeling Deirdre emerge, took his hands in hers. Fierce, violent energy rushed through his fingers into her palms, calming him, unsettling her.

"I saw it—" she said, reliving it, "just before—just saw it, when our fingers touched—over the spoon—I saw you—on your horse—I saw—I saw it all—the race—the accident—"

"Except it wasn't an accident." He shook his head in shame. "It was my fault, all my—"

"No." Jane Angelina whispered urgently, her eyes so deep, he could have plunged into them. "I don't know why, but I saw you—and you were sick, feverish. Your eyes. I saw your eyes. They were glassy, unfocused. I saw it—felt it—in one of those flashes I get sometimes, that make time stand still—I saw—*everything*." She shivered.

"Not everything," Miggsy confessed, desperately wanting her friendship and whatever might follow, but not under false pretenses. "You didn't see how I failed—"

He hadn't meant to say that. But sitting hand-in-hand with her, feeling her draw it out of him, like venom from snakebite, emotions which had been bottled up too long, spilled out from his despairing soul into her radiant heart.

"Your horse," she said, when he finally ran out of ways to blame himself, "—Wilde—did he—will he—ever run again?"

"I—I don't know—" he said sadly, wanting to leave it at that. But he couldn't lie to her. "After the accident, I ran away because I was so ashamed—I just—I just couldn't face them—and I kept going—I never went back—I called right after I left because I had to know that Wilde was hanging on but I never called again because—" He looked at her with tears in his eyes, saying out loud to her, what he hadn't even whispered to himself, but of course, always knew, "—as long as I didn't call, I wouldn't know, and if I didn't know, then Wilde was still alive—*is*—still alive. I just kept moving from one city to another—changing my name every time I changed my address—so I would disappear, and Will could never find me, even if he wanted to."

"So, he has no idea how you are—what's become of you all these years—if you're dead or alive?" She was incredulous.

"I—I guess not," he said, shakily.

"He must be worried sick about you, don't you think?" She asked gently.

Miggsy's hands slipped from hers, and he stared at her blindly, as everything he thought he knew shattered around him, like the hall of mirrors it always was, and she was face to face with the truth: he'd been obsessing about them night and day for almost ten years, without really *thinking* about them even once.

"I have to call Will and beg his forgiveness," he said, finally. "I'm just—terrified about what he—what he—"

"You're not alone anymore," she reassured him, taking up his hands again, taking up his heartache.

But her voice was parched and faint, and even through the darkness, he could see how much paler she'd become.

It was such a bittersweet irony. He'd set out to save her from her nightmare, and yet here she was, drained from trying to save him from his. And so, he offered her the only comfort he could, tonight, his shoulder to lean on, his arms to lie in.

"We're a team, remember?" She yawned, drifting off again, nestled in his arms, her curls, golden spirals of starlight.

"Seeing the flickering flame of her framed by the star–studded sky would lift the spirits of a dead man, give a coward courage," Cowardice rhapsodized, on the wings of apple pie.

Mama smiled in her waking dream, reflecting on how the first fiery sizzle of time exploded into the very stardust of love songs.

BJ, having installed himself like a retaining wall between the desert and the sweethearts, grinned his signature grin, waking up, that is, if he was actually asleep. Because, asleep or awake, his mind was always on Mama and the café. And now, his two new friends were there too, permanently, in the great providence of his perception.

And he was looking out towards the sky beyond Nebo, into the future, not only his future, but everybody's, Mama's, and the angel's, and Miggsy's, and all the wayfarers and wanderers and strippers of the world who had lost their way.

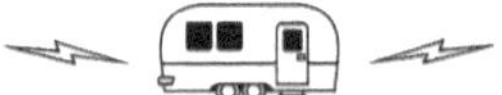

Mama blinked back from the clarity of her fog, and rotated forty-five degrees north-north-east, luxuriating in the first swig of sunlight, synapses snapping.

According to the communiqués she'd been furiously downloading through the blow-hole permanently engraved in her cranium, the universe had gotten itself jump-started from a blowout much like the one in her noggin. One minute nothing. No time, no space, no universe, except for one imperceptible, infinitesimal, vastly overcrowded dot of molten, roiling potential, in the middle of absolute nowhere, fomenting escape. One great belch later, and the seeds of the stars and absolutely everything else pinged and ponged outward, from where they were imprisoned, to the farthest reaches of eternity, much like the aroma of her momma's apple pie was, at that present moment, gallivanting to points unknown.

"Is it Sunday?" Jane Angelina asked sleepily, because she was hearing prayers.

"*I want a Sunday kind of love,*" the Doo Wops confessed.

"I can make coffee." Miggsy volunteered, feeling well-rested for the first time in maybe forever.

"I'll help." Jane Angelina unwound herself from his lap then gave him a hand up.

And right after the two, too vivid, almost clashing blues of their eyes flashed in the new morning light, causing a different set of sparks to fly, they both saw it, still piping hot, still steaming with fresh-from-the-oven flavor, still bursting with still bubbling apples—still whole!

Cowardice, permitting himself a glimpse at it in its current incarnation, or more to the point, *reincarnation*, was about to hypothesize how it had gotten that way, putting it down to some sort of pie trompe l'oeil, or pastry prestidigitation, perpetrated by BJ and Mama in the dead of night. But on second thought, decided to take it on faith.

Mama, on the other hand, knew from her "little jaunts" across the universe, that like space, time, once unfurled, was an infinite but invisible pie, and that every single incident in the history of the universe, no matter how great or small, was a slice of that time-pie, unchanging and always there, as real as any point in space.

Mama knew there were many reasons for her Momma's apple pie to be whole again, the best being that it had always been whole, and would always be whole somewhere on the time/space continuum. So why not here? Why not now?

Just then, BJ enwrapped the bubbling pie in his gigantic mitt, handed it, mitt and all, to Mama, kissed her full on the lips, said, "Hang on Mama, darlin'."

And flexing his monumental muscles, BJ hoisted the lounger, with Mama on it, high over his head like the grandest grand prize you could ever win and headed right back up the hill towards the café.

"Hang on, Miggsy!" Deirdre giggled, in hot pursuit. "We're going for the updraft!"

BJ vaulted uphill, racing the sun, holding Mama, so resplendent, glorious, sublime, and supine, and so high, that of course, she saw it first.

There, shimmering in the nearing distance, like a star on a Christmas tree, *ma's* was in sight! Mama watched her precious café rise above her, shining like it used to in its halcyon days, and the next thing she knew, her heart took flight, and the rest of her just had to go along for the ride.

Basking in her molten chaise, her chariot of fire, held aloft by the man she loved, her momma's ambrosial pie swaddled in her arms, Mama was so excited to be reunited with her café, BJ and her falling angels, so over-joyed to be open for business again, that flashes of elation and sparks of sheer delight burst forth from her hot-wired noodle, sizzled through her high voltage lounger, ricocheted off her scorched soup can conductors, and fractured the bone-dry sky above her, ripping through it.

Jane Angelina was sailing along on BJ's back draft, Miggsy at her side—re-laxing her relaxed hold on him a little, then a little more, then a little more, until only the tips of their fingers were touching—when she heard the ce-lestial commotion and looked up just in time to see the sky above Mama flapping back and forth in the blistering breeze like torn scenery.

And then, right behind the fluttering sky—in the split-second between mirage and miracle—she caught a glimpse of the infinite universe in all its glory. And it was dark and vast and endless and it had so many stars in it that she could not begin to count them

But she could hear them.

"Pretty little angel eyes," they tintinnabulated all the way from the begin-ning of time, illuminating their gift to her—just one moment from their road trip from there to here, their drive-through down the space/time continuum,

the Route 66 of the cosmos—one moment that took her breath away, because it was the one moment that answered her one and only prayer for herself.

There, behind the thinly veiled curtain of time, was her father, pushing her on the swing he had made for her, under those very stars. But unlike a memory, or a wish, or even a dream, she was really there with him in the shelter of that moment. And, the stars were whispering in her ear, she had never not been there with him. All those precious moments with her father were not just then, but now and always.

"Pretty little angel eyes," they crooned, welcoming her with open arms, just the slightest trace of apple pie mingling with the stardust on their breath.

"I know you were sent from heaven above," Miggsy harmonized whole-heartedly.

BJ reached the top of the hill and kept going, right up the ramp he'd installed earlier, to the roof, where Mama held out the still bubbling pie, sheltered in BJ's oven mitt, to Jane Angelina and Miggsy, who caught it on the fly-by, held it between them, hammocked in Jane Angelina's apron, landed it safely, and put it back on the windowsill where it belonged.

Jane Angelina glanced up to give the okay sign and beheld Mama glinting in her lounger, like she was her own constellation. But Jane Angelina knew Mama was much more than a bunch—or even a galaxy—of stars. Mama was a universe.

Soup cans flashing with incoming signals. Lifted up, high atop the mountain by BJ, her mountain of a man, her Atlas, who held up her world. Closer to heaven than ever before. Shining like a beacon in the ever-rising sun, Mama watched the steamy spices of her momma's pie waft up from the windowsill and drift down the road in search of her poppa.

Irma was filling in for a vacationing hoofer on the chorus line of Olive
Oyls at *"Popeye's on the Strip"* in downtown Vegas, getting ready for the
afternoon show, having the time of her life. Though she was now head
choreographer and all-around den mother to the newest batch of over-the-
hill, spaghetti-limbed Rockettes, and it had been ages since she'd left her
café in young Norma Lee's capable hands, there was no doubt about it, she
still had it in her, all the oomph, spice, and vinegar of her personal hey day.

She was doing the deadly kick, kick, double kick, without missing a
beat, when she got a Western Union from times gone by, and without a
second thought, she high-kicked it right out of there and down to Route
66, the entire chorus line of Olive Oyls—who could certainly afford the
carbs, suddenly caught in the thrall of all things apple pie—in tow behind
her, kick, kick, double-kicking, arm-in-arm, like leggy paper dolls.

How Irma and company made it through the seventy-five miles southwest on the I-15 to Route 66, and then on to New Nebo, was a matter of
speculation, especially since Irma herself cryptically attributed it to the
time-tested kick, kick, back kick, double kick routine, because, as she put it,
"it really separates the men from the boys." But what kept them kicking high
and kicking strong, she freely admitted, were the Calliopes, or more specifically, the inimitable Calliope stylings of the incomparable Carson City
All Girl Calliope All Star Band, tearing down Route 66 on their red, white,
and blue flatbeds, thumping out their prize-winning, signature medley, a
magnificent blending of "Happy Days Are Here Again" and "Forget Your
Troubles Come On Get Happy" all the way from St. Louis, Mo, where, immediately after winning the nationals for the fifteenth year in a row, they
all experienced a simultaneous craving for apple pie, and before you could
say "Jenny Craig", the renowned former Weight Watchers accepted their
trophy and hit the road.

Mrs. Judith Blumenthal Malone Epstein and Mrs. Christine Stevens Young, formerly Ms Judy Blue Thighs and Ms Crystal Night, put their seal of approval on the finishing touches for the Meet 'n Greet Breakfast in the fabulous Grand Gardenia Ballroom at the Amarillo International Hotel, before kicking off another of their wildly successful "Self-Esteem for Strippers and Showgirls" seminars, now in its—can you believe it?—twenty-fifth year.

Although they were no spring chickens by any stretch of the imagination, those still sexy grandmas sashayed onto the stage, like the strippers they once were, heads and breasts held high, thanks, in equal parts, to self-respect and modern science, and were greeted by riotous applause.

Quieting their adoring audience with a well-rehearsed-to-appear-to-be-totally-spontaneous bump and grind, they welcomed everyone warmly with the true anecdote they always told about how they came to be in the self-esteem business to begin with, because of a young bouncer at the "La Strip Joint," in Tallahassee, who was wise beyond his years.

"So," Judy concluded, "when Krystal came back that night with a shiner from her no-good boyfriend, who made her feel like she deserved it—"

The riveted audience rippled with rousing variations of "I've heard that before."

"BJ looked right into her black eye, even though it was stuck shut," Judy went on.

"That boy shined some kind of light right past my shiner and into my brain," Krystal added, dabbing a tear, "when he said, in that deep, rumbly voice of his that made the room vibrate and certainly shook some sense into me, 'You're a good person, Krystal, and you don't have to take shit from no one!' And that was it! My eyes were opened!"

They were about to add the punch line, always a crowd pleaser, that BJ had punctuated his pep talk by beating the shit out of the good-for-nothing boyfriend, and to enjoy breakfast, when the delectable aroma of apple pie deluged the room and they changed their plans.

"Someone call for a fleet of limos!" Krystal announced, sniffing the air with purpose. "We're heading west!"

Major General Bruce Alan Murdoch, Retired, was back at the old Nebo base after a dozen years, reviewing the troops in advance of a special breakfast honoring him, when a barrage of familiar flavors bombarded his senses, ordering him to order all troops to reconnoiter at *ma's Café* for a real breakfast, in zero-thirty minutes, and maybe stay for lunch, if a certain herb crusted Coca-Cola basted ham was on the menu. And, by the time he'd barked his orders, there was already a convoy of hungry Humvees, at least a mile long, tailgating in that direction.

Beaming down from his new altar, at his scruffy, dear congregation, now sitting comfortably on upholstered seats in real pews, cozy in the warmth of the recently refurbished church, compliments of an anonymous donor, Father Joaquin was about to say a silent blessing for the person who had provided so beneficently for his needy flock, when something strange happened. Without warning, a bitter wind came whistling in through an open window, intruding on the toastiness manifested by both the new heating system and the saintly father's profound generosity, bringing with it the shock of winter, the slight undertones of apple pie, and the unmistakable image of that strange yet helpful young man who had disappeared as mysteriously as he had appeared, standing under a glittery awning resplendent with stars that shined like a beacon in the desert night, offering respite from the cold.

Invoking the Good Lord, who was making this so, Father Joaquin smiled at his gathering of misfits and misfortunates, and told them it was time to get the chill from their bones and head west.

Meanwhile, all the way down town, well past midnight, calcifying in the warren of aisles of newspapers, X-rated magazine, and dubious, "exotic" smokes, Edwin H. Hughes, nasty proprietor of Hughey's News & Smokes, involuntarily took a moment from his permanent state of begrudgement to put down the gin and savor the scent of apple pie fighting its way through the mustiness on a beeline to him.

Then it occurred to Edwin H. Hughes—not really out of the blue—that it was time to take that well-needed vacation he never seemed to get around to, grab his now dusty journal, and journey into the desert to be a writer again.

No one knew exactly when the line had stretched as far back as Chicago, and then kept on going east to the Atlantic Ocean, or when they got wind of it west to the Pacific. But those splendid, jaunty flavors that made up that one unmistakably, irresistible aroma that could only be apple pie rising from the oven—Mama's momma's simple offering—coasted along the disappearing highway that once was Route 66, and in the time it takes to take a pie out of the oven and place it on a window sill to cool, anyone who cared to look, could see all along the once defunct Mother Road, a calliope fueled, rag-tag conga line of people, who, somewhere deep inside their hearts and souls, yearned for home.

"I'm telling you, BJ," Mama chuckled, "once you've stuck your finger in the socket of enlightenment—there's no going back!"

It was high noon on Mount Nebo. The sun was at its summit. The heat was at its hottest. And Mama, melded as she was to her beloved lounger, felt herself expanding along the universe, floating toward the edges of time and space, like a founding member of the Big Bang Band, part and parcel of the primordial kaboom, a piece of everything in her, a piece of her in everything.

"Just think," she said, when she spied the smiles overtaking the faces of the first weary travelers to cross the threshold into *ma's Café*, seeking sanctuary, even if they didn't know it yet, "my momma was right."

"Life could be a dream."
"Sh-Boom."

EPILOGUE

High in the mountains, in the dark pith of the woods, in an immense stone house, chiseled from the mountain itself, unreachable by ordinary men, BJ's father, Big J, who still thought of his only son, big as he'd become, as Little J, came in from the cold, shucked off his heavy coat, and settled into the oversized, overstuffed easy chair in front of the gigantic fireplace.

Warming in the fire's massive blaze, he felt the weariness of all big men, if they were lucky enough to get as old as he was. On days like this, he missed his son. But they had different paths to follow. Little J had to be in the world. It was his path.

Laughter echoed throughout the house and across the thousand-acre woods outside his door. Big J breathed a sigh of deep contentment that all was well in this private, sheltered world, and when he did, he caught the faint whiff of something wonderful that wasn't coming from the enormous kitchen in the back of the great house.

"Hey!" He called out to his fellow giants, "anyone up for apple pie?"

And with one gigantic intake of breath, which some have said actually stopped time, they simultaneously agreed that indeed they were.

He was at her grave again. This time, not barking orders, ensuring its highest maintenance. This time, not rigorously double checking that she was always surrounded by blooming magnolias. This time, just kneeling to her in death as he never knelt to her in life, once again, begging her forgiveness for the sin of banishing their son from their lives.

He remembered loving her with a passion that drove him to have her at all costs. He remembered torturing her for the sin of loving him, or was that it at all? Wasn't it the sin of bearing a defective son? It was so hard to remember anymore.

Mills Donald Miggston was trying to remember, forcing himself to face every pain he'd ever inflicted, when the ghost of her shivered through him and he knew she was the lucky one, to be at last at peace. It crossed his mind then, that he couldn't remember a time in his life when he'd had a moment's peace, no matter how drunk he got.

And, reaching for his flask, he almost missed the warm breeze carrying the spicy sweet perfume of apple pie wafting up the well-manicured hill.

Lily Preston Murphy woke up in the middle of a too bright room, so bright, she was blinded and couldn't quite remember where she was. Was she still in that room at the Hotel Eden, with the man who went down as smooth as Scotch? Was it the day after, when she awoke to blinding white sheets, and all alone, except for her new suit, her crown, and her bourbon glasses? She had a faint remembrance of that not being the end in that room, although she'd wished it had been. She needed a drink. Where was that girl? Where was that Janey, that Janey Angelina? Not that she'd give her old mother a drink. Although to be fair, she did put a little of the hair of the dog in that vitamin soup concoction she made to keep her alive, when Lily Preston Murphy really just wanted to die every time she looked into her daughter's eyes and saw the man who went down as smooth as scotch, then disappeared.

Something strange was going on. Because strange smells were coming from somewhere, maybe the kitchen, strange, wonderful smells that made her think of something she hadn't thought of for years—since she denounced Satan and all his temptations—apple pie.

Will De Longpre, a man of deeply imbedded habits, was doing what he'd been doing every morning and every evening for the last ten years. He was in the private barn listening to Mozart, reminiscing with Wilde about their lad, praying for his safety. They were about to whip up some pulpy apples in loving tribute to him, when the aroma of homemade apple pie popped in from out of nowhere and changed their minds.

"Ya wouldn't happen to have a recipe for apple pie, would ya?" He asked Wilde.

But before Wilde could reply, the phone rang.

Deep in the woods, down a narrow, windy path, where he had retreated long ago, when the scent of apple pie vanished from the air, and he could no longer find his way back to his dear Lee-Ann, Norman Walters was sitting on the makeshift pier behind his cabin, trying to catch breakfast, marveling at how strong some memories turned out to be, thinking that if only Norma Lee were there, the trout would be swimming to her,

And he was sure his senses were playing tricks on him, which they tended to do more and more these days, because just when he felt a tug at the end of his line, he also felt a tug at his heart.

And, breathing deeply, he was sure they had found him again, those tender, doting spices, beckoning him to follow them home one more time.

About the Author

A lover of words and meanings hidden in plain sight, Karen Gottlieb has taken the circuitous route through life, or perhaps it was a straight line, before landing on this page. As a lyricist, her songs have been recorded by artists like the incomparable Michael Feinstein and the iconic Olivia Newton John, and are available on iTunes, YouTube, and Spotify. She's been commissioned by major corporations to write songs for their conventions, had plays performed in NY and LA, run a successful corporation, and as a writing coach, helped transform young people's lives. But her greatest accomplishment is her exquisite/radiant daughter, Alexandra. Karen lives in Los Angeles, California with her eternally supportive husband, Leonard, and their imperious cat, Lolita.